"Tired of glamorous private investigators so svelte they could be fashion models? Has author Selma Eichler got a heroine for you."
—*South Florida Sun-Sentinel*

"Desiree is a doll—fat, fun, late to everything."
—*Mysterious Women*

Raves for Selma Eichler and the Desiree Shapiro mysteries . . .

Murder Can Mess Up Your Mascara

"Tantalizing meal descriptions, old-school New York charm, and even a touch of romance make this book worth gobbling up." —*Publishers Weekly*

Murder Can Botch Up Your Birthday

"A highly engrossing read that shouldn't be missed."
—*Rendezvous*

Murder Can Rain On Your Shower

"An exciting private investigator tale that is fun to read . . . delightful." —*Midwest Book Review*

Murder Can Cool Off Your Affair

"A laugh-out-loud riot. I love Desiree's sense of humor." —*Mystery News*

continued . . .

Murder Can Upset Your Mother

"Eichler scores again. . . . [A] delicious cozy."
—Publishers Weekly

Murder Can Spoil Your Appetite

"Desiree Shapiro is a shining creation."
—Romantic Times

Murder Can Singe Your Old Flame

"Witty dialogue . . . hilarious characters."
—Publishers Weekly

Murder Can Spook Your Cat

"Queen-sized entertainment!" —Barbara D'Amato

Other books in the Desiree Shapiro mystery series
in the order in which they were originally published

MURDER CAN RUN YOUR STOCKINGS

A Desiree Shapiro Mystery

Selma Eichler

A SIGNET BOOK

SIGNET
Published by New American Library, a division of
Penguin Group (USA) Inc., 375 Hudson Street,
New York, New York 10014, USA
Penguin Group (Canada), 90 Eglinton Avenue East, Suite 700, Toronto,
Ontario M4P 2Y3, Canada (a division of Pearson Penguin Canada Inc.)
Penguin Books Ltd., 80 Strand, London WC2R 0RL, England
Penguin Ireland, 25 St. Stephen's Green, Dublin 2,
Ireland (a division of Penguin Books Ltd.)
Penguin Group (Australia), 250 Camberwell Road, Camberwell, Victoria 3124,
Australia (a division of Pearson Australia Group Pty. Ltd.)
Penguin Books India Pvt. Ltd., 11 Community Centre, Panchsheel Park,
New Delhi - 110 017, India
Penguin Group (NZ), cnr Airborne and Rosedale Roads, Albany,
Auckland 1310, New Zealand (a division of Pearson New Zealand Ltd.)
Penguin Books (South Africa) (Pty.) Ltd., 24 Sturdee Avenue,
Rosebank, Johannesburg 2196, South Africa

Penguin Books Ltd., Registered Offices:
80 Strand, London WC2R 0RL, England

First published by Signet, an imprint of New American Library,
a division of Penguin Group (USA) Inc.

First Printing, February 2006
10 9 8 7 6 5 4 3 2 1

PUBLISHER'S NOTE
This is a work of fiction. Names, characters, places, and incidents either are
the product of the author's imagination or are used fictitiously, and any resemblance to actual persons, living or dead, business establishments, events, or
locales is entirely coincidental.
   The publisher does not have any control over and does not assume any
responsibility for author or third-party Web sites or their content.

If you purchased this book without a cover you should be aware that this
book is stolen property. It was reported as "unsold and destroyed" to the
publisher and neither the author nor the publisher has received any payment
for this "stripped book."

To my husband, Lloyd,
for his continuing help and forbearance—
and because Desiree wouldn't have it any other way

ACKNOWLEDGMENTS

Many thanks to—
Antoinetta Monaco and Michael Betman, whose beautiful wedding served as a model for the wedding of Desiree's niece.

My knowledgeable editor, Ellen Edwards, whose guidance, as always, is much appreciated.

My assistant editor, Serena Jones, who helped in so many ways—and always so cheerfully. Serena has since moved on, and I'll miss her. Much good luck, Serena!

Chapter 1

I was frozen with fear.

I gulped. Then I gulped again.

But that didn't keep my stomach from doing somersaults. Or prevent my heart from pounding so hard I thought it would burst out of my chest. That's not all, either. My mouth was totally dry, and my palms were so wet they slid off the armrests.

God! I hate flying!

I suppose I looked as terrified as I felt, because the man seated next to me murmured reassuringly, "It'll be all right. We've just hit a couple of little air pockets, that's all."

Little air pockets? I'd like to know what he'd consider *big* air pockets!

A short time later, when the turbulence finally subsided, the man turned to me again. "Are you all right?" he said kindly.

I eked out what was meant to be a brave smile (but probably came across more like an insipid grin). "I'm fine. Thanks for asking, though."

"You don't seem to care much for air travel," he observed.

"How can you tell?" We both laughed.

Now, this gentleman and I had been sitting side by side for over a half hour. But other than exchanging hellos right after we boarded, we hadn't communicated with each other by so much as a single syllable until our Boeing 767 started jumping up and down.

With those "little" air pockets behind us, however, we began making up for that prior lack of dialogue.

"Are you headed for New York on business or a vacation?" my companion—a tall, balding man of about fifty—inquired.

I told him I lived here, that I'd gone out to Minneapolis to attend a wedding. (My old and dear college friend Christie Wright—a widow like yours truly—had finally said yes to the determined suitor who'd been putting the pertinent question to her for years.)

"What do you do in New York? If you don't mind my asking."

"I don't mind at all. I'm a PI."

"As in private investigator?"

"That's right," I answered curtly, bristling at the incredulous tone. I mean, so what if I'm only five-two? Or that the scale—whenever I'm foolish enough to step on one—proclaims that my weight isn't precisely what the charts dictate it should be? And the fact that I'm slightly more mature than the phony celluloid version of the female PI doesn't say diddly about my ability to do the job, does it?

"I'd never have guessed," the man told me. "I'm an attorney—the name is Ben, by the way, Ben Berlin—and I've hired female investigators on occasion. Believe me, you don't resemble any of them—even remotely. You're so . . . so . . ."

Watch it, buster, I warned him silently.

". . . *soft.*" He wrinkled his forehead for a moment. "What I'm trying to say is that you appear to be much more feminine than the other women investigators I've met up with."

Well, I was okay with that, so patting my glorious hennaed hair, I decided to favor him with another smile. "I should introduce myself, too. I'm Desiree Shapiro. But please call me Desiree. Anyhow, what about you? Are you also from New York?"

"No, from Minneapolis. I'm flying in to attend the funeral of my favorite aunt," he informed me somberly.

"Oh. I'm sorry to hear . . . that is, I'm . . . um . . . very sorry for your loss," I commiserated, struggling for the words. (When it comes to anything like that, it's points when I'm even intelligible.)

Ben's "thank you" was thick with emotion. "I still find it hard to believe she's gone."

"Her death was sudden?"

"Yes. Aunt Bessie is—*was*—no youngster, of course. But as far as I know, she was in good health—and I'm sure I'd have heard if she weren't. As a matter of fact, I spoke to her only last week, and she sounded very chipper . . . so *alive.*" His eyes seemed to be on the verge of filling up, and he shook his head as if to will away the tears. "I was shocked when Joel—her son—left a message on my answering machine last night that she died sometime earlier that day. Apparently it was the result of an accident. At any rate, she's being buried tomorrow."

Unable to come up with an appropriate response, I relied on the all-purpose nod.

"She was really good to me," my companion went on. "You see, my family was originally from Queens—our house was only a couple of blocks from Aunt Bessie's. But then my dad got this job offer in Minnesota, and he couldn't afford to pass it up. I was halfway through my senior year in high school when this occurred, and as you can imagine, I wasn't the least bit anxious to switch schools. Fortunately for me, Aunt Bessie—she was my dad's baby sister—insisted I stay with her until the semester was over. And I obliged her." The trace of a grin here. "Anyway, I've been living in Minneapolis since I graduated high school. My mother and father are both long gone, but my wife and I raised four kids out there."

Neither of us said anything for a few seconds, then Ben added softly, "I wasn't able to see Aunt Bessie as often as I'd have liked to, but we kept in close touch. I'll miss her a lot, Desiree. She was a wonderful woman. She . . ." He didn't finish. I suspect it had something to do with the lump in his throat.

It was just minutes later that this young flight attendant came down the aisle pushing a beverage cart. "Would you care for something to drink, ma'am?" she inquired in a voice that practically defined the word "perky."

"A Coke, please."

"And you, sir?"

Ben was wise enough to decline.

She poured my Coke and was in the process of handing it to me when the plane lurched. But ever so slightly this time—honestly. Still, you'll never guess where most of that drink wound up!

"I'm *awfully* sorry," the girl told me (anyone under thirty is a girl to me), her cheeks instantly becoming an identical match to my hair. As she was busy attempting to pat me dry, however, she evidently had second thoughts. "You really should be a little more careful, though, ma'am. And I do mean that for your own well-being."

"*I* should be more careful?"

"Well, you did jostle my arm a bit."

I was all set to protest. I mean, even my eyeballs had been immobile, for God's sake! But before I could say anything, Miss Klutz had moved on.

Have I mentioned that I hate flying?

I made a quick trip to the rest room to sponge myself off. I returned to find Ben fast asleep. He didn't wake up until we were circling La Guardia Airport.

Once we were on the ground and the plane had bumped its way to a stop, Ben rose and squeezed past me to collect his belongings. But before reaching into the overhead compartment, he glanced down at me. "It was nice meeting you, Desiree. Listen, it's not too likely that we'll be running into each other again, so take care of yourself, huh?"

"You do the same." I fumbled under the seat for a few seconds before making contact with my I LOVE NEW YORK tote bag.

When I raised my head again, my soon-to-be client was gone.

Chapter 2

It was only a week after I flew out to Minneapolis for Christie's wedding that my niece Ellen's lavish nuptials took place.

"Lavish" is no exaggeration, either. Margot, my beloved sister-in-law—and my tongue is planted firmly in my cheek when I call her that—had pulled out all the stops for her daughter's big moment. Or, at least, so I thought. I later learned that Mike's parents (Mike being Ellen's longtime boyfriend, then fiancé, and now—at last!—brand-new husband) had offered to split the cost of the gala right down the middle. And to Ellen's mortification (and, I suspect, her father's, as well), Margot didn't turn them down. More than three hundred gowned and tuxedoed people attended that affair, too, which was held at New York's legendary Plaza Hotel. "I think my mother's inviting everyone she's ever said hello to," Mike had once remarked. Well, apparently Ellen's female parent did the same. One woman I met that evening introduced herself to me as Margot's second cousin twice removed (whatever in God's name *that* is).

At any rate, you couldn't have asked for a more beautiful ceremony. I cried almost from the moment the minister opened his mouth to the second the rabbi wound things up. Which was pretty embarrassing. I mean, as matron of honor I was practically front and center, and there I was, leaking copiously from two facial orifices. To make things worse, the occasional accompanying snuffles provided a little unintended competition for the clergymen at some of the more touching moments of the service. At one point I glimpsed Ellen smiling at me in obvious amusement, my reaction being no big shock to her, since she's frequently caught me bawling during animated features. (Listen, I don't care what anyone says: *Shrek was* very moving.)

And speaking of Ellen, she was absolutely radiant. Her slim white lace gown—a mock turtleneck with long, narrow sleeves—couldn't have been more elegant. Or more perfect. It gave the impression of having been molded to her reed-thin figure. And the simple headpiece was the ideal frame for that lovely face of hers. I've always maintained that Ellen looks very much like the late Audrey Hepburn. But that evening the resemblance was almost uncanny!

As for the groom, Mike cut quite a dashing figure in his white tuxedo. The man is well over six feet tall and really attractive, with sandy hair and clear blue eyes.

Trust me when I tell you that it would be hard to find a handsomer couple. (And I'm certain I'd feel that way even if I weren't slightly prejudiced—and hadn't been the one who introduced them in the first place.)

At any rate, the instant the ceremony was over, I made a beeline for the ladies' lounge to touch up my mascara-mottled face. Following which I joined the rest of the guests in The Terrace.

After sharing hugs and kisses with the bride and groom at the entrance to this large, multi-tiered room, I had a warm exchange with Mike's parents—Allison and Wes Lynton—who were standing only a few paces beyond them. Then, as I was making my way to this long table toward the rear in order to get a closer view of the ice sculpture on display there—and maybe have a taste of one or two of the hors d'oeuvres surrounding the frozen artwork—I bumped smack into Margot. And before I'd had the chance to fortify myself with a glass of wine, too!

"Congratulations, Margot," I told her, forcing myself to peck her cheek.

"Thank you," she mumbled before returning the gesture. But her expression brought to mind that story about the little boy who while munching on an apple one day, discovered just *half* a worm.

Still, I opted for civility. "It was a beautiful ceremony."

"I could hear how much you enjoyed it," retorted the only sister of my late—and very dear—husband, Ed. Then, for good measure: "So could everyone else."

I have no idea how I would have responded if, at that moment, Ellen's father hadn't joined us.

"Desiree!" he exclaimed, handing his wife a cocktail of some kind. "It's been a long time—too long. And I'd like to add that you're pretty as a picture tonight." He stepped away for a better view of my gown—an ankle-length, pale yellow A-line with butterfly sleeves. "That's some dress! You've always had such wonderful taste, hasn't she Margot?" I doubt he actually expected confirmation from his spouse, however, because he was avoiding her gaze. I didn't blame him, either; she was skewering him with her eyes.

"Thanks, Max, and congratulations!" I enthused. "It's great to see you. How have you been?"

"Can't complain, can't complain."

"You look terrific." And he did. Some time ago most of Ellen's family members had relocated to Florida, and Max was sporting a very becoming golden tan. (The same could have been said of Margot, but I'd sooner have pulled out my tongue than say it.)

"Do you know where I can find Steve and Joan?" I inquired, referring to his son and daughter-in-law.

"They're around somewhere. Exactly where, I couldn't tell you. But take a little walk; you're bound to run into them. And wait till you get a load of our grandchildren, Desiree. They're all grown up now, the three of them. By the way, do you know that Minna and Sam are here, too?"

"They're *here*? Ellen must be so pleased. She told me Minna was in the hospital until about five days ago. Is she all right?" Ellen had been almost certain her paternal aunt wouldn't be up to making the trip from Florida.

"She had some surgery, so she's still a little bit weak. But she'll be fine. Anyhow, my sister would have come to this wedding if they had to schlep her here in her hospital bed."

I gave Max a kiss. "I'm going to try and locate everyone. See you both later," I said.

Margot piped up with a "yeah" that was anything but enthusiastic.

Notwithstanding the wall-to-wall people, I managed to acquire a glass of Merlot a couple of minutes later. And despite the frequent pauses I allowed myself in order to take a sip of the wine or sample one of the endless variety of teeny edibles the waiters persisted in tempting me with, I managed to locate Minna and Sam fairly quickly. In light of her recent illness, I was gratified to see how well the older woman looked. I hastily swallowed my shrimp-with-cocktail-sauce, and the three of us chatted for a few minutes. Then Sam pointed me in the general direction of Ellen's brother and his immediate family.

After a short but determined search I came across them. "Desiree! I just toured the room looking for you," Steve told me.

We all greeted one another affectionately. Max was right. The two kids were hardly kids anymore. *Two?* "Somebody's missing," I pronounced.

Joan enlightened me. "Justin."

"Twenty seconds after we walked in here, he zeroed in on a cute little blonde—one of Mike's relatives, I think," Steve said. "He's probably trapped the poor girl in a corner somewhere so he can pitch her."

"I doubt that he'll be successful," Joan put in. "She seemed like a levelheaded young lady to me."

"Wanna bet?" her husband countered with a grin.

He had spotted the approach of his middle son,

whose face was now distinguished by some bright pink lipstick—and a really goofy smile.

"That's my boy," Steve said proudly.

"Chauvinistic pig," Joan muttered, with a playful kick to her husband's shins. (But not so playful it didn't produce an "Ouch!")

I was soon adding to the teenager's colorful face with a little lipstick of my own (a lovely shade of coral, incidentally). Then after I'd visited with Steve and Joan and the three budding Kravitz adults awhile longer, a couple I didn't know rushed over to greet them. So I relinquished my floor space and moved on.

Almost immediately I ran into someone I'd met at Ellen's shower—a friend of Mike's mother's. We had a brief conversation, and the woman had just left me to search for her "gentleman friend" when I felt a hand on my shoulder. I turned around to see a frail, elderly man beaming at me.

"I'm Calvin Strong." (A misnomer if there ever was one.) "You're the maid of honor," he apprised me, sucking on his obviously false bottom teeth. I didn't bother to tell him I was the *matron* of honor. It would probably have been all the same to him anyhow. "What's your name?"

"Desiree Shapiro."

"You got a husband, Desiree?"

Now, considering that our acquaintance dated back less than a minute, I would normally have found a question like that pretty inappropriate. But in light of who posed it, I was amused. "I'm a widow."

"You kiddin'? What a coincidence! I lost my dear, sweet wife a year ago, and I've been a very lonely man ever since."

"I'm . . . uh, so sorry."

"What can you do?" Calvin responded with a shrug. "But, listen, since we're both unattached, you and me, maybe we could have dinner one night—I'll pay."

I can't figure out why I constantly manage to attract these randy old codgers. Maybe a special, undetectable magnet was implanted somewhere on my person one night while I was sleeping. "Um, I don't think so. But thank you for asking me."

"You're turning me down?"

"I'm sorry, but I have to. I'm very busy with my work and—"

"You gotta eat, don'tcha?" And tilting his head and squinting, he took a quick inventory of me. "You look like you got a real good appetite, too—if I might make that observation."

It was at this juncture that a tall, white-haired woman in a gorgeous silver gown joined us. "I've been searching all over for you, Calvin," she scolded. Then, smiling at me: "Aren't you going to introduce me to this lady?"

Calvin licked his lips, and his face turned the color of chalk. "Sure," he responded a couple of seconds later. "Margaret, this is Desiree. Desiree, uh, Margaret."

"His wife," the woman elaborated. And she extended her hand.

Dinner was served in the magnificent Grand Ballroom. I was seated at the head table with Wes Lynton—Mike's father—on one side of me and Steve on the other. Margot and I—fortunately—weren't even within sniping distance of each other.

The meal was delicious: crabmeat in puff pastry for starters, then a salad, then a sorbet, then a choice of prime ribs or fillet of sole. And the best was yet to come. A dessert table had been set up in a separate room across from the dining room—and what desserts it displayed! I couldn't decide between the chocolate mousse and the crêpes suzette. So following a great deal of agonizing, I had both. (After all, this *was* Ellen's wedding.)

Naturally, there was no shortage of champagne, either. And while I normally restrict my imbibing of anything alcoholic to a single glass, that night I more than tripled my intake. Which is the only thing that can possibly account for my sudden metamorphosis into a female Fred Astaire. I mean, I tangoed with Wes—and I had no idea I even knew *how* to tango. And later on, when I cha-cha'd with Steve, I didn't land on his toes. Not even once.

I was outdone in that department by my niece, however. Normally no lighter on her feet than I am (in fact, to tell you the truth, she's a four-star klutz), that night, in the arms of her new husband, Ellen seemed to float across the floor.

All in all, it was a truly magical evening.

One I'd been waiting—and waiting and waiting—for.

Chapter 3

I spent Sunday recuperating from the sensational time I'd had on Saturday. By Monday morning, though, I was more or less ready to get back to work—only unfortunately, at present I didn't have any. Work, that is.

Jackie—my secretary—was on the phone when I came in. (Her desk is right near the entrance.) She looked at me purposefully as she spoke into the mouthpiece. "One moment please, Mr. Berlin. I'll check to see if she's in." And once she'd put the man on hold: "Well? Are you here?"

Berlin . . . Berlin . . . I had to rack what was lately a sorely undertaxed brain before making the connection: the flight home from Minneapolis!

I nodded. Naturally I'd take the call. (But then, I take just about every call.)

I scurried back to my office and picked up. "Well, hi, Ben," I said, doing my best to conceal my surprise at hearing from him.

"I'm so glad I was able to locate you, Desiree," he told me, sounding troubled. "For the past two days I've been trying to remember your last name. It finally came to me about five minutes ago."

"Is something wrong?"

"I believe my aunt Bessie may have been murdered."

"Murdered? What makes you think that?"

"I don't recall if I mentioned how she died."

"You said it was an accident, but you didn't get any more specific than that."

"My aunt broke her neck falling down the basement stairs. The police don't appear to suspect foul play, but right after it happened, the detective in charge of the case—a Sergeant Spence—informed Aunt Bessie's son Joel that they'd be conducting an autopsy. And I couldn't seem to get that out of my mind. So on Friday I contacted the sergeant to verify that this was merely routine. I didn't have the slightest inkling it was anything other than that, you understand, but I wanted reassurance. Well, Sergeant Spence said not to worry. An autopsy is normal procedure in cases like my aunt's where death wasn't due to natural causes. Probably she'd simply lost her footing, he told me. I was feeling relieved—until he remarked that he couldn't figure out why women my aunt's age insist on 'prancing around' in high heels.

"And this is when I began to suspect that Aunt Bessie's 'accident' might not have been an accident after all."

"I'm not following you."

"I'll explain. A year or so ago my aunt tumbled down those same stairs—they're pretty steep. Luckily, though, she was only about three steps from the bottom when she slipped. Still, she managed to break her ankle. What I'm getting at is that Aunt Bessie was wearing fairly high heels that day, which led to her admitting to herself that she was no longer as steady on her feet as she once was. And she swore that, from then on, whenever she went to the basement, it would be in flat shoes."

"Maybe she needed something in a hurry, and she didn't stop to think about what had happened to her before," I speculated.

"I suppose that's possible, but I don't consider it likely. She suffered a lot with that ankle—it didn't heal properly."

"What was in the basement anyway?"

Ben laughed—in spite of himself, I'm sure. "You name it. There's a finished office with the usual files and other office paraphernalia. Joel set it up when he lived at home, and Aunt Bessie appropriated it when he moved out. Just beyond the office—which is fairly small—is a large bookcase filled with books of every variety—encyclopedias, histories, mysteries, children's stories. . . . When I visited her last August I remember seeing a couple of bikes around, too, along with an ancient phonograph and a bunch of records. Oh, and a big box of CDs that Joel kept assuring her he'd pick up and take to his own apartment one of these days."

I assumed Ben was through, but a second later he piped up with, "Wait. I almost forgot. Aunt Bessie had a cedar closet built in the basement about twenty years ago, and she kept a lot of her clothes in it. But let me concentrate for a minute." There was a brief pause, after which he added to the list. "I believe I spotted Donnie's old trombone down there, as well—Donnie's Aunt Bessie's older son; he lives in San Francisco now. There was also a beat-up refrigerator and a stove that was in equally bad shape—both of them still in working order, though. Aunt Bessie stored a supply of canned goods in that place, too."

"How often would you estimate your aunt went to the basement?"

"Maybe once every week or two, maybe less, maybe more—I can't actually say. I heard a sharp intake of breath now. "Listen, I'd really appreciate it if you'd look into this for me, Desiree. It could take a month or longer before the autopsy results come in. And even if the findings confirm that my aunt died of a fall, what would that prove? Can the report tell us whether or not anyone pushed her?"

I had to concede that it probably couldn't. "Do you know of anyone who might have wanted to harm your aunt?" I inquired gently.

"Aunt Bessie was such a good woman that it's not casy for mc to imagine anyone's having that sort of animosity toward her. But there *was* one person who couldn't have been overly fond of her."

"Who was that?"

"I don't have the man's name, but he was a developer who was interested in buying this property my aunt owned in Aubrey, a little town at the New Jersey shore—she and my uncle had purchased a summer home there in the seventies. At any rate, this developer contacted her a few months back. Apparently he wanted to build a shopping mall in Aubrey and acquiring that lot was crucial. He was willing to pay a very good price for it, too.

"Well, Aunt Bessie was actually on the verge of selling—it's been a long time since anyone's made use of that house. But suddenly she changed her mind. What was the rush to get rid of it? she said to me. Suppose she decided one day that she could use a vacation at a nice, restful spot. Or suppose Joel should suddenly want to spend some weekends at the beach. She even managed to convince herself that when Donnie and his wife and kids came East during the summer, as they almost invariably did—he and his wife are both high-school teachers—they might enjoy a week at the Jersey shore. I believe the truth is, though, that when my aunt began thinking about the happy times the family used to have in that house, she became too sentimental to part with it."

"This developer wasn't too pleased with her decision, I gather."

"Evidently her turnaround was really hurting him financially. She told me only a few weeks ago that he was still pressuring her to sell, phoning her regularly with all sorts of inducements. Well, it could be that the man finally concluded that he'd have better luck with one of her heirs."

"But you can't give me his name?"

"I'm afraid I've forgotten it. Either that or Aunt Bessie never mentioned it to me. But I'm pretty certain Joel can tell you how to reach him."

"Is there anyone else your aunt might have had some unpleasantness with? And I'm talking about *any* unpleasantness, no matter how minor."

There was a prolonged silence before Ben responded. "This may not qualify as unpleasantness exactly, but Joel became engaged in October, and Aunt Bessie wasn't thrilled with his choice of fiancée. Not that she said as much, but she did tell me that Frankie isn't Jewish, and I have no doubt this was troubling to my aunt. If anything else about the woman disturbed her, though, she never spoke about it. And incidentally, I'm not altogether sure Frankie was even aware that my aunt had reservations about her."

"Aunt Bessie had no problems with anyone other than the developer and Frankie?"

This time Ben came up empty. "None that I heard about," he said, sounding dispirited. Then suddenly he brightened. "But you might want to talk to one of Aunt Bessie's neighbors, a Mrs. Ross. She and my aunt lived two houses away from each other for almost forty years, and they were very close. If Aunt Bessie confided in anyone, it would be Mrs. Ross." And now, without so much as pausing for breath, Ben put to me, "Well, Desiree, will you take the case? Will you find out what *really* happened to my aunt?"

"I can only promise that I'll do my best."

"Listen, I should probably keep my mouth shut— but how many lawyers are able to do that?" he said with a self-conscious little chuckle. "The fact is, though, that I strongly believe you were predestined to uncover the truth about Aunt Bessie's death, that fate put you on that particular plane on that particular day."

I had to bite my tongue hard to keep from blurting out, *Fate, my tush! Christie's wedding put me on that plane!*

"I don't pretend to be a mystic or anything," Ben went on. "It's just that I have this . . . call it a sixth sense . . . so—" He broke off. And while he managed another chuckle, he was plainly embarrassed. "Anyway, if you think I'm nuts, you're not alone. Last night I shared my feelings about this with my wife, and she's threatening to have me committed."

Wanting to put him at ease, I responded lightly, "I hope you're right; I hope fate *is* involved. I have a sixth sense, too, and it's telling me I'll need whatever help I can get."

At this point Ben inquired about my fee. I quoted my usual reasonable rate (after all, I'm not exactly in the Bo Dietl category), and Ben promptly boosted it a couple of notches.

With a grand total of one client having darkened my door in weeks (said client hiring me to search for a missing teenager—who then decided to return home before I could even begin my investigation), I couldn't bring myself to voice more than a mild protest over the pay raise.

Which, lucky for me, the man elected to disregard.

Chapter 4

I started with the dead woman's son—Joel Herman.

Ben had given me both Joel's office and home numbers, and I tried him at work.

"Lana Stevens Apparel."

"Mr. Herman, please."

"Sure, hon, and *whom* shall I say wishes to speak with Mr. Herman?" inquired this voice that's kind of hard to explain. All I can tell you is that it was low and gravelly, and that my mind instantly conjured up a middle-aged female with inch-thick makeup and bloodred lipstick. I could also envision a neckline that plunged down to here and a skirt that hiked up to there when she crossed her legs. (Which, according to my mental picture, she was doing just then.) And if the lady had long, fake red nails, bleached blond hair (henna, for your information, is not the same as bleach), and a wad of gum in her mouth, it wouldn't exactly have shocked me.

"My name is Desiree Shapiro. Please tell Mr. Herman that his cousin Ben asked me to get in touch with him."

"Cousin who?"

"Ben."

"Would you mind spelling that, hon?"

I couldn't believe it! "B-e-n. Ben."

"Oh, I thought you said 'Bin,' " the woman told me, tittering. "Hold on a sec." And with this, I heard the unmistakable crack of chewing gum. (See? I was

right about that!) Then before putting me on hold:
"Hey, Joel! There's a—"

Moments later Aunt Bessie's younger offspring was
on the line. "Joel Herman speaking. Ben asked you
to call me?"

"Yes. And I'm very sorry to . . . to have to contact
you about something like this, but your cousin believes
that your mother may have . . . that there's a possibility she . . . uh . . . that she was the victim of foul play.
I'm—"

Joel's voice shot up about an octave. "What did you
say?" And before I could respond: "For chrissake!
How did he come up with *that*?"

"Well, he phoned the detective who's handling the
case—a Sgt. Spence—because he was concerned about
the reason an autopsy was being conducted. The detective assured him it was strictly routine, but right
after that he made a comment Ben found very
disturbing."

"What *kind* of comment?"

"It's really too complicated to go into on the telephone, Mr. Herman. I was wondering if we could possibly meet and—"

"Hey, don't play games with me; this is about my
mother! I want to hear what the detective told Ben.
And who *are* you, anyway?"

"My name is Desiree Shapiro, and—"

"Bebe already told me *that*," he snapped. (Bebe, I
took it, being the woman with the gum.)

"I'm a private investigator, Mr. Herman. Ben hired
me to look into your mother's death."

"You're kidding!"

"Look, as you're no doubt aware, Ben loved your
mother very much. And he can't shake the idea that
someone may have intentionally harmed her."

"That's why they're doing an autopsy—to verify
how she died," Joel asserted.

"It could be weeks before the report comes in—
maybe longer. And it's always better to investigate

something like this as soon as possible. With the passing of time, memories fade and the facts have a tendency to become distorted. Plus, it's highly unlikely an autopsy would be able to tell us whether your mother had an accidental fall—or somebody pushed her."

"Listen, Miss Whatever-your-name-is, nobody did anything to my mother. Nobody would want to. She was a very good person. She tripped going down those lousy cellar stairs and broke her neck. Period. I don't want to be rude, but I'm going to call my cousin Ben right now and tell him to find something else to do with his life besides getting everyone all worked up for no reason." And with this pronouncement, the man hung up on me.

God! I hate that!

Later that morning I left my desk for a short while. I hadn't been back for more than a second or two when my secretary and dear friend (ninety-five percent of the time, anyway) buzzed me.

"Where were you?" Jackie demanded.

"In the ladies' room."

"You have yourself a new case?" She was plainly irritated.

"What makes you ask?"

"Somebody named Joel Herman phoned a couple of minutes ago. And since he's the second stranger to call you this morning . . ."

Who was the detective here, anyway? "Well, as a matter of fact, Mrs. Holmes, I did just take on a murder investigation."

Jackie ignored this feeble attempt at levity. "You never said a word to me," she scolded. (I swear, the woman has this talent for making me feel as if I'm about eight years old and she's the one who gave birth to me.)

"I haven't had a chance to. I was going to tell you later. Honestly."

"Sure you were," she retorted before deigning to hang up so I could return the call.

Joel opened the conversation with an apology. "I'm sorry I was so, well, rude before, but even the *thought* that my mom may have been murdered . . . that somebody might actually have . . ." His voice trailed off.

"I understand."

"Ben told me about the high heels. I still believe she needed something from the basement that day and forgot for a minute that she was wearing them."

I viewed this explanation as making perfect sense. (After all, it had also occurred to me.) "It's very likely that you're right," I conceded, "and I hope you are. I'm only trying to determine, to the best of my ability, whether there's anything—besides the shoes, I mean—to add substance to Ben's concern that your mother's death was other than accidental."

I'm not at all certain Joel even heard me. "Or maybe she *didn't* forget what shoes she had on," he mused, "but she didn't want to take the time to change them. So she figured she'd just be extra-careful." Then with a sigh: "Anyway, Ben tried to convince me that this business about the heels—which even he agrees isn't really *proof* of anything—at least raises some doubt as to how my mom died. But if you want my opinion, he's making a lot of fuss for no reason. Still, I suppose it can't hurt if you check things out. Anyhow, he gave me your number, and I promised I'd call you back and answer your questions. So go ahead, ask away."

"It really would be better if we spoke in person—and as soon as you can manage it. We could meet anywhere you say."

"I might as well do it today—this afternoon. Where are you located?"

I gave him the address.

"That's convenient at least. I work right across town, on West Thirty-second and Broadway. I have to stop off and see a customer in a little while, but I could be at your office in about an hour, an hour and a half, if that's okay."

"That would be great."

"But listen, because of what happened, I've had to take a lot of time off from work lately, so I hope we can do this fast."

"I won't keep you long, I promise—only a few minutes."

This, of course, was a big, fat lie. I've never questioned *anyone* for "only a few minutes."

Not by choice, at any rate.

Chapter 5

It was well after twelve when I got off the phone, so I ordered a sandwich and a Coke and ate in. Then I straightened up my office a bit. (The term "office" is a euphemism here; the truth is, it's more like a cigar box with chairs.) And after that I decided to talk to Jackie and see if I could unruffle her feathers a little.

But when I went out to her desk, it was occupied by another woman, who informed me that Jackie was in Elliot Gilbert's office taking dictation, Elliot being one of the partners in the law firm that rents me my workspace. The other partner, by the way, is Pat Sullivan. So take a guess at the name of the firm. (Hint: Think operetta.)

Anyhow, while admittedly the size of my business quarters is nothing to brag about, I *am*—thanks to those two dear souls—in a desirable area, as well as a very nice building. And if I wrote down how little they charge me, just about everyone would figure it was a misprint—everyone from Manhattan at least. That's not all, either. Without having to fork over a penny more, I get to share the services of the best secretary in Manhattan. And, believe it or not, I'm talking about Jackie, who—when she isn't pouting or nagging or attempting to take total control of my life—actually lives up to that designation.

At any rate, with Jackie presently unavailable, I went back to my cigar box to wait for Joel Herman, who showed up about fifteen minutes later.

The deceased's son was a nice-looking young man (not much past thirty, which still qualifies him as "young" in my book). He must have been about five-ten or so and thin, with dark, curly hair and the whitest, straightest teeth you're likely to see outside of a toothpaste ad. We shook hands, then I hung his trench coat on a hanger at the back of the door, while continuing to give him the once-over.

He was dressed in a brown suit, which, while it fit fairly well, was made of an obviously synthetic material. (The shine gave it away.) On the plus side, though, his yellow shirt was neatly pressed. His brown-and-yellow striped tie coordinated perfectly with the rest of the outfit. And his shoes were so highly polished you could practically see your reflection in them.

Joel took the chair next to my desk—his only option, really—and flashed those perfect teeth at me. "So what do you want to ask me, Ms. Shapiro?"

"It's Desiree."

"Okay. And I'm Joel."

"Before I start 'grilling' you"—I was, of course, smiling when I used the word—"can I offer you something to drink? Or cat?"

"Thanks, but I grabbed a bite before heading over here."

"All right, then here goes. Are you aware of anyone who had reason—or *thought* they had reason—" I quickly amended, "to dislike your mother?"

"Ben told you about that real estate developer, right?"

"Yes, but Ben wasn't able to give me the man's name."

"It's Cliff Seymour. He's something, that guy. He was hot for this property my mom owned at the Jersey shore—apparently that land was very important to him. Even after my mother decided not to sell, he wouldn't let up. He kept right on calling and calling her." And now Joel immediately inserted, "But that doesn't mean he killed her. I don't believe *anyone* did."

"And I'm not disputing you. I'm only trying to examine all the possibilities."

"Yeah, I understand," my visitor murmured grudgingly.

"Can you tell me how I can reach Mr. Seymour?"

"I'll go through my mom's papers—she may have his number in her address book. And I'll get back to you tomorrow."

"I'd appreciate it. Was there anyone else your mother had problems with?"

"Well, I suppose I should tell you about Sylvia Vine. She was a distant cousin of Mom's, and until they got into this big argument, they were very close. In fact, when I was growing up, Mom made me call her *Aunt* Sylvia. I think they were that tight because they had so much in common, you know?"

"How do you mean?"

"They came here from Russia at about the same time. They both married men who went into their own retail businesses—my father had a hardware store in Queens, and Uncle Moe, Sylvia's husband, owned a children's clothing store. My brother Donnie and I are around the same age as Sylvia's two sons. Plus, Mom and Sylvia were widowed within a year of each other."

"Do you have any idea what caused the trouble between them?"

"What happened was, in August—or it could have been September—my mother said she'd lend Sylvia's son Richie a few thou to help him buy into this little company. But then, less than a week later, he was arrested for—" Scowling, Joel stopped cold. "I'm not exactly sure *what* they got him for," he admitted, plainly irritated with himself. "Fraud, I think. He never did time or anything; he ratted out this other guy who was also involved in whatever it was, and he copped a plea. The fraud thing had nothing to do with the company Richie was interested in, but Mom reneged anyway; she said she didn't want to invest in someone who wasn't honest."

"And I take it this ended the women's friendship."

"Yeah. Mom was heartbroken about the split, too, and for a while she wouldn't let up about it." Then, shaking his head, Joel mumbled bitterly, "Sylvia didn't even bother to show up at the funeral."

"Incidentally, this Richie—were you and he friends?"

"Uh-uh. I never really liked him."

I moved on. "Is there anyone else your mother had been feuding with? It needn't have involved a world-class argument; I'll settle for a few harsh words."

"No, not that I know of."

And now I leaned across my desk. "Uh, please don't be offended, Joel, but I have to ask." He was peering at me warily as I said the words that were bound to inflame him: "How did your mother feel about your fiancée?"

Joel's eyes narrowed to mere slits, and he spat out his response. "What did Ben tell you?"

"Nothing, actually. Only that you became engaged in October and that he couldn't say how your mother and your fiancée got along."

"Why the hell did he have to start all this?" Joel all but shouted. "Hey, she wasn't *his* mother. He shouldn't have gotten you involved without checking with Donnie and me first. As far as we were concerned, my mom's death was an accident. And it still is—unless the police say otherwise."

"Your mother meant a great deal to Ben, Joel. And, rightly or wrongly, he has this strong suspicion that she was a homicide victim. As I mentioned on the phone, the reason he was so anxious to bring in an outside investigator is because it's not too probable the autopsy can determine whether your mother fell or was pushed down those stairs. And if she *was* pushed, it certainly won't establish who did the pushing."

"Yeah, I know all that," the young man responded sourly.

"I'm sure that it wasn't his intention to bypass you and your brother. It's only that in his determination to see that his Aunt Bessie's killer is brought to justice, he didn't stop to consider that he should have consulted with her sons before hiring a PI."

"He had no business going ahead on his own," Joel insisted. "But since he already did, I guess I might as well cooperate with you; I don't seem to have much choice." He let out a sigh. "Okay, you asked about Frankie. I won't b.s. you and claim that my mother was crazy about her from the get-go. She was upset about Frankie's not being Jewish. But it's not like Mom had anything personal against her. How could she? I brought Frankie there a big two times."

"And your fiancée's feelings toward your mother?"

"She sensed that being Protestant wasn't winning her any points with my mom. But in spite of that, Frankie actually *liked* her. And Frankie's a very positive-type person. She didn't have any doubt they'd eventually wind up friends—and she would have been right, too. Before she died, Mom had already begun to soften toward her." Almost instantly Joel added a vehement postscript to this, accompanying it with an unmistakably hostile expression. "So if you're thinking Frankie had anything to do with my mother's death, you're out of your head."

"I wasn't thinking that at all. Let's start with the iffy premise that a crime was even committed in this instance. Well, it's my job to gather all the facts about the victim's interaction with various people. But believe me, the purpose of my questions isn't only to establish who might have had a motive for assaulting your mother; they're also designed to help me figure out who didn't."

"If that's the truth, then I apologize for blowing my stack. I wanted to straighten you out about Frankie, that's all."

"You say your mother had softened toward her?"

"That's right. The day Mom died? I got a call from Frankie. She sounded really pleased, you know? She had just been to my mom's, and we were invited to have dinner there that night. I asked what was going on, and Frankie said she wasn't really sure, but she felt that things might be looking up.

"*Looking up?*" he sputtered. "When I got to the house I found my mother dead!"

"How terrible for you! I'm so sorry."

Joel appeared to be close to tears when he murmured his thanks.

I waited until I was reasonably confident that his emotions were under control, then inquired gently, "Um, you said *you* found your mother. Frankie wasn't with you?"

"No, we went there separately—Frankie had a couple of errands to run first. Besides, we each have our own place"—he made a face—"a tiny studio. We've been hunting for a nice one-bedroom so we can move in together, but everything we like we can't afford. And everything we *can* afford we hate."

"So . . . uh . . . Frankie reached you at your apartment to notify you that you were expected at your mom's that evening?"

Joel nodded. "I was there all day setting up my new computer."

He was apparently still too shaken to recognize that I was attempting to learn whether he had an alibi for the time of his mother's death. Nevertheless, I was aware that I was pushing my luck when I proceeded with the follow-up question. "Can anyone verify that you were at home all afternoon? A neighbor perhaps? Or maybe there were some phone calls?"

"No neighbors, no calls. But I didn't kill my mother." He said it between clenched teeth.

"Please don't be offended, Joel," I put in hastily, fearful that any moment now he might make a run for it. "I only asked because I need the information for my records." He didn't respond, but at least he was still sitting there. "Um, what time did you arrive at your mother's?"

"Seven, seven-fifteen."

"You have a key to the house?"

"Yeah, but I didn't use it. First I rang the bell—

three, maybe four times. She was expecting us, but I didn't want to just barge in on her like that, you know? Anyway, I was about to take out my key when I noticed that the door was a little ajar."

"And you went in."

"Yeah. There was a light on in the kitchen, so I headed straight back there. The door to the basement was wide open—it's in the kitchen—and I called out to my mother. When there wasn't any answer, I walked over there and called out again. Then I looked down—the light was on—and I saw her lying at the bottom of the steps. It was . . . it was awful, the sort of thing you never forget." Joel swiped at his eyes with the back of his hand before continuing.

"Anyhow, I ran down the stairs and put my ear to Mom's chest. But her heart didn't seem to be beating. I remembered seeing something on TV about being able to tell whether someone has a pulse by placing two fingers on their neck, so I tried that, too. Nothing. I wanted to put her head in my lap, but if there was any chance she was still alive, my moving her like that could have added to her injuries, you know? So I took out my cell phone and dialed 911, praying all the while that I was wrong, that she wasn't dead after all. Then I sat on the floor with her until Emergency Services arrived. Frankie got there about five minutes after they did. It was an awful shock to her, too." He managed a brave smile. Following which he looked stricken again.

"Are you all right?"

"I guess so."

"By the way, your mother's dinner invitation—was there something special that prompted it?"

"Like I told you, Frankie had been to see her that afternoon. She thought that if Mom realized how committed she was to me, it could—"

"Excuse me. Your mother was aware your fiancée would be stopping by?"

"No. Frankie said afterward that she couldn't stand my being so unhappy because of this . . . this problem with my mom. She was certain my mom must be hurting, as well, so she decided it might help if she went over there and they talked things out. Frankie offered to convert to Judaism that day, too—something that had to mean a lot to my mother. In fact, Mom's whole attitude was different after that. The upshot was that she told Frankie she wanted us both to come to dinner later. She was going to make us beef Stroganoff."

At this point I breathed deeply, stiffened my spine, and took the plunge. "I imagine you must have been pretty angry with your mother for feeling as she did about your fiancée."

Surprisingly, Joel seemed unperturbed by the comment. "Maybe a little," he answered thoughtfully. "But more than that, I suppose I was hurt. I was always sure that when I made the important decisions in my life, Mom would be in my corner—no matter what. But after I got engaged, whenever I spoke to her on the phone the two of us would start arguing about Frankie. That changed a few weeks ago, though. We both cooled it a bit, you know? It was like we had a kind of truce—only neither of us had declared one. And, of course, at the end . . ." He didn't finish. He didn't have to.

"You felt you had cause to be optimistic."

"Definitely."

"Something's been puzzling me, Joel." And I posed the question that had been on my mind ever since Ben had asked me to investigate Aunt Bessie's fall. "Did your mother usually walk around the house in high heels?"

"Of course not. A friend of hers was supposed to pick her up at one-thirty that afternoon. They'd planned to drive into Manhattan to do some shopping, and then Mom was going to treat Mrs. Ring to dinner—she's the friend, and it was her birthday. But Mrs. Ring called about two o'clock to say her car had broken down and they'd have to make it another time. Frankie rang the doorbell before my mother had an opportunity to change her clothes."

"And you know about your mother's plans—how?"

"Mom explained to Frankie that this was why she was all dressed up."

"When you found your mother, was she still wearing the same clothes she had on when Frankie was there earlier?"

"I can't say for sure. But it wasn't the kind of outfit she normally wore unless she was going someplace, so I suppose it was the same."

I pondered this for a moment. "It would appear that your mother tumbled down those stairs soon after Frankie left her. Otherwise, she would have put on more comfortable clothing."

"Unless she got a telephone call before she had a chance to run upstairs," Joel proposed. "The conversation could have lasted an hour or longer—my mom was quite a talker. Or," he said thoughtfully, "now that she was having Frankie and me over for dinner, she might have needed something at the store—it's only a block away—and she decided she'd change when she got back. Or maybe it was both: She received the call, then went to the store. Or vice versa. And it wasn't until *after that* that she fell down the stairs."

"I guess any of those things could have kept her in her good clothes for a while," I conceded. "Uh, listen, Joel, it might be helpful if I had a look around your mom's house. Would it be possible for me to see the place?"

Joel responded with a shrug. "When did you want to do it?"

"Is tomorrow okay with you?"

He reached into his pocket and removed a key from a leather case. "Here," he said, placing it in my open hand. "Stick it in the flowerpot on the back porch when you leave. And let me know if you change your mind about going over there tomorrow."

"I will, Joel. And thanks a lot. Oh, by the way, did you happen to notice any cooking aromas or food in the kitchen—perhaps something on the stove—when you walked in that night?"

"No. There was nothing like that at all. And I remember this struck me as sort of strange. The table was set, though—like for company."

Well, with beef Stroganoff's requiring only a half hour to prepare, it was conceivable, although not very likely, that Bessie had planned on waiting until six-thirty or so before starting dinner. Which didn't do all that much to narrow the time frame for her death.

"One more thing. Can you think of any reason your mother might have had for going to the basement that day?"

"This cop asked me that, too—the one who came to the house with the ambulance. I told him my mother went down there pretty often. She'd store stuff in that refrigerator when the one upstairs got too crowded. I said maybe she had to take something out or else put something in it. Frankie told him the same thing."

Highly agitated now, Joel ran his fingers through his hair. "I suppose it's occurred to you that it's possible—*very* possible—Mom had that fall because she was on her way downstairs to take out the meat for our dinner—Frankie's and mine. God! I *hate* to think that could be it!"

I was trying for some words of consolation when Joel checked his watch. "Look at the time! I gotta get going!" And he sprang from the chair.

Glancing at my own watch, I feigned astonishment. "Oh my! I had no idea how late it was. Give me one more minute, though. I need you to tell me how I can get in touch with Frankie and with Sylvia Vine and her son."

Joel grabbed his coat. "I'll call you in the morning."

"I was hoping to contact them today," I protested.

But Joel had already made his exit—or, more accurately, his escape.

Chapter 6

No one had mentioned Frankie's last name. I didn't know where the developer was located or what his company was called. And I hadn't a clue how to contact Sylvia Vine, either.

No problem, though, I consoled myself; I'd start with Mrs. Ross. There wouldn't be any difficulty getting in touch with *her*—her house was just a couple of doors away from the home of the deceased. Then it dawned on me: While I'd been told Aunt Bessie had lived in Queens, I had no idea *where* in Queens. I mean, there were dozens of towns in that borough. So finding the right Ross in Queens shouldn't be any more of a hassle than finding the right Chan in Chinatown.

I called Ben Berlin.

"Aunt Bessie's place is in Ozone Park," he informed me, after which he supplied the address. "Joel didn't get in touch with you?"

"Yes, he did. As a matter of fact, he came to my office this afternoon, only he had to leave in a hurry. He said he'd phone me tomorrow with all the particulars, but I'm anxious to start setting up appointments today if I can. Would you happen to know how to reach Joel's fiancée—Frankie?"

"All I can say for certain is that her surname is Murray. I understand she has her own apartment, but don't ask me where. And I believe she works in a dress shop, but unfortunately, I don't recall the name of the place." He managed a halfhearted chuckle. "What else can't I help you with?"

"Do you know how I can contact Sylvia Vine?"

"Sylvia Vine? That sounds vaguely familiar. Who is she?"

"A former friend and distant relative of your aunt's—no doubt of yours, as well."

"Sylvia Vine?" Ben repeated. A second or two of silence followed, after which he said uncertainly, "You don't mean Sylvia *Levine,* do you?"

"It's very possible I do. She could have knocked a couple of letters off her name."

"Now I remember! That's exactly what she did!"

"Apparently there was some recent animosity between this Sylvia and your aunt. Did your aunt ever talk to you about it?"

"No, she didn't. Actually, it was a long while back that Aunt Bessie even mentioned Sylvia's name to me. Last I heard, though, the woman was living somewhere on Long Island. But I couldn't say which town. I really have to apologize, Desiree. I'm not making your job any easier, am I?"

What a nice man! "Don't worry, Ben. I can try Mrs. Ross this afternoon. And Joel will probably give me most of the other information I need in the morning."

"You'll keep me advised on how the investigation's going, won't you?"

"Of course."

As soon as the conversation with Ben ended, I called Information.

There was a listing for a Cassie Ross in Ozone Park with an address on the same street as Aunt Bessie's. I wasted no time in dialing the number.

"Hello, this is Cassie," a raspy female voice announced. "We can't take your call just now. At the sound of the beep—"

I hung up without leaving a message; I'd phone her again later. In the meantime I thought it might not be a bad idea, in the interests of peace and tranquility, to set things right with Jackie. Although what she regarded as my latest transgression was, as my transgressions go, definitely of the minor variety—even from her perspective.

I went out to her desk. "Hi, Jackie," I said in what I hoped was a tone that conveyed contrition, sincerity, and warmth. But I guess this was too much to expect two little words to deliver.

She looked up from her typing. But there was no pleasant smile. No friendly greeting. Only a blank stare.

"Can we talk for a minute, Jackie?"

She hunched her shoulders. "Go ahead."

"I'm sorry for not mentioning my new case to you, but—"

"Listen, Desiree, last week you were carrying on like crazy about not having any clients, and I really felt for you, too. In fact, I *worried* about you. What happens when things improve, though? You're struck dumb. Obviously you can't be bothered sharing the good stuff. Not with me, anyway."

I recognized that she might have a point there. I did mention my lack of business to Jackie—although I absolutely deny "carrying on like crazy" about it. To the best of my recollection, I'd merely made a couple of comments on the subject in passing. I wasn't about to challenge her, however. The truth is, it takes a braver woman than I am to go toe-to-toe with Jackie. "You're absolutely right. I should have told you about the case—and I intended to. I haven't had much of a chance, though." She was frowning now, so before she could respond, I added quickly, "But I should have made sure I got to you regardless."

"Okay," Jackie said benevolently, "let's forget it. But I want all the details later." And she went so far as to favor me with a kind of semi-smile before she resumed her typing.

A short while after returning to my cubbyhole, I tried Mrs. Ross again. This time she picked up. I explained who I was, and she agreed to see me the following morning at ten.

* * *

It was around six o'clock when I walked into the apartment. I'd just locked the door behind me when the phone rang. I rushed over to the desk so I could grab the receiver before the answering machine kicked in. (The damn thing makes me sound like Minnie Mouse—no doubt due to some malfunction in the instrument.)

"Hi, Dez." The instant I heard the voice, I broke into what must have been a very stupid-looking grin. Then I started to tingle.

I suppose it might be a good idea to backtrack a little here and fill you in on my relationship with Nick Grainger. . . .

The man is bright, considerate, articulate, funny. . . . He has all sorts of admirable qualities. As to his appearance, he's short and skinny, with pale skin and thinning hair. And, oh yes, his teeth are slightly bucked. In other words, looks-wise he's just about perfect—at least from where I sit. You see, I seem to have this nurturing thing (it's the only way I can explain my penchant for the needy-looking types), and Nick gives the impression of urgently requiring a nourishing, home-cooked meal. Along with some world-class—but unobtrusive—mothering, of course.

Our relationship—or whatever you want to call it— hasn't exactly been ideal, though. Almost from the beginning I recognized that the physical aspect needed work. (There *wasn't* any physical aspect.) Still, I was willing to hang in and see what developed. But then I discovered that the man has one major flaw: It's called Derek.

The first time I met Nick's nine-year-old son was when the three of us went to dinner together. At the outset, things appeared to be extremely promising. I was actually under the impression that the kid and I were bonding—until Nick left us to go to the men's room. This is when Derek informed me—very pointedly—that his divorced parents would be remarrying. "You wait and see," he said. And he punctuated this declaration by deliberately spilling his frozen hot chocolate in my lap! When Nick returned to the table, though, the little bastard was all tears and apologies regarding the "accident." I played along with him, too. Listen, what choice did I have? Who was Nick going to believe: a woman he'd been dating casually (too casually, if you want my opinion) or his own darling child?

The worst, however, was yet to come.

Sometime after that I invited Nick to dinner at my apartment. It was my intention to put a famous old adage to the ultimate test that Sunday evening: I was going to find out if this particular man's heart could be reached via his stomach.

But the Fates played me dirty.

A shrill and incessant ringing jolted me out of a sound sleep on Sunday morning at an ungodly nine a.m. (It *was* a weekend, for heaven's sake!) Nick was calling to inform me that his ex had just notified him she wouldn't be retrieving her son later today as planned. Derek, she'd said, was all Nick's until Monday morning!

Well, this being the case, Nick suggested we go out to eat. The thing is, though, I'd spent hours in the kitchen the night before, and much of the dinner was already prepared. What's more, earlier on Saturday I'd launched a vicious attack on my apartment, scrubbing and vacuuming and polishing until every square inch of it was positively twinkling—and all the long-neglected muscles in my body were screaming out in protest. I wasn't about to let my efforts be for nothing, so I insisted that Nick come over with Derek. I mean, considering that I was on red alert, what could The Kid From Hell possibly do to me?

I'll tell you what he could do: sneak into the kitchen and dump a bottle of pepper into my boeuf Bourguignon, that's what! Naturally, the dish was inedible. But I wasn't willing to see what would happen if I were to level with Nick about his progeny's latest little caper. So I tossed the stew into the sink and told Nick

I'd intended to pour off some of the fat but had lost my footing.

Nevertheless, things came to a head that night.

The three of us had adjourned to a Chinese restaurant. We were sitting there, waiting for the check, when a casual remark from another patron caused Derek to throw a tantrum, during which he wound up blurting out his true feelings toward me. And, take my word for it, they were hardly of the warm and fuzzy variety. That sweet boy was in great voice that night, too; just about everyone in the Black Pearl turned around and stared. I ran out of the place as fast as my abbreviated and underused legs would permit, Nick calling after me that he'd phone the next day.

I didn't hear from him the next day, though. Or the next. Or the next . . . However, that disastrous get-together had finally convinced me that there was no point in our continuing to go out. I mean, I couldn't imagine this thing's having a happy ending—not when it was so apparent that Nick's beloved little heir would enjoy nothing more than attending my funeral. Nevertheless, I was disappointed in the man. I mean, he could have at least called to commiserate with me a bit and then we could have said a proper goodbye and wished each other well.

It was more than two weeks before Nick finally picked up the receiver. He'd been mortified by his son's conduct, he told me, and he hadn't called because he hadn't known what to say to me.

Men!

Anyway, being that I'm of such resolute character, I allowed Nick to persuade me to see him again. (To be honest, it didn't require all that much persuading, either.)

We had dinner last Wednesday, and except for some initial awkwardness, it was a very pleasant evening. Not only that, it ended with a kiss. And I'm not talking about the piss-poor, perfunctory little busses he'd been planting on me until then. This one was the real thing!

But to get back to Monday night's phone call . . .

Nick and I inquired politely about each other's health. Then once it was established that he was fine and that I was also fine, he asked about Ellen's wedding. (Considering the tentative nature of our relationship, I hadn't invited him to escort me.)

"It was beautiful. The ceremony was beautiful. *She* was beautiful. Mike was beautiful. And the food was sublime."

"I'm glad you didn't tell me the food was beautiful, too."

"As a matter of fact, it was." We both laughed.

"Listen, I called to wish you a Merry Christmas and a Happy New Year. Derek and I are leaving for Florida tomorrow." (Nick's parents spend part of the year in Boca Raton now.)

"Yes, I know; you mentioned it last week. Anyway, I wish you the same. And I hope you have a great time down there. Your folks must be very anxious to see the two of you."

"Especially their grandson—who deserves a vacation in Siberia. But I promised my parents months ago that I'd bring him down for the holidays—my mom's really big on holidays. And I wouldn't feel right punishing *them* for Derek's atrocious behavior."

"Of course not. Incidentally, who's minding the store?" I meant that literally. Nick owns a florist's shop on Lexington Avenue, six blocks from the apartment building where we both live.

"Emil—my helper—will be looking after things. And Emil has a nephew—a very nice boy—who's home from college, and he'll be lending a hand." There was a pause here that was long enough to prompt me to try to fill the vacuum. But while I was floundering around for something to say, Nick spoke again. "Uh, Desiree?"

"Yes?"

"I could really kick myself for agreeing to stay at my parents' until after New Year's," he said softly. "I'd have liked to spend New Year's Eve with you."

I was still toying with the idea of admitting I'd have liked that, too, when I realized that Nick was no longer on the line.

Chapter 7

Cassie Ross's house was so . . . so *Christmasy* that I came close to blubbering.

I'd been doing my best to banish the holiday from my head, since there was no one around to share it with. Nick, as you know, was off to Florida with The Kid From Hell. And Ellen and Mike were spending Christmas in Greenwich, Connecticut, with Mike's parents. I'd been invited too, but although I like the Lyntons a lot, I wouldn't have been comfortable joining them now. Maybe it's because it would have made me feel like a pity case.

I also had to cross out all of my friends. A couple of days ago Pat Wizniak (who not that long ago was Pat Martucci) left town with husband number four to go skiing in Vermont. And both tonight and tomorrow Jackie would be in the company of her elderly and practically forever beau, Derwin, the silver-toupee-topped gentleman for whom the term "skinflint" must have been invented.

I couldn't hang out with any of my buddies in the building, either.

This afternoon Harriet and Steve Gould, who live directly across the hall, were driving out to Yardley, Pennsylvania, home of the parents of daughter-in-law Hyacinth. (And you snickered at "Desiree.")

As for Barbara Gleason, whose apartment and mine share a common wall, there's good news and not-so-good news. I'll begin with the good news. After orchestrating I don't know how many colossal failures, this past week her ninety-year-old matchmaking Aunt Theresa had finally arranged a blind date for her that could actually have potential. Now, if the man met all of Barbara's usual criteria, this would mean that he was intelligent, kind, generous, personable, and the earner of large bucks. In this instance, however, it seemed that Barbara had dumped one of the requirements. Like her, the guy was a teacher, so I couldn't quite see him zipping around in his own plane or setting up residence at Trump Tower. At any rate, the not-so-good news (as far as I was concerned) was that he was taking Barbara to dinner tonight, and tomorrow she was preparing a meal for *him*. Which meant she'd be tied up both Christmas Eve *and* Christmas Day. Okay, call me selfish. The truth is, I'm really, *really* happy that my friend has met someone she cares about. Only would it have hurt Aunt Theresa to wait another week or two before testing her matchmaking skills again?

But to get back to Cassie Ross and that house of hers . . .

As soon as I pulled up in front of the small wood-and-brick dwelling, who did I see waiting on the front lawn to greet me? A plaster of Paris Santa, along with all eight of his stupid reindeer! And naturally, when I walked up the front steps, there was a huge wreath on the door. Then once inside, Cassie said proudly, "Come see our tree."

Oh, shit! But a "no thanks" was out of the question.

The tree was something, all right. Standing in the center of the living room, it was gigantic, completely dwarfing everything around it. But the decorations were what made the tree really unique. I'm not talking tinsel and balls here. What seemed to be miles of popcorn had been strung together and draped over its branches. There were all-day suckers hanging here and there. And little bags of cookies and snacks were fastened to colorful ribbons and strewn just about everywhere. I had to look away. The tree not only depressed me further, it reminded me of how hungry I was, besides.

"This is really so creative . . . so . . . so *artistic!*" I gushed to a beaming Cassie once the mandatory viewing was over. And now I followed her into a cheerful green-and-white kitchen that smelled of baked goods and coffee.

"Sit," she commanded. I sat, delighted to note that the table was set for two and that at its center was a platter of what had to be fresh-from-the-oven blueberry muffins. "I hope you drink coffee," she declared. "If not, I'll make you some tea."

"Coffee's fine, thank you."

"Good." Cassie glanced at the muffins, then back at me. "Uh, you're not on a diet or anything, are you?"

"Do I look like I am?" I put to her quite reasonably.

"Not exactly," she responded with an embarrassed little titter. She poured us both some coffee. After which she took a seat herself.

Cassie was something of a surprise to me. I had figured Aunt Bessie to be somewhere in her seventies and had taken it for granted that her good pal was about the same age. But this lady was certainly years younger—although just how many years I couldn't say. A tall, vigorous-looking woman, she was dressed in a coral turtleneck sweater and a pair of fashionable beige Capri pants (the latter barely managing to contain her more than ample curves). Her dark curly hair had only a few gray strands. And the olive skin didn't give away any secrets, either—it was virtually unlined.

"Help yourself," she said, passing the platter to me. I was only too happy to oblige her. (I had overslept that morning, so all I'd had time for were two slices of toast and jelly—one consumed on the way out the door—and a few sips of coffee.)

"Eat! Eat!" Cassie instructed after I'd placed a muffin on my plate.

I buttered the muffin (it's the only way, really), then

took a bite. "This is delicious," I told the watching Cassie—right before getting in another bite.

"Yeah, well, I'm not as good a baker as Bess was—she was fantastic, may she rest in peace—but I do okay." It was a couple of seconds before I realized—quick-witted individual that I am—that she was referring to Aunt Bessie.

I sneaked in bite number three before saying, "Um, I'd like to ask you about Bess, if you don't mind."

"I expect you to. That's why you're here, isn't it?" But my first question hadn't even made it past my lips when Cassie put in, "You mentioned on the phone that her nephew, Ben, thinks she was *pushed* down those stairs."

"He thinks she might have been, yes. But we can't be certain. Not yet, at any rate."

"I can't believe anyone would do a thing like that to Bess. You've never met a sweeter person. Next to my husband and kids, I was closer to her than to anyone else in the world."

"I'm so sorry. Her death must have been a terrible loss to you. Were you friends for a long time?"

"Since I was a young bride. She sort of adopted me when I moved into the neighborhood, and ever since then . . . Well, all I can say is, I miss her like hell." Cassie's lower lip began to quiver, and I was afraid I might be in for a crying jag. But she picked up her napkin and dabbed at her eyes. She seemed to be okay then; still, I held off for a bit before continuing.

"Did you spend much time in each other's company?"

"It depends on what you mean by 'much.' Every week or two we'd get together for 'coffee and'—either she'd come over here or I'd go over there. I did tell you what a terrific baker Bess is—I mean *was*—didn't I? Anyhow, we'd sit around for about an hour chatting and stuffing our faces. We went shopping together once in a while, too. And we never had any kind of celebration in this house without including Bess and her family—and vice versa."

"I'm hoping she might have confided something to you that could help me with my investigation. Did she ever speak to you about any disagreements she had?"

"Not the kind that would make someone want to kill her. At least, not someone normal. Although how can you tell who's normal? Especially nowadays."

"I understand Mrs. Herman had an argument with another good friend of hers pretty recently. Did she talk to you about that?"

"You're referring to Sylvia."

"That's right. Sylvia Vine."

"It was 'Levine' when Bess first introduced me to her—she changed the name a few years back," Cassie informed me dryly. "The woman blew her stack because Bess decided not to lend her son Richie a few thousand bucks—I'm not sure of the exact amount."

"From what I hear, this was money Mrs. Herman had previously promised him so he could buy into some company."

"True. Only right after she agreed to help him out, the dumb kid—if you can call a person in his thirties a kid—gets himself busted."

"Joel said something about his being arrested for fraud."

"I don't know what they called it. All I can tell you is that Richie and this other sleaze were collecting money for a charity that didn't exist. The cops pulled the two of 'em in, but Richie was lucky. His buddy, who they say was the brains behind the scam, had been in trouble with the police before. Accumulated a nice little record for himself, too. The upshot was that Richie squealed on his pal and got off with doing community service. But once Bess learned what he'd been up to, that was that. And I don't blame her one bit. Now have another muffin. I got a ton of 'em."

"Thank you, but I—"

"Listen, Desiree—okay if I call you Desiree?"

"Please do."

"Good. I'm not a formal type person You call me Cassie. Anyhow, turning down one teeny muffin won't get you a shape like Halle Berry's. Trust me." And with this, she plucked another muffin from the platter and, leaning across the table, unceremoniously deposited it on my plate with the usual command: "Eat!" Then after restocking her own plate, she asked if I wanted more coffee.

"I'd love some, thanks."

Cassie got up to refill both cups, and I busied myself with obeying her dictate.

When she sat down again I had another question for her. "What do you know about a hassle regarding Mrs. Herman's decision not to part with some property at the Jersey shore?"

"All there is to know, I suppose. Originally, Bess intended to sell the house she owned down there, only she got sentimental about the place and changed her mind. But this real estate guy was after her to change it back again. He needed her land so he could build a mall in the area. Anyhow, he kept pestering the hell out of her."

"Was she afraid that he might physically harm her?"

"Oh, no. That never occurred to her."

"You wouldn't, by any chance, have any idea how I can contact this man?" (I'd left the apartment too early to get that information from Joel—presuming he carried through on his promise to phone me with it this morning, I mean.)

"Uh-uh. All I remember is his name was Rocky something-or-other."

I grinned. "It's Cliff. Cliff Seymour."

Cassie chuckled. "Cliff . . . Rocky. Same difference, right?"

"I don't imagine you're familiar with the name of his company, either."

"You got it."

"And Sylvia and Richie? Can you tell me how I can reach them?"

"I don't have Sylvia's address or phone number, but

she lives on Long Island—Great Neck. I have no idea where Richie lives, though."

"Er, one thing more. How did Mrs. Herman and her son get along?"

"Bess had two sons, you know. She had a great relationship with the older one—Donnie. And it didn't have anything to do with his living way out on the West Coast, either. They were always close; Bess was a very caring mother. As for Joel, she was every bit as devoted to him as she was to Donnie, although I could tell how disappointed she was when he didn't go on to college like his brother. Not that she ever came out and said as much—not in so many words, anyhow. Still, for a while I had this notion that the college thing was causing some friction between them. But listen, this was years ago. And I think it was the only thing her Joel ever did—or, in this case, *didn't* do—that really upset Bess. That is, until he got involved with that chippy of his   pardon me, fi*nan*cee," she amended, deliberately mangling the word.

"You've met Frankie?"

"No, but I heard a lot about her. Bess was concerned that she wasn't kosher. You know what I mean?"

Boy, did I! "She wanted Joel to marry a nice Jewish girl," I responded sourly, instantly recalling the frigid reception my like-minded sister-in-law had accorded that nice Catholic girl her brother brought home a long time ago—namely me. (Of course, it also didn't help that we'd hated each other on sight.) Years later, however, when Ellen became engaged to Mike—who's Protestant—Margot was straining at the leash to welcome him into the family. And while it's *possible* she'd altered her view on interfaith unions, no one will ever convince me that it wasn't the M.D. after Mike's name that actually made the difference.

"Well, she would have preferred it if Joel did marry someone Jewish," Cassie was saying. "She felt that there can be problems when you marry outside your religion. And I agree."

"There can be problems when you marry *inside* your religion, too," I reminded her.

"Sure," Cassie conceded, "but there's one less cause for friction when the couple are both the same faith, wouldn't you say so?" Apparently she wasn't that anxious to learn whether I would say so or not, because she went on without waiting for an answer. "Listen, I don't want you to get the wrong impression of Bess. I'm Episcopalian. I go to church every Sunday, too, rain or shine. Bess respected my religion, and I respected hers; we were best friends for thirty years. Anyhow, when I mentioned her having this sense that Frankie wasn't kosher, it had nothing to do with religion—it was just an expression. What I meant was, Bess believed that there was something about the girl that wasn't *right*, that she wasn't the type of person she was trying to present herself to be."

"How so?"

"The first time they met, Bess saw how Joel's new honey was leading him around by the nose: contradicting him, interrupting when he was trying to make a point, that kind of stuff. Only Frankie was real clever about how she phrased things. Also, she spoke in this sweet little-girl voice. Joel didn't even seem to be aware that half the time she was putting him down.

"And that wasn't all that bothered Bess. Both evenings they spent together, Frankie managed to get in how Joel was chomping at the bit to open his own clothing store, something he'd never said word one about to his mother. The girl also claimed that being in the same field—Frankie works in some dress shop— she could be a tremendous help to him. Bess said she made it sound like success was practically guaranteed. There was one catch, though, Frankie told Bess. She and Joel didn't have much in the way of liquid assets. *Liquid assets, my rear end!* Together, those two don't have a pot to piss in—excuse the language."

"Did Frankie actually ask Bess for money?"

"Not in so many words, no. But she wasn't bringing up that store business just for fun."

"What did Joel have to say about it?"

"He wasn't in the room when either of those conversations took place. If I remember right, one time it was after dinner, and Frankie was in the kitchen with Bess—giving her a hand with the dishes so she could hit her up for the dough."

"I assume from what you're telling me that Bess was well off financially."

"I never counted her money, but I believe she was fairly comfortable."

"Something puzzles me. According to what Bess said to Ben, her only real objection to Joel's fiancée had to do with the girl's religion."

"Look, Desiree, Bess figured her son would most likely wind up with Frankie, and she didn't want to bad-mouth his future wife. She wasn't about to take the chance that sooner or later—maybe even after there were a couple of babies in the picture—her real opinion of Frankie would get back to the two of 'em. The problem was, though, Bess just couldn't pretend to be happy about this marriage, and she felt she had to come up with a reason why. So she latched onto religion; at least that way she wouldn't be knocking the girl's character, you know? And like I told you, the religion thing *did* bother her—only not as much as she wanted us all to think."

"*Us all?* She opened up to you."

"Not at first. But one day we were having coffee at her place, and we got on the subject of the engagement. I told her I knew she was holding something back. At first she said I was nuts. But two chocolate chip cookies later, she finally let it out."

"How did Joel react to his mother's lack of enthusiasm for his girlfriend?"

"Bess said that it was driving a wedge between them. She finally made up her mind to try and avoid the subject."

"Did it surprise you to learn that she had invited Joel and Frankie for dinner on the night she died?"

"Not really. When Joel told me Frankie had dropped

in on her out of the blue like that, I figured she
might've somehow managed to soften Bess's feelings
toward her. Or it could be that Bess decided to take
one last stab at trying to warm up to that little gold
digger." And now Cassie slowly shook her head. "It
must have been terrible for Joel, finding Bess the way
he did . . . terrible."

Cassie and I said good-bye a few minutes later. But
before we did, I gave her my card, asking her to call
if she should think of anything else that might be helpful. Cassie, in turn, handed me a bag containing a half
dozen blueberry muffins. I was of the opinion I had
the best of the exchange until two seconds after I relieved her of her largesse—when she uttered those
three nasty words: "Merry Christmas, Desiree."

Bah, humbug!

Chapter 8

My next stop that morning was only steps away from Cassie's.

On entering the house that had been home to Bessie Herman for decades, I was immediately taken aback by how it managed to be both musty and cold at the same time—so cold, in fact, that I didn't even unbutton my coat during my brief stay. (Incidentally, I wasn't checking out the place because I expected to find a clue of any sort—especially not after all this time. It was simply that this was something I felt obliged to do.)

I began my tour of the premises in the small beige-and-brown living room, which was extremely neat and furnished with what I took to be comfortable, good-quality—although not particularly attractive—pieces. There were only two items of interest here, neither of them having anything to do with Bessie Herman's death. One was a cherry corner cabinet filled with beautiful crystal collectibles—a number of which I recognized as Lalique. The other was the good-size seascape above the sofa. It might have been an oil or an acrylic—or maybe a print, for all I knew—but whatever it was, the effect was lovely and tranquil.

Moving on, I poked my head in the adjacent dining room. And moments later I trudged upstairs.

The first thing to catch my eye in the master bedroom was a photograph on the dresser. The subjects were a pleasant-looking middle-aged couple—the woman with a warm, almost contagious smile—flanked by two preadolescent boys, the smaller of them unmistakably Joel. I glanced around. This room, too, was unusally tidy (to my way of thinking, anyhow), with no personal items draped over the chair or strewn on the king-size bed, which was carefully made up with a blue floral spread that matched the window curtains. The only hints that someone had retired here night after night were the wine-color velour bathrobe hanging on the back of the closet door and the matching slippers peeking out from under the bed. I gulped now, suddenly aware of the faint odor of Chanel No. 5 that lingered in the room. *No doubt it clung to Bessie's clothes*, I told myself. Still, while I wasn't exactly spooked, for a few seconds there I had this feeling that . . . well . . . it was kind of eerie.

I pretty much breezed through the rest of the upstairs rooms before returning to the first floor—and Bessie's kitchen.

The space was *huge*, particularly by Manhattan standards. Listen, it couldn't have been much smaller than her living room. I marveled at how effortlessly it accommodated a good-size Formica table and four vinyl-padded chairs, along with a number of appliances—including a washer and dryer! Then, with what I admit was a certain degree of reluctance, I sucked in my breath and trudged over to the half-open door opposite the stove. The door to the cellar.

Switching on the light at the top of the landing, I took a quick look at what lay ahead of me. Following which I kicked off my pumps, then removed a pair of flat shoes from my suitcase-size handbag and traded them for the pumps. And now, holding on tightly to the railing, I crept cautiously down the fourteen steep, narrow wooden steps.

Well, even though I had no problem making it safely to the basement, I could appreciate how easy it would be to slip or to catch your heel on one of those steps—and wind up with a broken neck without any outside help. But for this same reason, I could also conceive of that staircase as an ideal instrument of murder.

And here I stopped cold. *But what if the victim hadn't been considerate enough of her assailant to actually die?*

In that case, I responded instantly, *it wouldn't be too difficult to help her along with a not-so-gentle rap on the head.*

On the drive home from Ozone Park I agonized for a while over poor Aunt Bessie's fate. Seeing her picture had made her that much more real to me. Eventually, however—and to my disgust—I reverted to the self-pity I'd been infused with earlier in the day.

I mean, forget that I'd just visited the scene of that unfortunate woman's death—possibly *homicide*; I had no reason to bitch about my own situation regardless. After all, it wasn't as if I were ill, or destitute, or friendless. Still, I couldn't get past the reality that I'd be celebrating Christmas alone this year. I suddenly lamented the fact that I didn't have a pet waiting for me at home—and I'd have settled for a goldfish.

By the time I dropped the car at the garage near my apartment, I was in a deep blue funk (and Bessie Herman's fate was a contributing factor, too—honestly). I soon concluded that there was only one way to shake a mood like this: spend money. (And don't give a thought to the bills until they show up in the mailbox.) So I hopped the bus and went to Bloomingdale's.

The store was mobbed with last-minute gift-givers— of which I was one. The only difference being that the recipient of my largesse was me.

Braced to do battle, I elbowed my way through the handbag department, where I was able to snatch up a green leather clutch just as the woman next to me was reaching for it. It was really such a stunning bag that I refused to acknowledge that I had very little use for a green leather clutch. Or that it carried a price tag that might have inspired me to get a second job.

I narrowly escaped being crushed to death in my efforts to lay hands on my next acquisition: a puce cashmere scarf that had been marked down—twice! Never mind that it made me look sallow; it was *such* a great buy.

My final act of madness was to purchase an expensive silk print blouse—after deciding that once I got home, I'd figure out what to wear it with. (Which, incidentally, never happened.)

I'm sure you won't find it any big shocker that I wound up returning all three items a few days later. But at least they provided me with the momentary lift I was hoping for.

Anyhow, my shopping spree over, I stopped off for an early supper at a French restaurant a couple of blocks from the store. I had a glass of white wine, followed by a generous slice of quiche and a salad. I was going to end the meal with a cup of coffee, but then I heard my voice—almost of its own volition—ordering a peach Melba to keep the coffee company.

It was after six when I got back to the apartment. There was a message on the answering machine.

My heart started to pound. *Nick, maybe?*

But no.

"Hi, uh, it's Joel."

God! I'd forgotten all about him!

"Your secretary gave me your home number—she told me you weren't expected at the office today." He made it sound as if I'd been playing hooky. "Listen, I dug up the information you wanted on how to reach everyone—except for Richie. But you can get that from his mother."

And now he proceeded to rattle off Sylvia Vine's address and phone number, followed by those of Cliff Seymour and (reluctantly) Frankie. Joel spoke quickly, and I had to play back the tape three times in order to jot down all the facts. Plus, I'd scribbled so furiously that when I examined the paper shortly afterward, I couldn't decipher even half of what was on it. Fortunately, however, I hadn't deleted Joel's message, so I played it again—twice—and rewrote most of what I'd already written.

Minutes later I was in the bedroom slipping into something comfortable. Which in my case usually consists of the world's rattiest-looking bathrobe. I was just tying the sash when the doorbell rang. It was Barbara Gleason.

"I *thought* I heard you come in," she said.

I stared.

This was a brand-new Barbara. Her makeup appeared to have been done by a professional. And her dark hair, which, it was apparent, had made a very recent trip to the beauty salon, had been cut fairly short and set in soft waves, almost creating an oval of her long, thin face. Also, she was wearing a lovely beige faille suit that was styled so that it somehow gave her angular frame the curves it had never had before. Add to this that the woman was positively glowing. "You look sensational, Barbara!" I exclaimed.

"Do you really think so?"

"Absolutely. But if you doubt me, check the mirror."

"I have—at least a dozen times," she admitted, giggling. "Anyway, this was delivered to my apartment about an hour ago—the guy needed someone to sign for it." For the first time, I noticed the small package she was holding in her hand. But before I had a chance to react, she said impatiently, "Here. It's for you." And with that, she shoved the thing into my midsection.

"Oh, uh, thanks."

"I've gotta get going. Sandy will be picking me up any minute. He's taking me someplace special for dinner, only he won't tell me where. He wants to surprise me."

"Well, have a wonderful evening—wherever you spend it."

"I will. Uh, you didn't make any plans for tonight?"

"Of course, I did. I'm going to stay home and watch *Victor/Victoria*—I have the tape."

It was obvious that Barbara wasn't sure how to respond. "Uh . . . that's good." She sort of air-kissed my cheek. (Understandably, she wasn't about to smudge her lipstick.) "Well, uh, Merry Christmas, Dez. I'll talk to you soon."

"Right." I air-kissed her back. "And the same to you, Barbara." I wasn't quite able to utter the actual words.

As soon as I closed the door I began to tear the wrappings off the package; I could barely wait to see what was inside. *Could it be a gift from Nick?*

It couldn't.

Nevertheless, I can't say I was too disappointed. Inside the little white box was a beautiful pair of long sterling silver earrings set with coral stones. I was thrilled, earrings being a particular weakness of mine. And when I read the note that was enclosed, I was also touched. HAPPY HOLIDAYS TO THE MOST THOUGHTFUL AND LOVING AUNT IN THE WORLD, it said. It was signed, YOUR NEPHEW AND NIECE, MIKE AND ELLEN.

That's right! In addition to my wonderful niece, I now had a nephew—and he was a doll! Yet here I was, having all this *agita* just because I was spending a few days out of the year by myself. Big deal! I mean, I should have been concentrating on the good stuff, like Ellen's finally marrying her soul mate. Besides, there was a chance that things might still work out between Nick and me, too (maybe with a bit of divine intervention). So what was I crabbing about, anyway?

Hours later I settled into the sofa. Within easy reach was a bag of Cheetos, along with a Snickers bar that had been sitting in the freezer awaiting an emergency. And on the VCR was one of my all-time favorite movies.

Naturally, I couldn't guarantee that I'd be this easy to please on New Year's Eve—or even tomorrow. But I actually had a pleasant evening.

Hey, I was pretty good company after all.

* * *

On Christmas morning I woke up with some advice for myself: If I wanted to get through the next twelve hours or so without feeling totally forlorn, I'd better treat this like any other day. And with no tree or other holiday reminders in the apartment, that shouldn't be too hard to do.

I did draw the line somewhere, of course. I wouldn't be phoning any of my suspects. I could appreciate how a thing like that might not be too well received today.

Laying out my agenda, I figured I'd first tackle the apartment, which was practically screaming to be dusted and scrubbed and vacuumed. Then after that I'd transcribe my notes on yesterday's meeting with Cassie Ross.

I'd already taken out the cleaning paraphernalia when I decided to call Ellen and Mike at the Lyntons'. In fact, my hand was on the phone when it rang.

"Oh, Aunt Dez!" Ellen squealed. "The sweater is *exquisite*—and that *color!*" (It was turquoise.) "It fits perfectly, too!" (A size nothing.) "We got your presents yesterday, before we left to drive up here, but we only opened them about five minutes ago."

"I was just about to call and thank *you*—you and Mike. I love the earrings, Ellen."

"Honestly?"

"Honestly."

"Do they go with anything you have?"

"Sure. They go with a lot of my clothes."

"Really?"

I was spared having to come back with a "really," because Mike, who was evidently on the extension, spoke up at that instant. "Merry Christmas, Dez. And thanks for the great gift"—I'd gotten him a wallet with his initials stamped in gold—"you have no idea how much I needed a new wallet."

"Oh, yes I do." (His old one was, to put it kindly, not in the best of health.)

He chuckled, then said in that sincere way he has, "I am so sorry you're bogged down. My folks are, too. They were looking forward to your spending the holiday in Greenwich with us."

"I wanted to, honestly, but I'm up to my ears. I took on a new case, and I'm trying to get a handle on it."

"You'll figure things out," my biggest—and only— fan piped up. "You always do."

"I hope you're right, Ellen."

There was a second or two of silence. "It isn't another murder, is it?"

"Well, yes. That is, it could be. But the woman may also have been the victim of an accident. That's what I have to find out. Anyway, don't worry," I was silly enough to instruct my niece, the worrywart. "I'm not going to put myself in any danger."

"Promise me you'll be c-c-careful." (Ellen is apt to stutter when she's very nervous.)

"I promise."

"You mean it?"

Before I had to answer that one, Mike broke in. "She promised and she means it, Ellen. So why don't we let her get back to work."

I silently blessed him. "Give my love to your folks, Mike, and wish them a . . . a Merry Christmas for me." (Yes, I actually got it out.) And directly following this, I managed my escape.

For the next few hours I concentrated on making the apartment more livable. Then, after a short breather, I sat down at the computer to transcribe my notes. But being the pokiest typist I know, I hadn't accomplished a whole lot when my stomach loudly ordered me into the kitchen.

I had every intention of dealing with the rest of the notes once I had something to eat—no matter how long it took me to get through them. But then I got a call from Nick, who said he missed me.

And my work ethic flew out the window.

Chapter 9

How delirious was I when I got to work on Thursday morning? My feet barely made contact with the ground.

The call from Nick had been brief, since he was about to leave the house to take The Kid From Hell swimming. (I suppose it doesn't reflect too well on my sweet, forgiving nature that for a fleeting moment I embraced the thought of a drowning. Like I said, though, it was only for a moment.) He told me that he just wanted to say hi and wish me a Merry Christmas. I wished him the same. I even claimed that I hoped he was enjoying himself. And this is when he uttered the magic words: "I miss you, Dez."

Funny. I can't remember the rest of the conversation at all.

At any rate, as I entered the office, I practically chirped my "Merry Christmas, Jackie."

Then I noticed her face. She looked like Princess Black Cloud. The woman had the same sort of expression that I'd probably been walking around with for a good part of the week.

"What's wrong?"

She shook her blondish-brown head. "Nothing."

"I can tell you're upset."

"You would be, too, if your boyfriend took you to a crappy diner for Christmas dinner. You should have seen that place! I'm amazed that the Board of Health hasn't closed it down."

"Gee, Jackie, Derwin—"

"Don't you *dare* defend him! Do you know what kind of a gift he got me? A Crock-Pot! You heard me—*a Crock-Pot!* It was most likely on sale, too. Me, like a jerk? I bought that guy eighteen-karat-gold cuff links. Listen, sending me *six* roses for Valentine's Day was chintzy enough—but this? I've had it with him. We're finished. Kaput."

"Did you tell Derwin that?"

"No, he knew I was furious about the diner, but I'm sure he figures I'll get over it like I did all the other stuff he's pulled. Well, not any more; I'm—"

Jackie's buzzer sounded then, and she took the call, after which she grumbled, "Elliot wants me to come in for dictation. I'll talk to you later."

Heading back to my cubbyhole, I fretted about what to say when I spoke to her again. I concluded that I'd have to tread very carefully. I mean, true, Derwin was no Diamond Jim Brady. But the two of them had been going together for years, and despite periodic bouts of frustration with his . . . uh . . . *thriftiness,* Jackie really cared for this man. And it was obvious the feeling was mutual. I just didn't want to come out with something that might encourage her to break things off. Assuming, of course, that she wasn't as firm in her resolve as she was telling me (and—I suspected—herself) that she was.

As soon as I sat down at my desk—and with Joel's list of names in front of me—I picked up the phone. I elected to begin with Frankie Murray, mostly because I was so damn curious about her.

"Rad Rags," a woman announced.

Rad Rags? "Uh, I'd like to speak to Miss Murray, if she's available," I stated, once I'd gotten past that name.

"Hold on a sec." And then, at the top of her lungs: "Fran—kie!"

About a minute went by before I was informed by a thin girlish voice, "Frankie Murray, speaking."

"Um, this is Desiree Shapiro, and I'm—"

"Oh, yes, Ms. Shapiro. Joel mentioned that you'd be calling. He said there were some things you wanted to ask me about."

"That's right. I'd appreciate it if we could get together as soon as possible—wherever it's convenient for you."

"Oh. I thought . . . I was under the impression that you'd question me over the phone."

"It would be much better if we spoke in person."

"We-ell, if you think it's necessary . . ."

"I honestly do."

"I suppose I could make it tonight, after work," she suggested, none too enthusiastically.

"That would be great. Where is your store located?"

"The shop's downtown," she advised me, with a slight emphasis on the word "shop." (Evidently, my referring to the establishment as a store had been a no-no.) "In Tribeca," she elaborated, referring to one of Manhattan's trendier areas. "Joel mentioned that your office is in the Thirties, though."

"It makes no difference. We can do this anywhere you say."

"Is around here all right?"

"Sure. What time are you through with work?"

"I get off at seven on Thursdays."

"Is there someplace near the shop where we could have a bite?"

"Well, yes, but I'm meeting Joel for dinner later."

"How about if we just go for coffee, then?"

"Fine. There's a pretty decent coffee shop down the street—Sister Sue's." She gave me the address. "I can be there by about ten past seven, okay? Oh, and I'll be wearing a pink outfit."

Now, even considering that it was the dead of winter (when the few pink articles of clothing I myself own were packed away for the season), this didn't surprise me. Not from a girl who worked at a place called Rad Rags.

*   *   *

I was about to see if I could set up an appointment with another of my suspects when Jackie burst into my office, her face flushed.

I misread her expression. "What's wrong, Jackie?"

"Derwin called," she related excitedly. "He got us tickets to *The Producers* for January—and, Dez? They're *orchestra* seats!"

"You're kidding!"

"I swear!"

I jumped up and rushed over to give her a hug. A big mistake, because Jackie—a pretty fair-size woman—hugged me back with a little too much enthusiasm.

"The guy loves you, Jackie—a lot," I croaked when I was able to.

"Yeah," she murmured. And her smile could have warmed up an igloo.

I dialed Cliff Seymour next, for no particular reason. The phone was answered by a woman who singsonged, "Seymour Real Estate and Development Company. Good morning."

"Good morning. May I speak to Mr. Seymour, please."

"Which Mr. Seymour would you like, ma'am?"

"Oh, I didn't realize there was more than one. I want Mr. Cliff Seymour."

"May I have your name, please?"

"I doubt that he's ever heard of me. Just tell him I'm looking into the death of Mrs. Bessie Herman."

"Uh, hold on."

"Cliff Seymour," a deep, masculine voice announced almost at once. "Does the receptionist have it right? Did you say that Bess Herman is *dead?*"

"I'm afraid so."

"I'm very sorry to hear that. Nice lady, Ms. Herman. What happened to her?"

"Two weeks ago she fell down the basement stairs and broke her neck. It's possible she was pushed."

"*Pushed?* Who would do such a thing?"

"That's what we're trying to find out."

"And you are—?"

"My name is Desiree Shapiro, Mr. Seymour, and I'm a detective." You'll notice that I omitted the *private*. The way I saw it, if Cliff here should jump to the conclusion that I was with the NYPD, well, this was entirely his own doing. After all, it wasn't as if I'd *lied* to the man.

"You're a police officer?"

Damn! I had no choice but to own up to the truth. I mean, go around impersonating a member of the force, and you'd better be prepared to suffer some pretty unpleasant consequences. "I'm a private investigator," I admitted reluctantly.

"I see. But why are you phoning *me* about this? I barely knew the woman."

"I was told she reneged on a sale that was very important to you."

"True enough. But I don't kill people because they back out of a deal. If I did, at this point in my career I'd be a mass murderer."

I managed a little laugh. "You've got something there. Anyway, you're not under suspicion. The reason I contacted you is because you may be able to shed some light on a couple of matters that have been puzzling me."

"Trust me, Ms.—Shapiro, isn't it? I don't have any knowledge that could possibly clear things up for you."

Now, I hear this kind of protest so often that I was prepared with my response even before Cliff said what he did. "I've learned from experience that people often know more than they think they do, Mr. Seymour. Listen," I wheedled, "I could really use your input. We can get together anyplace you like." Then I quickly tagged on, "I promise it would only be for a few minutes." (A lie that has an almost fifty percent record of success. Cliff, however, was in that other fifty percent.)

"I wish I could accommodate you, Ms. Shapiro; I

honestly do. But I'm currently tied up with a new project, and I simply can't spare the time."

I wasn't ready to give up. "Look, Mr. Seymour, now that Mrs. Herman is gone, you have a good chance of acquiring that property you're so interested in, correct?"

"Hey, hold it a minute. I—"

"Believe me, I'm not accusing you of anything. All I'm trying to tell you is that Bessie Herman had two sons who, it's fairly safe to assume, are her principal heirs. And if they should learn that you refused to cooperate with the investigator who's checking into their mother's death . . . " I left it to Cliff to complete the sentence for himself.

He clucked his tongue. "I see that you're not above a little blackmail, Ms. Shapiro. Well, sorry to disappoint you, but I'm not biting. I'm certain the sons will be anxious to unload that property, and no one is going to match the price that I'm prepared to pay for it."

"As I said, Mrs. Herman had *two* sons. And while the younger one may be eager to sell regardless of whether you agree to meet with me or not, from what I've heard about Donnie—the older son—your unwillingness to help could put the kibosh on things."

Suddenly, Cliff Seymour laughed. "You're something else, you know that? I don't put much credence in this threat of yours. But on the smallest, the most *infinitesimal* chance that you're not just shooting from the hip—okay. I guess I can spare you ten, fifteen minutes."

"Thanks, Mr. Seymour; I appreciate that. Where are you located?"

"Near the Jersey shore. And you?"

"Manhattan. But I'd be happy to do this at your place of business."

"Actually, that won't be necessary. The fact is, tomorrow evening I'm having dinner in Manhattan with a friend. The reservation is for eight o'clock, but I *could* make it into the city a little earlier and stop by your office first. What's the address?"

I told him.

"That's very convenient to the restaurant I'm going to. Why don't we set something up for about seven-thirty."

Well, this meant that before I'd even have a chance to warm up to my chore, the man would be out the door. I thought fast. "I'm afraid I already have an appointment then. Would it be possible for us to get together at a quarter to seven?"

"*A quarter to seven?*" Cliff griped. "Christ! I'll have to leave here practically in the middle of the day."

"Suppose I drive down to *your* place tomorrow, then. It's no problem, and I can be there whenever you say."

"Well . . ." He thought this over for a couple of seconds. "No, that doesn't make sense; after all, I'm going to be right in your neighborhood." And grudgingly: "I imagine I can manage to be there at a quarter to seven."

For some stupid reason, I felt I should make the gesture one final time. "I really don't mind doing this at your office if that would be better for you."

There was some slight hesitation; I'll give him that. "Frankly, that *would* be a help. Can you be here around two?"

Crap! He wasn't supposed to take me up on the offer! "Two it is."

I stopped cursing myself just long enough to jot down the directions he provided.

Chapter 10

The instant I set foot in Sister Sue's, I felt like an antique. I wasn't merely the oldest one there, I was the oldest *by far!*

It was a small place and fairly well packed with what appeared to be a young, hip crowd. But according to the excruciatingly thin, ponytailed waiter who approached me, I was in luck; they still had one empty table. He gestured vaguely toward the rear.

I didn't realize until I walked back there that said table was practically on top of the men's room. I mean, if I had pushed my chair back another foot or so, I'd probably have been parallel to the urinal!

Anyway, within a few minutes—at exactly seventen—this teeny person with long blond hair hurried in. I had no doubt as to her identity. She was in head-to-toe pink: pink jeans, pink knitted cap, pink wool pea coat. I noticed later that even this kid's suede boots were pink!

Her eyes began searching the room, and I stood up and waved. She acknowledged me with a nod and hurried over.

"You're Ms. Shapiro, right?" she asked in the little-girl voice I recognized from the phone.

"Desiree," I corrected. "And you couldn't be anyone but Frankie." We smiled at each other.

Frankie held out her hand. "It's nice to meet you," she said. This was immediately followed with "But not under these circumstances, of course."

She wriggled out of her pea coat, underneath which

was—you guessed it—a pink sweater. Then only seconds after she'd draped the coat on the back of a chair and sat down, we were joined by a waitress with the name tag CINDY. Looking painfully bored, Cindy—who must have been about eighteen years old—greeted my companion with a lack of animation that was no doubt typical of her. "Oh, hi, Frankie. You guys know what you want, or should I bring youse a menu?"

"I'll have an espresso. Decaf, please, Cindy," Frankie told her.

"A slice of strawberry cheesecake with that?"

There was the slightest bit of indecision before Frankie answered, "Uh-uh, better not. I'm meeting my fiancé for dinner."

Cindy shrugged. "And you, ma'am?"

"I'll have an espresso, too. Only regular. And I'll have a slice of that strawberry cheesecake Frankie turned down."

"Gotcha." She had begun to walk away when Frankie called out, "Uh, Cindy?"

The obviously put-upon waitress retraced her steps. "Yeah?" she demanded, hands on her hips.

"I've changed my mind about the cheesecake."

Cindy nodded, then made a hasty retreat, mumbling something that sounded like, "Figures."

"So what is it you'd like to ask me?" Frankie said now, focusing an enormous pair of Wedgwood-blue eyes on me. She was, I determined, an unusually pretty girl.

"Um, can you tell me a little about your relationship with Joel's mother?"

"Frankly, it wasn't exactly what I'd hoped for. I thought she was a nice person—honestly. But, unfortunately, she wasn't too fond of me."

"I understand that religion entered into her feelings toward you."

"Actually, I believe it was her only objection to me, especially considering that I'd been in her company all of two times—I'm not including the day of the . . .

the fall. But apparently it meant a great deal to Ms. Herman that her son settle down with someone of his own faith."

"Did she ever say that to you?"

"No, but she did say it to Joel."

"You must have been terribly upset to hear that."

"Not enough to push her down the basement stairs, if that's what you're intimating. The fact is, I don't believe anyone was responsible for what happened. I'd probably break my neck, too, if I tried walking down those steps in high heels."

"I'm not suggesting you had any involvement in Mrs. Herman's death, Frankie. It's very possible that it *was* an accident. Still, I was hired to check into what caused her to take that header, and conducting an investigation of this type requires that I get a fix on the character of the deceased. It's crucial that I find out what Mrs. Herman was like and how she related to people."

It took a few seconds for Frankie to respond. "I suppose I can understand that. Well, as has already been established, she was very much opposed to my marrying her son. And the reason for it made me really angry. After all, this is the twenty-first century, for heaven's sake. But then I realized that it was unfair to be so judgmental. Ms. Herman was an old lady, and she'd grown up with a different set of values."

How understanding of the girl, I decided. *How adult.* But almost immediately I cautioned myself to consider the flip side: *How resourceful of her to provide me with such a self-serving rationale.*

It was at this point that Cindy brought over our order.

Frankie and I both had a few sips of espresso, which was passable, and a forkful of cheesecake, which was like lead. I mean, God forbid it should land on some unfortunate's toe!

"The sad part is that Ms. Herman and I were actually starting to work things out at the end," Frankie went on, the blue eyes moist now.

"You paid an unexpected call on her the day she died."

"Yes. I consider myself a pretty confident, take-charge woman, Desiree. When there's a problem, I don't sit there crying about it, I *do* something. Poor Joel was distraught about his mother's reaction to our engagement, and it broke my heart to see him that way. He adored her, you know—he adored us both. But he had no idea how to remedy the situation, how to make it right. So he allowed things to fester." And leaning toward me, her voice not much above a whisper, Frankie confided, "My fiancé is a wonderful man, truly he is. But when faced with any sort of adversity, he has a tendency to bury his head in the sand." Then in what I took to be a halfhearted defense of her betrothed, she added, "It's been my experience, though, that this is the nature of men in general."

It's been my experience! I wasn't able to suppress a smile. "How old are you, Frankie? If you don't mind my asking."

"I don't mind. I'm going on twenty-six. You were under the impression I was younger, weren't you?"

"To be honest, if I were judging on looks alone, I'd have figured you for a teenager."

"That's one of the reasons I was hired at Rad Rags. For the most part, their clientele is quite young, and Irene—she's the owner—felt it would be a good idea to bring in a salesperson the kids could relate to."

"Speaking of Rad Rags, how did the woman come up with a name like that?"

"Rad stands for radical—some of the things we carry are a bit way-out—and Rags is slang for clothing, of course."

"Of course," I echoed. "But to get back to why we're here . . . What happened when you dropped in on Mrs. Herman?"

"Her initial reaction, when she saw me standing there on the porch, didn't appear to be too promising. 'Uh-oh, what am I doing here?' I said to myself. In fact, for a moment I was certain she was going to close the door in my face. Naturally, I should have realized that this wouldn't have been Ms. Herman's style. She was too classy an individual to do such a thing, no matter how displeased she might have been by my visit. At any rate, she asked me in—she even made a fresh pot of coffee for us—and after that I explained why I'd come.

" 'Look, Ms. Herman,' I put to her. 'We both love Joel very much, and we want to see him happy, true?' She said that yes, this was true. 'I can't change the fact that I'm Protestant by birth,' I told her, 'but I *can* convert to Judaism.'

"Well, she was taken aback. 'You'd really be willing to do that?' she asked me. I assured her I would, that it was actually no great concession since I'd never been a churchgoer anyway. Now, I'm not claiming that she softened to the point of throwing her arms around me, but I did detect a major difference in her attitude."

"And this is when she invited you and Joel to dinner?"

"That didn't happen until we were at the door. She thanked me for coming to see her. I was about to say good-bye when she said she wanted us to have dinner there that night. She told me she had some meat in the fridge and that she would make a Russian specialty for us—beef Stroganoff. And then she smiled and even squeezed my shoulder."

"It certainly sounds as if your relationship with Mrs. Herman was headed in the right direction, Frankie. How long did you spend with her that afternoon?"

"Let's see. I got to the house about two, I believe—I'd taken the day off from work. And it must have been three-thirty when I left—maybe slightly before. So I'd say I was there approximately an hour and a half."

"Do you live in Queens, too?"

"No, in downtown Manhattan, not far from the shop."

"This means that practically as soon as you got home, you had to turn around and go back."

Frankie laughed. "Not quite. I took the subway, and I was in my apartment not much more than an hour later. Ms. Herman *had* asked if I wanted to stay until dinnertime, but this way I had a chance to shower and freshen up. She told me to try to get there by seven-thirty."

"Incidentally, while you were with her, did she say anything about having to go down to the basement for something?"

Frankie shook her head. "No, she didn't."

"One more question," I lied. "Can you tell me what sort of shoes Mrs. Herman had on when you were with her?"

"I didn't notice the style, but I'm almost certain she was wearing heels—either high or medium."

"Uh, there's something else I wanted to check out with you."

"What's that?"

"I understand that you tried to induce Mrs. Herman to finance the purchase of a clothing store for Joel."

Frankie's pink cheeks (yes, they were *that* color, too) instantly turned crimson, her lower lip began to quiver, and for the first time since she'd sat down here, she raised her voice. "Who *told* you such an awful thing?"

"I'm honestly not sure. Somebody mentioned it in passing. Are you saying you never had such a discussion with Mrs. Herman?"

"I believe I did tell her that it was Joel's objective to own his own shop someday but that currently we didn't have the resources to make it happen. I only shared this with her because I had the idea she'd be pleased to hear that her son has ambition, a direction in life." And now, in a tone about an octave above her normal range, she declared, "But as far as her supplying the funds—my God!—I promise you, that didn't even occur to me!" She made an obvious effort to collect herself, then added more calmly, "Apparently Ms. Herman completely misread my intention. And to be frank with you, while I didn't delude myself into thinking that she was eager to have me for a daughter-in-law, I'm disappointed in her for misjudging me like that."

I attempted to mollify the girl. "In all fairness, it's conceivable that it was the person who passed the story on to me who put the wrong interpretation on your talk with Mrs. Herman."

"Maybe," she conceded. But it was obvious she was far from convinced.

"Uh, you spoke with Mrs. Herman about this only once?"

"As far as I can remember."

I was about to wrap things up when Frankie's cell phone rang.

"Three guesses," she challenged playfully. Then, a wide grin on her face, she politely excused herself to take the call.

A second after her hello, she mouthed "Joel" to me.

Now, I want you to understand that unless I'd stuck my fingers in my ears, it would have been impossible to tune out the ensuing conversation—Frankie's contribution to it, at least. At any rate, she listened for a moment, following which she said into the phone, "Yes, I realize that, but I believe we're just about through." And tilting her head, she fixed her eyes on my face for confirmation.

I nodded.

Frankie did a little more listening, and it was evident she heard something that displeased her. Because it didn't take long for her to complain in this honey-dipped tone of hers, "I realize you've had an awful lot on your mind lately, sweetie. Still, I did tell you a number of times that I don't care for Indian food, but you never pay attention." Joel had no chance to respond to this, because she proffered an instant apology. "I shouldn't have said that—not with all you've been going through. Forgive me, baby?"

There was a pause here, during which Frankie must have been forgiven, because afterward she all but purred to her intended, "You know exactly what I want to hear, don't you? Anyhow, French would be fine. But so would Italian. Or sushi. You choose the restaurant—you always find such marvelous places."

Once Joel had had his final at bat, Frankie concluded with, "That sounds wonderful, baby. I'll meet you there in about ten minutes." She hung up with a smile.

I smiled back. I'd just had the privilege of witnessing a master manipulator at work.

Chapter 11

Frankie may have had someone eagerly awaiting the opportunity to take her out for a nice meal, but I, unfortunately, did not. And by the time I got to my apartment, my stomach was giving me what-for. I mean, how long was a lousy, barely nibbled on piece of cheesecake supposed to hold a person?

The first thing I did after getting out of my clothes was to make myself some bacon and eggs. I followed this with a cup of vile coffee—a specialty of mine— accompanied by a dish of Häagen-Dazs macadamia brittle, to which I am totally addicted. Then after pouring myself a second cup of coffee (luckily, after all these years I'm immune to this assault on my taste buds), I conducted a post mortem on the evening's get-together with Frankie Murray.

Bessie's neighbor, and apparently number-one confidante, had painted a picture of a conniving young woman—a description Frankie had lived up to in spades. Still, she wasn't what I'd been expecting. I mean, having previously met with Joel, I hadn't figured that his intended would be quite so bright. Or articulate. Or polished.

Don't get me wrong. I'm not implying that the dead woman's son was stupid. But in the brains department, he was definitely no match for the lady of his choice.

At any rate, it goes without saying that I wasn't about to accept as gospel everything Frankie had just imparted to me. *Did she actually offer to convert?* I wondered. *And if so, was Mrs. Herman's reaction as*

*positive as the girl would have me believe? And whose
version of that conversation about Joel's pining for a
shop of his own was closer to the truth, anyway—hers
or Cassie Ross's?*

I pulled myself up short. Even if Frankie had been
fabricating to beat the band, this didn't make her
guilty of murder. She might simply have been motivated by a desire to remove herself from suspicion.

At this point I forced myself to abandon all of this
speculating—which, if it continued much longer,
would doubtless wind up in the usual way: with the
only thing I had to show for my efforts being an Extra-
Strength Tylenol headache.

I had no sooner cleaned up in the kitchen and settled on the sofa when the phone rang.

"Hello, Ms. Shapiro? This is Don Herman. I hope
I'm not disturbing you."

"No, no. Not at all." It took a couple of seconds
before I realized that the caller was Bessie Herman's
older son—heretofore always referred to as "Donnie."

"I understand you're looking into my mother's
death," he was saying.

"Uh, yes, I am, Mr. Herman," I responded, while
preparing myself for the anticipated protest. "And
you, uh, have my deepest sympathies. From all that
I've . . . um . . . heard, your mother was a wonderful person."

"Yes, she was. Listen, Ms. Shapiro—"

"Desiree," I corrected automatically.

"All right, and I'm Don. I just want you to know
that Ben and I spoke a few days ago, and I've since
concluded that he's right. My mother's tumble down
those stairs *should* be investigated. To be honest with
you, I've begun to vacillate between being virtually
convinced that she tripped to seriously considering the
possibility she was pushed. On the one hand, you see,
it *is* conceivable she didn't stop to change her shoes—
perhaps at that moment she was either very preoccupied or in a terrible hurry. On the other hand, my

mother was a cautious person. And the last time she attempted to negotiate those steps in high heels, she stumbled and incurred an extremely painful injury. Which leads me to believe it's also conceivable she'd have taken an extra few minutes and put on more sensible shoes—no matter what.

"At any rate, Desiree, it has become increasingly difficult for me to live with this kind of uncertainty, so I'm pleased that Ben has persuaded you to try to ascertain what really occurred that day. Although, naturally, I'm hoping you'll come to the determination that my mother was the victim of a grievous accident."

"I'm hoping that, too, Don." (I had no problem absorbing this name change, since with his precise, almost pompous, manner of speaking, the man sounded nothing at all like a Donnie.) "But I should make it clear that there's always the chance we'll never know for sure how your mother died. I promise you, though, that I'll do everything I can to find out the truth."

"I appreciate that. Uh, I don't suppose you've uncovered anything of consequence as yet."

"No, I'm afraid I haven't. Right now I'm in the process of gathering information. And I still have people to talk to and questions to ask."

"Yes, well, that's pretty much as I surmised. And it isn't the reason I telephoned you. I picked up the phone this evening because it's occurred to me that I should touch base with you in the event there's some way that I might be of assistance."

"Maybe you *can* help. Are you aware of anyone your mother might have been having problems with?"

"Actually, I am. We have this relative—Sylvia Vine; she was a cousin of Mom's about half a dozen times removed. This woman and my mother had been friends for years. But then Sylvia's younger son— Richie, his name is—decided to buy into a business of some sort, irrespective of the fact that he was short on funds. My mother very kindly offered to lend him five thousand dollars. However, before he had an opportunity to cash the check she sent him, Richie was arrested—apparently the fellow was an unconscionable swindler. And, quite properly, when Mom learned of his true character, she was no longer of a mind to finance him.

"Sylvia was just livid at my mother for what she regarded as welshing on a promise, which led to their having a very nasty argument. My mom was so aggravated, so preoccupied with the falling out, that for a while it was difficult to move her on to another subject."

Well, by now this was such a familiar story that I'd been tempted to put my fingers in my ears. Still, I felt obliged to respond in some way. "And you think this Sylvia might have been responsible for your mother's death?"

"That's certainly a possibility. However, it's Richie I have in mind. The altercation with Sylvia took place back in August. But less than a month ago Richie himself telephoned my mother. It was the first she'd heard from him since the unpleasantness with Sylvia regarding the money. Mom told me he sounded as if he was either drunk or on drugs. He was dreadful to her, she said, going so far as to call her a—how can I put this delicately?" Don took a moment to go over his options. "This is the best I can do," he finally informed me, his tone apologetic. "The little lowlife referred to my dear, generous mother as an 'effing lying bitch.' Of course, Mom hung up then, but the episode left her shaken. She couldn't believe he'd spoken to her in that manner—she'd known him since he was a baby. And what was likely even more troubling to my mom was that Richie's animosity toward her pretty much put an end to any hope of a reconciliation with Sylvia."

"Was your mother afraid for her safety after that conversation?"

"I tend to doubt that," Don replied. "She was in tears when she recounted it to me, however. For some reason that I was never able to fathom, she'd always been fond of Richie. At any rate, I assured her that this would not happen again, that I was about to have a brief dialogue with the fellow. It was my intention to warn him that if he should bother my mother again, if he should ever utter even a single syllable to her, I'd beat the crap out of him. Excuse the language."

The words sounded so out of character for this man that I had to smile. "It's excused," I said. I didn't volunteer that I myself have, when appropriate, resorted to a few terms that could put a blush on the cheeks of a longshoreman. (This X-rated vocabulary being employed only under the most stringent of circumstances, you understand.)

"Mom wouldn't hear of my contacting him, however," Don continued. "I had to swear I would let the incident drop. But if I should ever discover that Richie bore any responsibility for . . . for her death"—there was a catch in his voice now—"I'd never be able to forgive myself for not pursuing the matter."

"According to what you've told me, Richie never actually threatened your mother, though. Correct?"

"Correct. Still . . . " He let the word dangle there.

I suddenly wondered why Joel hadn't mentioned that call. "Uh, how did your brother feel about Richie's tearing into your mother like that?"

"He never knew about it. My mom was very anxious to keep this quiet; she didn't want to exacerbate the situation. Nevertheless, she needed to talk to *someone*, and I turned out to be that someone. Cassie Ross—her best friend—must have been out of town at that time," he joked. "Anyway, I had to promise that whatever she communicated to me would remain our secret."

"Why did she elect to share this with you and not with Joel?"

"For one thing, my brother has a temper—we both do, only Joel's boiling point is slightly lower than mine. But I believe it was primarily because Mom felt it was more prudent to confide in the son who lived in San Francisco, rather than the one who was right there, in New York. After all, I could hardly rush over to Richie's place to confront him."

"You believe that's what Joel would have done?"

"All I can tell you is that it would have pleased me no end to take a well-aimed swing at that punk myself."

"You mentioned Richie's 'place.' Do you know where he lives?"

"No. But it shouldn't have been too difficult to track him down."

"Tell me, Don, was your mother on bad terms with anyone else?"

"Nigel—her dry cleaner," he answered promptly.

"Her *dry cleaner*?" This was a new one on me.

"Approximately a year ago my mother took her favorite outfit to Dependable Cleaners. Now there's a misnomer for you! That suit didn't have a single spot on it when she brought it in. She'd been invited to some fancy luncheon, and she merely wanted it freshened up—she hadn't worn it in some time. Unfortunately, a few days later when she picked up the garment and brought it home, she noticed a large discoloration near the hem of the skirt, something she was positive hadn't been there before.

"Well, she returned to the store with the suit, and Nigel—he's the owner—insisted that the stain had been on the skirt all along and that they'd expended every effort to remove it, but nothing could be done.

"Now, ninety-nine percent of the time my mother was a sweet, gentle seventy-two-year-old lady, Desiree. But that man had not only ruined this outfit she was so fond of, but he was, in effect, calling her a liar, as well. He even had the gall to insist that the suit was out of style anyway and that she couldn't have paid more than fifty dollars for it at the outset. Incidentally, the original price was *two hundred* and fifty. My mother bought it on sale, and even then it cost well over a hundred dollars.

"Mom was incensed at the man's handling of the situation, of course, and she advised him to prepare to be sued. He all but threw her out of the shop."

"Did she follow through? And sue him, I mean."

"No. Those of us she spoke to about this told her we understood how frustrated, how *infuriated* she must be by Nigel's refusal to accept responsibility for the condition of the outfit. At the same time, however, we cautioned her that it would be fruitless to file a lawsuit over damage to clothing that was at minimum five years old. I was under the impression we'd prevailed upon her to put the entire experience behind her, too."

"But you hadn't?"

Don answered my question with one of his own. "Are you familiar with a television program called *The People's Court,* Desiree?"

"I watch it whenever I play hooky from work."

He chuckled. "Ditto. And not that long ago my mother also discovered the show—and became an instant *People's Court* junkie. She *loved* Judge Marilyn! She was even glued to the set during reruns.

"Well, evidently the unpleasantness with Nigel must have been festering all this time, because less than a week before her death, Mom resolved to bring him on *The People's Court.* According to the last report I received from her on the subject, she'd paid another visit to the shop to let Nigel know what he could expect. She informed him that her purpose in airing their dispute was to alert the citizens of Ozone Park to the sort of person he was. Following this, she lectured him about treating his customers with respect. Her parting words to the fellow were to the effect that a *sensible* businessperson would have made an effort to reach an amiable settlement with any party who had a legitimate grievance. It was certainly preferable, she pointed out, to placing one's reputation at risk."

"How did Nigel reply to this?"

"He didn't. My mother didn't give him the opportunity. As soon as she'd had her say, she turned around and marched out."

"Your mom could be pretty feisty," I murmured admiringly.

"That's true. However, only when pushed."

"Do you have any idea if she ever contacted the show?"

"No. But with Nigel aware of her plans, I don't imagine it makes a difference whether she'd taken any action yet or not. The more I think about it, the more feasible it is to me that Nigel went to the house that Saturday to induce Mom to change her mind—but without success. You have to appreciate how strongly my mother felt about retaliating against this individual, Desiree. That's why I seriously doubt that she could have been persuaded to back down. And as a result, I can see where the situation might have gotten out of hand. From what I've gathered, my brother Joel is a pussycat compared to this Nigel."

"Speaking of Joel, I would assume he knew nothing about your mother's quarrel with Nigel. And for the same reason she opted not to tell him about Richie's phone call."

"Exactly. And as for that *People's Court* business, I don't believe she talked about that to anyone other than Nigel and myself—and, of course, Cassie. The truth is, my mother acknowledged that her determination to take the man to court bordered on the obsessive—although she never used the word—and it was clear that she was somewhat embarrassed by this. So she planned on keeping pretty quiet about her intention until she was absolutely certain the case would be televised."

"I'm looking forward to having a talk with Nigel," I said then, "along with everyone else who was causing your mom some difficulty."

"I'm aware of one other person who might fall into this category, Desiree: a realtor who was trying to pressure her into selling her vacation home. But Ben must have already discussed him with you."

"Yes, he did."

"Ben views the man as the prime suspect. But this is because as yet my cousin isn't familiar with the telephone call from Richie. And most probably he's all but forgotten about Nigel. That altercation took place quite some time ago, and he has no idea that my mother was now determined to broadcast their dispute on *The People's Court.*"

"You didn't enlighten him with regard to either Richie or the TV show when the two of you spoke the other night?"

"No. At that juncture I wasn't ready to even *consider* the premise that someone could actually have pitched my mother down those steps."

"And evidently your mom had continued to keep both matters between the two of you. I met with Cassie Ross a few days ago, and she didn't appear to be aware of them either."

"It couldn't have been easy for my mother to withhold the news of her intended television debut from Cassie," Don remarked with a laugh. "In fact, I'd be willing to wager that Mom was only a day or two from spilling the beans to her."

And now Bessie's older son was silent for a moment, after which he put in somberly, "Only she didn't live that long." I was attempting to come up with a sensitive response of some sort when he added, "I *am* surprised that she never broke down and told Cassie about Richie's telephoning her, though. But she'd eventually have gotten around to that, too. Perhaps of late her concern about my brother's marrying out of his religion hadn't left much room in their conversations for other topics."

I was thinking that Bessie's misgivings about Joel's pending nuptials weren't based on religion alone. But either this was all she'd shared with Don, or it was all he chose to share with me. Anyhow, it was then that he declared, "Well, I think we've covered just about everything. This has been some marathon phone call, hasn't it?"

I agreed that it had—and so did my numb right arm.

*   *   *

I was thoroughly exhausted after that long, *long* talk with Don, and he probably wasn't in any better shape than I was. But at least we'd accomplished a thing or two.

I now had a brand-new suspect in the person of Nigel, the unprincipled and abusive dry cleaner.

And then there was Richie Vinc, who—while on my list almost from the beginning—had suddenly emerged as a much more possible possible.

Chapter 12

I didn't see any point in going to the office Friday—not with a two o'clock appointment at the New Jersey shore. So on Thursday I'd dutifully notified Jackie that I wouldn't be in the next day. Listen, one of the woman's strictest unwritten commandments is that you keep her apprised of your whereabouts. I'd sinned on a handful of occasions in the past (unintentionally, of course—I'm not brave enough to challenge a commandment of Jackie's), following which I'd paid a heavy price for my negligence. And I wasn't about to let it happen again.

Anyhow, prior to leaving the house on Friday morning, I made a couple of phone calls. First I tried Dependable Cleaners in Ozone Park. I was informed that Nigel, the deceased's evidently formidable adversary, was on vacation and wasn't expected back until January sixth.

After this, I got in touch with Sylvia Vine.

I wasn't in the mood to play one of my favorite games just then—you know, the one that might lead her to assume I was with the NYPD. I told her right off the bat that I was a private detective.

"*A private detective?*" she repeated. Her voice was husky, with a pronounced foreign accent.

"I'm investigating the death of a relative of yours," I explained.

"Vut relative?"

"Bessie Herman."

"How come? She fall down cellar stairs, no?"

"That's very likely the case. But there's also a slight possibility that Mrs. Herman was pushed."

"No kidding," Sylvia murmured, making no attempt to contain her glee. Then before I could assure her that, in fact, I wasn't kidding, she added, "Not dat it vould be surprise if somevun *did* give her little shove. Believe me, Missus Sternberg, Bessie vas terrible person. But it took stupid me forty years to find dis out."

"Uh, it's Shapiro," I corrected.

"Vut is?"

"My name's Desiree Shapiro."

"Oh, hokay. Anyhow, vhy are you calling me? Is months since I last seeing Bessie—lucky me."

"I'm aware of that. But considering that you two went back such a long time, I thought you might be able to answer some questions I have."

"Vut questions?"

"This is hard to do over the telephone. I'd really appreciate it if we could get together—wherever it's convenient for you, naturally." I added the standard reassurance clause: "I promise it will only take a few minutes."

"I vould be very happy to do dis"—I'd just breathed a sigh of relief when Sylvia went on—"if I knew even vun tiny ting could maybe help you."

"You can't be certain that you don't. It's been my experience, Mrs. Vine, that the key to resolving a case often proves to be a small, seemingly unimportant piece of information."

"I haven't such a piece. And right now I got to hang up. I am not rude type individual, Missus . . . Missus . . . ?"

"Shapiro," I supplied again.

"Oh, hokay. Look, I got gentleman friend who is coming to house in a few minutes. Ve got train to catch."

Gentleman friend—as in lover-type gentleman friend? This was the first I'd heard of a romance in Sylvia Vine's life—if that's what it was. Possibly I'd find out more on the subject when I met with the lady, I speculated, choosing to ignore that she'd just turned me down cold. "I was thinking that perhaps we could do it tomorrow," I put to her. After which I hastily added, "Or Sunday, if that's better for you."

"I vill be in Vashington for whole veekend."

"How about Monday then? Or Tuesday? The sooner the better, of course."

"It von't be sooner—*or* later. Is not going to be at all. I don't know notting about how Bessie died; I just feel glad she is dead."

"Apparently you weren't too fond of the deceased."

"I hated her. I had good reason, too. Plenty good. Only don't get no ideas; it vasn't me gave her push. But if somebody did, whoever it vas got my congratulations."

Obviously, I had to do *something* to persuade Sylvia to see me. I reached into my stockpile of lies. "No doubt you have an explanation for this," I began, "but—"

"An explanation for vut?"

"I understand you were seen in the vicinity of Mrs. Herman's home on the day of her fall."

"*Vut?* Somebody lying to you. Or else maybe is you doing lying."

"I assure you, this is what was said to me," I retorted, all injured innocence.

"Hokay, hokay. So somebody make up—vhy, I don't know. Unless . . . Vas it dat rotten son of hers?"

"Joel?"

"Yeah, Joel. Donnie—he is older son—is all right, considering who vas his mama."

"I'm afraid I can't reveal the source of my information."

"Fine by me. It don't matter anyhow; I am still not permitting you should take up my time for no reason. And listen, I got to get going—I mean it. So goodbye and good luck."

"Just one more minute." And I quickly rummaged around in my stockpile of lies again. "I should tell you, Mrs. Vine, that if you refuse to speak to me, you'll wind up being interrogated by the police."

"*The police?*"

"I'm not sure you're aware that this is an active case we're talking about. An autopsy is presently being conducted, although it may be a while before we have the results. At any rate, as a good citizen, I really *should* step forward and report everything I know to the authorities—including the fact that you and Mrs. Herman had a terrible argument with regard to your son."

"Is not nice you should blackmail people, Missus Sternberg. Your mama—she never tell you dis?"

I didn't reply. I sat there holding my breath, waiting for her next words.

Sylvia finally capitulated before I turned purple. "All right," she groused. "You come Monday, ten o'clock." She gave me the address.

"Thank you," I said politely.

She mumbled something then that I didn't catch. I had the impression, though, that it still had to do with blackmail. And my mama.

Chapter 13

The trek down the shore wound up being a long one. But having the foresight of experience, I'd started out at eleven for what Cliff Seymour had described as about an hour-and-a-half trip "but definitely not more than two hours—even if you drive like my grandma Birdie." Forget his grandma Birdie. The man could hardly be aware that I've been known to get lost going around the block. The plain fact is, I can't seem to follow directions. I tell myself it's because I'm always immersed in such productive thinking. But most of the time I don't manage to believe me.

At any rate, after so many wrong turns that I stopped counting, along with all the backtracking these mistakes necessitated, at five to two I finally pulled into the parking lot of Seymour Real Estate and Development Company.

The firm was housed in a modern, single-story white building located directly off a highway in West Aubrey, which, I felt it safe to assume, was somewhere west of Aubrey—and Aunt Bessie's coveted property. I got out of the car and, anxious to leave the afternoon's frigid ten-degree temperature behind me, sprinted inside. (Well, my version of "sprinted," anyhow.)

And now I was in a large, sparsely decorated space containing six desks, three of them occupied at present. Gracing the desk closest to the entrance was a pretty blond cheerleader type with large baby-blue eyes and impossibly long dark lashes. I took the girl to be in her early twenties.

"May I help you?" she inquired in the singsong voice I'd heard on the phone.

"I have an appointment with Mr. Cliff Seymour. I'm Desiree Shapiro."

"Oh, yes, Ms. Shapiro," she all but trilled. "Please have a seat, and I'll tell Mr. Cliff you're here." She gestured toward a small room approximately seven or eight feet behind me.

Following her instructions, I sashayed over to what was evidently intended as the reception area—and was immediately faced with a crisis. Should I plunk my derriere on the sea green ultramodern sofa or on one of the two matching sea green chairs? Either choice could prove disastrous. I mean, all three pieces were so low to the floor that it was even money whether I'd ever be able to stand up again. Nevertheless, I took a deep breath and—with a courage that's uncharacteristic of me—lowered myself cautiously onto the sofa, perching on the very edge of the cushion.

It was less than a minute later when—wouldn't you know it?—Miss Singsong Voice appeared in the doorway. "Mr. Cliff will see you now."

To my relief, the telephone rang at this precise instant, and the girl raced back to her desk. I was, therefore, spared the embarrassment of having someone witness my intense struggle to hoist myself to a vertical position, which fortunately, with the assistance of the armrest, I was able to accomplish before sundown.

All in all, however, I'd hardly reflected the sort of elegance and grace that three years of ballet lessons should have endowed me with—irrespective of the fact that my training at Winifred Werthheimer's School of Ballet, Tap, and Acrobatics ended before I turned twelve.

"Ms. Shapiro, Mr. Cliff," the pretty blonde announced, standing on the threshold of her employer's office. Then she stepped aside to allow me to enter the room and promptly shut the door after me.

The man at the paper-strewn desk rose and murmured, "Thank you, Ms. Kranepool," to what was by now a closed wooden door.

It took only an instant for the buzzer inside my head to go off: I was once again in a hostile environment. The black leather couch and bright red leather chairs were striking, all right. But much, *much* too modern (from my viewpoint, at least). I mean, the thought of sitting only inches from the floor for a second time that day intimidated the hell out of me.

Cliff Seymour walked over to greet me, right hand extended. Somewhere in his forties, he was on the short side and stocky, with slick dark hair (he must have used half a tube of gel on it that morning) and a broad, toothy smile that didn't ring true. "Well, well, so you're the woman who's so anxious to give me the third degree," he remarked as we engaged in the obligatory handshake. After which, with what seemed to be an effort, he invited me to have a seat.

Uh-uh, buster, not on your life, I retorted in no uncertain terms—but only to myself. The protest to my reluctant host was infinitely more restrained. "Umm, I wonder if it would be at all possible for me to have a regular chair—you know, with a straight back. I, uh, hate to trouble you, but I have a bad spinal condition."

"No trouble." And spinning around, he leaned over his desk and pressed the button on the intercom. "Have Herbie bring one of the kitchen chairs to my office, will you Ms. Kranepool? Oh, and hold my calls, please."

I had barely finished the self-congratulation that I felt such creative thinking merited when Cliff inquired, "So how long have you had this physical problem of yours, anyhow?"

"For . . . quite a while."

"What is it—a spinal curvature?"

"Yes, actually."

"Is it very painful?"

"Umm—"

A soft knock on the door saved me any more mental strain. And in response to Cliff's "Come in," we were joined by a very tall, very thin young man with the most prominent ears I'd ever seen. They were pointy and stood straight out on either side of his head—butterfly wings immediately sprang to mind. He was toting a straight-backed wooden chair with a padded vinyl seat, which Cliff directed he place alongside the desk.

"I trust you'll be comfortable on this," Cliff said sarcastically. (But that could have been my imagination.)

"I'm sure I will. Thanks very much." Then, tearing my eyes away from Herbie's ears, I thanked him, as well.

Once we were settled in our respective chairs, Cliff announced, "This is a very busy day for me, Ms. Shapiro, so I suggest you cut to the chase. Just start asking your questions." He refrained from tagging on, "And then get the hell out of here," but it was implicit in his tone.

"Fine. But please call me Desiree."

"Why not." The instruction to address him as Cliff followed by a good few seconds—and was tendered with obvious reluctance.

"Um, how long had you been attempting to buy Mrs. Herman's house in Aubrey?" I began.

"Since sometime in August."

"At first she agreed to sell, but she changed her mind before the deal went through. Have I got that straight?"

"You got it."

"I was told you were counting on acquiring that property in order to construct a mall in the area. So Mrs. Herman's change of heart must have really rankled."

"You got that right, too."

"I was also advised that you made frequent tries at persuading her to reverse her decision again."

"Guilty. I wasn't ready to throw in the towel yet. Especially since I was in a position to sweeten the pot during virtually every conversation we had." Cliff's voice took on a decidedly defensive edge here. "I don't know what you've heard, but where I come from, that's called negotiating. Not harassment. Not intimidation. And certainly not a warm-up for murder—assuming that Ms. Herman was pushed down her basement stairs in the first place."

"Oh, I didn't mean—"

"Of course you did. But forget it. What else do you want to know?"

"Did you, uh, feel you were making any headway with her?"

He shrugged. "Who could tell? Sometimes I thought she was beginning to come around. Other times, no. But I intended to keep on trying. Even if things didn't work out there, though, I wouldn't have had much of a motive for killing the woman. In this business you miss out on opportunities all the time, but others always seem to crop up. For months we've been exploring alternate sites for that mall in the event Bess Herman couldn't be moved off the dime. And as it turns out, one of them appears quite promising. My brother actually prefers that backup spot. Me, on the other hand, I still lean toward the original location. But only a wee bit," he added with a smirk. "Not enough to kill for, I assure you."

"Tell me, Cliff, when was the last time you spoke to Mrs. Herman?"

"Almost three weeks ago. Probably only days before she died."

"Had you seen her recently?"

"Not since late September or early October."

"I'd appreciate your giving me your impression of her—as a person, that is."

Cliff shrugged again. "In spite of all the grief she gave me, I'd say she was probably nice enough. But it's not as if I bothered to analyze her character. I don't happen to be in the market for another mother.

And I'm not into playing around with little old ladies, either—at least, not yet."

Well, for a while I'd been working up to *the* question. And at this point I stiffened my spine (which, luckily, was minus the professed curvature) and dived in. "Do you recall where you were between, say, three-thirty and seven p.m. on the Saturday Mrs. Herman took that spill?"

Now, although it was conceivable that the Medical Examiner had been able to narrow the time of death a bit, for the present I preferred to avoid any involvement with the police. So I focused on the period between the time Frankie left the deceased's home and the hour her fiancé arrived there for dinner—according to the lovebirds, that is, and I could see no reason to doubt them. Anyhow, at this stage of my investigation, their information was all I required. "It's for my records," I threw in hastily in response to Cliff's deep scowl.

"Yeah, sure," he replied, his tone heavy with sarcasm. And a moment later: "That was two weeks ago, you said on the phone."

"Yes, she died on December fourteenth—two weeks ago tomorrow."

Without another word, Cliff flipped open the leather-bound book on his desk and riffled through it until he came to the appropriate page. "All right," he said, tracing the entries with his finger. "I spent most of the day looking at possible sites for a motel we're planning to build over in Pennsylvania. It must have been four-thirty or five when I got back to the office."

"And how long did you remain here?"

"I can't tell you exactly. I had to take care of a number of matters, though, so I'd estimate that it was easily two hours."

"Is there someone who can confirm your presence in Pennsylvania?"

"I didn't meet with anyone, if that's what you're asking. I was just driving around, checking out locations."

"Um, can anyone verify when you arrived at the office?"

"My brother was most likely still around," Cliff responded testily. "He spends more time at work than he does at home. But maybe you'd prefer someone other than a blood relative to corroborate my . . . *alibi*. So let me see if I can find a more neutral party for you." He pressed the button on the intercom again. "Would you mind stepping into my office now, Ms. Kranepool?"

I heard a faint, "Be there in a minute, Mr. Cliff."

And she very nearly lived up to her word, too.

"Do you remember seeing me in the office on the fourteenth of the month?" Cliff put to the girl.

"The fourteenth?" she echoed, screwing up her forehead.

"It was the Saturday before last."

"Oh"—she slapped her forehead—"that was the day after my mom's operation."

"Right. I forgot about that," Cliff said to her. Then to me: "I called Ms. Kranepool on Saturday morning to find out how her mother was doing, and she said everything had gone well, thank God. Anyhow, Valerie—Ms. Kranepool—volunteered to come in later so we could clear up a little work. She'd taken some time off before the operation to be with her mother, and things had started to pile up. I let her know I might not be able to make it in much before five, but she insisted that she didn't have any plans for the evening."

"I told him that whenever he got here was okay," the secretary interjected.

"Would you mind if I asked Miss Kranepool a few questions, Cliff?"

"Be my guest," he replied with a wave of his hand.

I kicked off with, "Do you have any idea what time you arrived?"

"I'm positive it was past four," she answered, "because I was aggravated. I'd planned on being here by four in case Mr. Cliff came in earlier than he expected to, but I ran into a lot of traffic."

"When did Mr. Cliff show up?"

"At about twenty-five to five. I'm certain of this because of Mr. Chad—Mr. Cliff's brother. You see, Mr. Chad practically lives at the office—even on Saturdays he usually stays until eight, sometimes nine o'clock. But that particular Saturday when he said good night to me, it was so early for him to quit that I automatically checked my watch. It was four-thirty. And Mr. Cliff missed him by maybe five minutes."

"Was anyone else around then?"

Miss Kranepool shook her head slowly, as if reluctant to disappoint me. "Uh-uh. Only me."

"What time did you leave?"

"I left when Mr. Cliff did. It was a few minutes before seven, I think."

"Something just occurred to me, Ms. Kranepool," Cliff said here. "Unless I'm mistaken, I dictated some letters to you that afternoon. Would you mind bringing me the copies?"

"Of course not."

"Nice girl," he murmured after she'd gone on her errand. "Not the smartest, I grant you, but she does brighten up the place. Know what I mean?" The jerk actually winked at me! (Good thing I wasn't seated any closer to him; he'd have poked me in the ribs for sure.)

I was in the process of forming my next question when there was a loud knock on the door. It was flung open before Cliff had an opportunity to respond.

I twisted around in my seat. Framed in the doorway was a tall, curvy brunette with a short skirt and very red lipstick. She was attractive in a "seen it all, done it all" kind of way. I figured her to be early fortyish.

"What is it, Janet?" Cliff demanded, glowering at the woman.

"I didn't realize you were in with someone. Sorry about that," she said, a glance in my direction including me in the apology.

"Well, you can see now that I am," Cliff retorted.

Janet was either a consummate actress or she was wearing invisible armor, because she didn't appear to be affected in the least by the reception she was receiving. "We have to talk, Cliff. Stop by my office later." And turning on her heel, she strode off, allowing the door to slam ever-so-slightly behind her.

"Our bookkeeper," Cliff grumbled. "She's been with the company for so many years that she tends to forget *she* works for *me*."

With Jackie for a secretary, I knew exactly what the man was talking about.

"Um, there's one more thing I wanted to ask you."

"Then ask it," Cliff said wearily.

It was at this moment that Miss Kranepool returned, clutching a few sheets of paper. "You dictated these on December fourteenth, Mr. Cliff."

He took a quick look at the typewritten pages, thanked her, and promised to return them later. Then, after dismissing Ms. Kranepool, he passed the papers over to me. "See for yourself."

There were four letters, each of them bearing that all-important date.

"Satisfied?"

"Satisfied," I told him, placing the letters on his desk.

"Good. I believe you wanted to question me about something else before we wrap this up," he reminded me. (No doubt deciding this was preferable to receiving a phone call from me tomorrow.)

For the life of me, though, at that instant I couldn't recall what I'd had in mind. "Yes, I did—I do. But I seem to have forgotten what it was."

"In that case it couldn't have been too important, could it?"

"You never know."

"And I never will, either. Listen, according to you, this was only going to take a few minutes. *A few minutes, my ass!*" he said with what might have been mistaken for a sneer. "Oops. Hope I didn't offend you, Desiree."

"Not at all," I assured him between clenched teeth. "But I just remembered the question. Have you contacted either of Mrs. Herman's sons about the property since her death?"

"Come on, Desiree. I only found out what happened to her when you phoned yesterday. But I plan on getting in touch with the younger one next week. I have no idea where to reach the older brother." And so saying, Cliff pushed back his chair. "I think it's time we called it a day, don't you?" He wasn't actually asking for my opinion.

"I suppose it is." And now I started to dig around in my suitcase-size handbag. "I'm going to leave my business card with you, though, on the outside chance something should occur to you."

Rising, he walked over and stood alongside me as I continued to mine for the thing. Then he began to tap his toes on the floor (and very likely let loose with a couple of silent screams, as well).

I finally located the card, and after delivering it to Cliff with a little flourish, I got to my feet.

"It's a shame you went to so much trouble trying to get ahold of this, Desiree," he said, casually tossing the card on his desk. "As I've been attempting to convince you, I know very little about Ms. Herman herself and nothing—zero—about her death."

He escorted me to the door of his office then, and we shook hands. "Thank you for your time," I told him politely.

"Sorry I couldn't help. Oh, and good luck with the investigation," he added dismissively, evidently certain he'd seen the last of Desiree Shapiro.

How wrong he was.

Chapter 14

Even with a fair amount of traffic, it was quicker driving home from West Aubrey than it had been driving down there. Probably because I only got lost twice.

When I walked into the apartment, the answering machine was winking at me. There was a single message.

"Ms. Shapiro, my name is Eleanor Frey. My mother lives in your building, and apparently she has a package that was meant for you"—this information delivered at rat-a-tat speed by an irritatingly cheerful voice. "I'll be at her place until around eight. But if you get in any later than that, don't worry; I'll be back here early tomorrow morning." She left her mother's telephone number.

Well, there was still more than ample time to reach her at her mother's today, but being extremely curious (make that nosy), I wouldn't allow myself the few seconds it would have taken to slip off my coat. I returned the call at once.

"Oh, Ms. Shapiro, it's Eleanor," I was told before I could finish giving my name. "All right if I bring down your package now?—I assume you're phoning from home."

"Yes, I am. But I wouldn't want to put you to any bother; I'll come upstairs."

"No, no. I'll see you in three minutes," Eleanor insisted.

And almost exactly three minutes later, there she was on my doorstep—a formidable-looking middle-aged woman in much-too-tight pants and an oversize top. She handed me a tiny white box.

"I'm really sorry about this, Ms. Shapiro. There was a mixup. I don't know if you've met my mother—she moved into the building about six weeks ago—but her name is Shapiro, too: *Sophie* Shapiro. And on December twenty-fourth she received this delivery. I can't understand how it happened—the correct apartment number was printed right there, in black and white. But I suppose things were pretty hectic this week, what with all the Christmas presents. . . . Anyhow, as near as I can figure it, the deliveryman must have asked my mother if she was Desiree Shapiro. But she doesn't hear too well—my mother's no spring chicken—so she probably thought he said *Sophie* Shapiro. Or maybe he just wanted to know if she was *Ms.* Shapiro. She tells me she signed for the package, too, although nowadays you can't place too much stock in *anything* she says." Eleanor paused for a moment (maybe to inhale) before continuing. "Then again, I suppose she'd have had to sign. I can't say if the man looked at the signature or not, but he probably wouldn't have been able to decipher her handwriting if he did—lately she mostly scribbles.

"At any rate, Mother called me the next day to tell me she'd gotten this *beautiful* gift. I asked her who it was from, and she said it was from somebody named Nick."

Nick! Nick sent me something for Christmas! It was the closest my heart had ever come to singing.

"I wasn't familiar with any Nick," Eleanor rattled on, "and I didn't remember my mother's ever mentioning the name, either. But I couldn't be a hundred percent sure the package was meant for someone else—not until I went over there this afternoon and saw the card. Then I was positive. Fortunately, my mother hadn't bothered to throw away the wrapping—among other things, she's turned into a regular pack rat—so I was able to find out who the intended recipient was.

"Well, that's the whole story." Suddenly Eleanor chuckled. "Even now, though, my mother isn't totally convinced that isn't *her* present"—she gestured toward the box in my hand. "You know how they get when they reach a certain age."

"Thanks very much for your trouble; I really appreciate it," I said. But pushing the words out of my mouth wasn't easy. I mean, once she'd shown herself to be so intolerant of her aged parent, I was hardly kindly disposed toward the woman.

"Or maybe dear old mum's sharper than I give her credit for," she told me then. "Could be she hates to part with that little item. Go take a look; it's *just gorgeous*!"

The second I closed the door I put the distasteful Eleanor Frey and her poor, confused mother out of my mind.

I was so anxious to see what was inside that box that I opened it where I stood. The card was on top of the tissue paper. It read DEZ, I HOPE YOU'LL ALLOW ME TO REMAIN IN YOUR LIFE LONG ENOUGH TO FILL THIS UP FOR YOU. OR BETTER YET, EVEN LONGER. It was signed MERRY CHRISTMAS, NICK.

I parted the tissue. Underneath lay a double-link gold charm bracelet with a single charm: a gold-and-ruby heart. I was so moved, I wanted to cry. But I decided the tears could wait. Right now I was going to model my gift.

I was holding out my arm and admiring the bracelet when it hit me: I hadn't sent anything to Nick! Frankly, at this point in our relationship, I hadn't so much as considered it. And to make matters worse, when I spoke to him the other day, he must have been expecting that I'd mention his present to me, which, naturally, I hadn't. Well, I would rectify that this minute—provided I could get ahold of his parents' phone number.

Information had two listings for a Grainger in Boca Raton, and I jotted down both.

On my first try the telephone was answered by an obviously prepubescent male with a disturbingly familiar voice. (I don't have to be any more specific than that, do I?) I hung up as if the receiver were scorching my hand. The thanks would have to wait until I heard from Nick.

It was then that I took another look at his card—I couldn't help myself. And this is when the bubble burst. The man hadn't signed it "Love"!

Still, I reasoned, *you don't send a bracelet like this to someone you only like. That sort of gift is certainly prompted by a stronger emotion than "like."*

A nice thing about bubbles. All it takes to get one aloft again is a little positive reinforcement.

I went back to Bloomingdale's on Saturday, right after breakfast. Which means I got there around one.

Returning two of Tuesday's acquisitions was pretty easy. It was a little more difficult to part with the green leather clutch. But I kept telling myself it was crazy to keep a bag I couldn't afford in order to wear it with a wardrobe I didn't own.

I managed to avoid any further temptation that day by marching straight ahead and refusing to allow my eyes to wander either to the left or the right.

It was late in the evening when I finally got around to reviewing my meeting with Cliff Seymour.

I had to concede that I didn't like the guy. To give you some idea of *how much* I didn't like him, the words he immediately brought to mind were snide, rude, and smarmy. Listen, I didn't even care for Cliff's face—although I grant you this was unfair. After all, his looks weren't his fault—apart from that hair gel, I mean.

I thought it best to remind myself that it wasn't my job to assess him as a human being, but as a murder suspect.

I concentrated on motive.

Acquiring the property of the deceased was important to Cliff, all right. And how much stock could I put in his claim that he felt she might still be persuaded to sell? Everyone else I'd spoken to seemed to believe Aunt Bessie was inflexible about retaining her house at the beach.

The man did talk about having found what appeared to be another suitable spot for the mall, though, which would pretty much have eliminated his reason for doing in Aunt Bessie. But who could say if he was telling the truth about this "promising" new location? Still, a point in his favor was the fact that he continued to prefer the original site—the one that included Aunt Bessie's property. I mean, why would he admit to a thing like that if he were her killer?

You poor, pathetic jerk, I shot back. (I wasn't in the mood to pull any punches.) *Could be he said that to induce you to think exactly what you're thinking,*

There was another, far more important consideration, however. Frankie told me she'd left the home of her almost-mother-in-law at three-thirty. (And as I pointed out before, I'd had no cause to question her word on this.) Which meant that even if Cliff entered the house directly on her heels, he wouldn't have had time to give Aunt Bessie that fatal shove and make it back to West Aubrey at twenty-five to five. And if he'd remained at work until almost seven . . . Well, it's a real challenge to be in two places at the same time.

Of course, I mused, there was always the possibility that he'd somehow persuaded that cutie-pie secretary of his to lie for him. But since I hadn't given him any indication as to when Aunt Bessie might have taken that spill—I was certain of this—he wouldn't have known what hours he'd be asked to account for— unless, that is, he'd helped her along.

Has it occurred to you that someone else might have clued him in on the time frame? I countered.

But what about those four pieces of correspondence dated December fourteenth?

And here I *really* lost patience with myself. *How stupid can you be? He could have dictated those letters at, say, eight p.m. Or the previous day. You've never heard of something being dictated one day and tran-*

scribed the next? Hey, he could even have had the girl type up those letters on Thursday, solely in anticipation of your visit.

This was about all the thought I devoted to Cliff Seymour that Saturday. My mind kept returning to Nick—and my bracelet.

I'll let you in on a secret. That night I even wore it to bed.

Chapter 15

I devoted most of Sunday to my work. In fact, I only took two breaks: one for lunch at about two o'clock and a second when Ellen phoned at a few minutes past four.

"Did I interrupt anything?"

"Yes—and thank you. I was transcribing my notes, and I *hate* transcribing my notes. How was your Christmas in Greenwich?"

"Great. Mike's parents are wonderful people."

"True."

"They felt *so* bad that you couldn't be with us—Mike and I did, too, of course."

"I wanted to come—I'm sure I would have enjoyed it. But I had so much to do that I'd have felt guilty taking off like that."

"How's the new case going?"

"Ask me in a week or two."

"Nothing yet, huh? What's it about, anyway? You didn't go into any of the details.".

I proceeded to provide a brief synopsis.

Ellen clucked a couple of times when I'd finished. "That's so sad," she murmured. "Aunt Bessie must have been a really nice person—I mean, for her nephew to care about her the way he did. So what do you think? Was it an accident—or . . . what?" I had the feeling Ellen couldn't quite manage to get out the word "murder."

"Well, naturally, I have to look into this as if it were a homicide, but I haven't actually formed an opinion so far."

"What do you *think,* though," she persisted.

I laughed. "You're not going to let me off the hook, are you?"

"Nope." Then she giggled, as only Ellen *can* giggle.

"Okay. Right now I'm leaning toward Aunt Bessie's having been pushed down those stairs—but that's at this particular moment. Five minutes from now I could change my mind. The thing is, I haven't uncovered anything that would convince me to sign on to either alternative."

Ellen was very encouraging—as always. (I suppose you could categorize it as blind loyalty.) "You'll find out what happened to her; wait and see. But be really, really careful, will you?"

Uh-oh. Here we go.

For once, though, she didn't wait to be reassured. "Something just occurred to me, Aunt Dez. Let's say that at some point you decide—erroneously—that the poor woman tripped. After all, you've been known to jump the gun every once in a while." Following which pronouncement she immediately tagged on, "Even though you invariably solve the case in the end. Anyhow, promise me you won't let your guard down prematurely."

"I promise." Then, desperate to change the subject, I blurted out the first thing to occur to me: "By the way, will Mike be off New Year's Eve?" (Ellen's new husband is a resident at St. Gregory's Hospital.)

"No, unfortunately. I was about to ask about *your* plans."

"I don't have any."

"You're not going out with Nick?"

"He's in Florida, visiting his parents. He'll be ringing in the New Year in Boca Raton."

"What about that disgusting child of his—is he down there, too?"

"You mean the devil's spawn?"

Ellen tittered. "I like that one. But I think I'm still partial to The Kid From Hell—or TKFH, in its abbreviated version." And then, her tone reflecting her concern: "You must be so-o disappointed. But I'm sure he'll make it up to you when he gets back."

"Ellen?" I said softly. "Nick sent me the most beautiful Christmas gift—a fourteen-karat-gold charm bracelet with a gold-and-ruby heart."

"My God, Aunt Dez! And you didn't *tell* me?"

"I *am* telling you," I reminded her. "I didn't receive it until Friday night; it was originally delivered to the wrong apartment. And since then I've been so caught up in this investigation that I even forgot to have supper yesterday. But I was going to call tonight and let you know—I swear."

Okay, so I did a little fudging here. I *had* had my supper yesterday—spaghetti with mushroom-and-tomato sauce. What's more, I hadn't intended to say a word to Ellen this evening about that very special present from Nick. I wanted to quietly savor the fact of it for a day or two—if this makes any sense to you. But as is no doubt fairly obvious, I'm not any great shakes at keeping secrets—my own, at any rate.

"Do you want to get sick?" Ellen was scolding. "You need to take the time to *eat*. And while we're on the subject of eating, I thought that in case you weren't doing anything special on New Year's Eve, you might like to come over for dinner."

Well, since I couldn't celebrate the arrival of 2003 with Nick, I wasn't in the mood to celebrate it with *anybody*—even my wonderful niece. "Thanks, Ellen, but I'm going to stay home; I've set aside the evening for pampering myself. What I have in mind is a nice, leisurely bubble bath—say, with a good book in one hand and a glass of champagne in the other. Then— assuming, naturally, that I'm not too crocked to function—I'll massage this magnificent body with a new body cream I have. And after that I'll give myself a facial and maybe a pedicure, too."

"You can do those things anytime," Ellen protested, the merest trace of a whine in her voice. "Anyhow, think about it. If you decide to come, you can even let me know at the last minute. It's not as if I'd be putting in any extra hours in the kitchen."

It wasn't exactly necessary for her to apprise me of this, since I've partaken of enough of Ellen's meals to be aware that the only thing she'd be making for dinner that night would be a telephone call. (Luckily, Mike has no objection to Chinese takeout, or after all these years with my niece, he wouldn't weigh much more than my pinkie by now.) "All right, I'll phone you if I change my mind. But I should tell you that I'm pretty firm about spending New Year's Eve in my own apartment this year."

"You haven't seen most of our wedding gifts yet," Ellen wheedled, taking one last stab at inducing me to weaken.

"I know. And believe me, I can't wait to have a look at all of that booty. But if I don't make it over on New Year's Eve, I'll be there soon afterward. Count on it."

"Well, it's up to you," she conceded reluctantly. "Anyhow, remember what I said earlier."

The switch in topics threw me. Regardless, Ellen being Ellen, I should have realized instantly what she was referring to. "About what?" I inquired foolishly.

"About looking after yourself. Swear you'll be careful."

"I swear."

"And that you'll eat."

"I have no objection to swearing to that, too."

"Those things are important, Aunt Dez. And sometimes I don't believe you take me seriously. You should—"

"Uh, Ellen? I have to hang up. Someone's at the door."

I couldn't think of any other way to terminate the lecture. And it worked. But it's the kind of ploy you can't use too often, otherwise the individual on the other end of the line could get suspicious. So I keep it in reserve for those times it's either "Someone's at the door" or a good, loud scream.

Chapter 16

On Monday I got up at an obscene six a.m. to ensure that I had plenty of time to eat, dress, and make it to Great Neck for my ten o'clock appointment. Naturally, I also factored in this talent I have for getting lost whenever I'm behind the wheel. Anyhow, I was all ready to leave and pick up my Chevy—in fact, I was out in the hall, poised to put the key in the lock—when I remembered.

"Oh, shit," I said aloud before I could censor myself. Then I dashed back inside and reached for the phone.

"It's me. I'm meeting with someone this morning, but I'll see you in the afternoon," I informed Jackie's voice mail. After which I cursed myself for a good couple of seconds for being such a wuss.

Now, my drive out to Sylvia's that day will no doubt go down in my personal history as a first—and probably last. The only way I can explain what happened (or more correctly, what didn't happen) is that the instructions I got from Stretch, one of the attendants at my garage, must have been positively foolproof (pun definitely applicable). I mean, I didn't miss a single turn or shoot past even one exit. Which is why, when I got to Great Neck, I stopped at a luncheonette for coffee and a Danish—and followed this with a second cup of coffee I didn't really want. But, the thing is, I had the feeling Sylvia Vine wouldn't be likely to drag out the welcome mat if I showed up on her doorstep even a few minutes in advance of the mandated ten o'clock.

Aunt Bessie's cousin—and former beloved friend— lived in a small, gated community, which I later learned was restricted to adults of fifty-five-plus years of age. Her modest white house, I noted, was almost an exact replica of the houses on either side of it— and the ones on either side of *those,* for that matter.

My hostess-in-waiting must have been watching through the window, because even before I rang the bell, she flung open the door.

"Missus Shapiro?" (Well, she finally got the name right, anyway.)

The woman couldn't have been Bessie Herman's junior by more than a couple of years—if that. But she was obviously determined to put a lot more distance than this between her own date of birth and Bessie's seventy-two. The result was that her appearance flirted with the garish. Her short, curly hair had been bleached to an almost white-blond, and she was heavily—and not very skillfully—made up, with bright blue eye shadow, dark red lipstick, and a large blob of rouge on each wrinkled cheekbone.

"You must be Mrs. Vine," I said. She nodded her confirmation, and I held out my hand. But she had turned away by then.

"Come," she instructed over her shoulder.

Following her into the living room, I became aware that, like me, the lady was vertically challenged, standing maybe an inch or so below my five-feet-two. Also like me—and this I'd established at first sight—she was on the full-figured side. But that, unfortunately, is where we parted company, since a decent portion of Sylvia's fullness was concentrated in the chest area. The low-cut, semi-sheer white overblouse she was wearing did an excellent job of trumpeting this fact—although it didn't quite manage to cover the visible panty line under her too-tight black spandex toreadors.

She indicated the sofa with a toss of that almost white-blond head. "Sit."

"Thank you," I murmured, obeying the dictate.

And now she adjusted the chair adjacent to the couch so that we'd be facing each other. But she hesitated before sitting down herself. "You vanting drink, maybe?" she offered. "Got tea, coffee, and Coca-Cola."

"No, thanks, I'm fine."

"Hokay." She plunked her well-rounded derriere on the chair. "So? Who tell you lie I vas in Bessie's neighborhood on day she die?"

"I'm sorry, but I really can't disclose—"

"Yeah, yeah. You make up so I seeing you, yes?"

"Of course not," I protested. But I could feel my face redden, and I cursed myself for it. "I can't reveal the name of the person," I said. "It's certainly possible, though, that the individual was mistaken."

Sylvia's next "yeah, yeah" was accompanied by a sly grin.

"Umm, would you mind telling me where you were between three-thirty and seven p.m. that day? It was on December—"

"I know ven happen." Then, her voice sharp with indignation: "I don't kill Bessie Herman."

"Oh, please don't misunderstand. I just need the information for my records."

"I vas here whole day cleaning up house, account of friend coming for dinner seven o'clock."

Her Washington companion? I wondered idly before inquiring, "Is there anyone who could verify that you were at home before seven? A neighbor, perhaps? Or someone you might have spoken to on the phone? It's just for my records," I quickly reiterated.

"I not see nobody. I probably speak on telephone, but who can remember now who I speak to?"

"It *has* been a while," I agreed. "But in case something should occur to you, would you mind giving me a call? I'll leave you my card."

"All right. So vut else you vant ask me?"

"I would—" A ringing telephone postponed the question.

"You vill excuse, please," Sylvia said, reaching for the portable phone on the large glass cocktail table between us. "Hello?" she murmured into the mouthpiece. And then: "Ahh, is you," she acknowledged softly, almost seductively, following which she jumped to her feet and hurried into the adjoining dining room. She talked quietly—too quietly for me to eavesdrop with any success.

The boyfriend, no doubt, I informed myself. With nothing better to do, I glanced around the room. It wasn't exactly what you'd call tidy. Magazines were piled on both end tables and strewn on the cocktail table, while a *Sports Illustrated* and a *Playboy* were the joint occupants of a club chair. The furniture was of decent quality, I decided, but it was obvious that nothing here was of recent vintage. Much of the upholstery was faded, and one of the sofa cushions had a very visible tear. Plus, the light beige rug proved the perfect showcase for any number of timeworn stains, a few of them fairly prominent.

I had just about finished surveying my surroundings when Sylvia resumed her seat.

"Do you live here alone, Mrs. Vine?" I asked (the *Sports Illustrated* and *Playboy* having prompted the inquiry).

"Yes, is only me. Both boys got own place now."

(Well, either she had strange tastes for a woman, or I was looking at the consummate hostess.) "Uh, I'd appreciate hearing from you exactly what it was that soured your friendship with Bessie."

"Her sons did not say to you already?" I was about to answer when Sylvia held up her hand. "Never mind. I tell to you anyvay. I tell to you da true."

She proceeded to relate pretty much the same story I'd gotten several times before—but with a slightly different spin to it. "My son, Richie, he had opportunity to be partner in automobile business, but he vas short money. Dat voman—my *friend*"—this was punctuated by a sneer—"*offer* to lend to Richie five tousand dollar. And on account of dis offer, Richie figure is all right to give two tousand dollar deposit and sign paper to buy into company. But den Bessie change mind and put stop on check. Vare dis leave my son, I ask you?"

"Uh, she must have had a reason," I responded cautiously.

"Reason is I talk too much. Bessie call me on telephone just vun day after Richie is arrested. Naturally, I am very upset. Richie and dis friend vas collecting money for some charity, see, but friend—Flip is name—he keep money for self. Richie not have no idea Flip doing dis, of course, but I say to myself, 'Suppose dey send my Richie up river anyhow?'

"Vell, Bessie tell from my voice dat someting boddering me. 'Vut is matter?' she vanting to know. I say notting is matter; I have little cold is all. But Bessie don't believe, and she not letting me alone. She ask and ask until I starting to cry. Finally, I tell to her. I explain dat Richie, he believe money going for very good cause, but instead is going in pocket of Flip. I find out later Flip is nogoodnik—been in prison already, and is alvays in trouble vit police. Anyhow, Bessie say not to vorry. 'Everyting vill be hokay,' dat liar promise me."

"Mrs. Herman didn't mention that she intended to stop payment, I gather."

"No. I not find out until Richie take check to bank. I not understand how such good friend—a *cousin*, even—could do such a ting. So I telephone to her. 'Vhy?' I say. She say she not vanting to make loan no more because Richie is not honest person. She claim she hear from somebody he and his buddy *splitting* charity money dey collected."

"Did you ask Mrs. Herman where she got that from?"

"Is not really important. 'Vhy you not at least calling to tell me you going to do dis?' I ask. She say she is sorry; she vas trying to vork up nerve to pick up telephone, but I not give her chance. Baloney! She had plenty chance—plenty!"

At this juncture the phone rang again, and again Sylvia retreated to the dining room and spoke in whispers. But I could swear I heard the word "tiger" at one point and that this was followed by a low, throaty growl.

On her return she shrugged and said plaintively, "Vut I can do? Got many friends."

"No problem. Uh, tell me, Mrs. Vine, was Richie able to get out of his commitment to buy into that business?"

"You tink dey let him off hook? Ha! Some joke! But dat's vut he have mama for. I borrow five tousand to give to son. Like I tell you, got friends."

"How is the company doing?"

"Is bankrupt, dat is how doing. My husband, Moe— he should rest in peace—his store is bankrupt vun time. Only vas after lotta years, not two, tree monts like Richie's place."

"Um, are you aware, Mrs. Vine, that just a few weeks ago Richie telephoned Mrs. Herman?" That was as far as I got before yet another call came in.

When Sylvia reentered the living room after this third brief absence, she was grinning sheepishly. "Got *too many* friends, I tink sometime." I had the impression she was blushing when she made the statement, but with all of that rouge it was hard to tell.

"There's no such thing. You're a fortunate lady."

Her bottom had barely made contact with the seat cushion when Sylvia, looking troubled, revisited the subject we'd touched on just prior to this latest interruption. "You tell me my son Richie, he telephone Bessie?"

I nodded. "Last month."

She shook her head. "Make no sense. How you hear dis?"

"From Donnie, Bessie's son. He informed me that Richie was very abusive to Mrs. Herman, that he called her some terrible names. She finally hung up on him."

"No," Sylvia declared emphatically. "I not believe dis."

"I intend talking to Richie to try to find out if that actually occurred."

"Good. He vill explain is big lie. He vill tell to you da true. Is how I raise my sons."

"Uh, the thing is, I need to know how to reach him."

She hesitated then.

"You're not concerned that what Donnie told me was a fact, are you?" I challenged—but gently.

"I write down number for you," Sylvia said by way of a denial. And jumping to her feet, she went over to a scarred little desk in a corner of the room. She came back with a piece of paper containing Richie's address—he was living in Brooklyn—and telephone number.

"So it vas Donnie who hire you, huh?" she mused, sitting down again.

"No, it was Mrs. Herman's nephew—Ben Berlin."

"I should have guess. Ben tink his aunt is such vunderful person. *Nyet!* Bessie Herman vas big pain alvays. But ve born same small town in Russia, and ve know each other since young girls. Also, our husbands, dey come to be like brudders. So all dese years I overlooking tings. Plenty tings."

"Such as—?"

"She alvays sticking big nose vare it don't belong. Ever since I come to dis country, Bessie boddering me I should go school and learn better English. But how I speak good enough for husband—he should rest in peace—so vhy she care, I asking you? She vant I should keep kosher home, too, and join synagogue. And she say I must buy new furniture. 'Fine,' I answer her, 'but whose money I should use?' She also instruct me how I should dress and how much makeup I should put on face. And listen, after my Moe pass avay, Bessie even tell to me how long I must vait before I have date. She not giving damn I vas poor lonely vidow." Sylvia's eyes seemed to throw off sparks. "Everyting vas her business. I svear to you, vas like having prison matron for friend."

Immediately after this, as I was preparing to leave on my own, Sylvia glanced at her watch and announced, "You got to go now. Have beauty parlor appointment in half hour." And with a self-satisfied little grin: "Got big date tonight."

I was smiling to myself when I walked out of the house. The poor lonely widow certainly didn't appear to be lonely anymore. When I reached the sidewalk, two women were slowly passing by, arm-in-arm, the younger one, who was somewhere in her middle years, obviously supporting her frail, much older companion. Suddenly the latter stopped in her tracks, turned around, and looked me square in the face.

"You're friends with that *courva*? Shame on you!"

I didn't respond. Mostly because I was so astonished by the outburst.

And what the hell was a *courva*, anyway?

Chapter 17

Courva . . . courva . . .

The word was vaguely familiar, but I had no idea what it meant. And although I had the feeling it was Yiddish, I wasn't really sure. One thing I *was* sure of, however: It was definitely not a compliment.

The trip home from Great Neck didn't turn out to be a repeat of the miraculous drive out there. In fact, I got lost not once, not even twice, but a ridiculous three times. Worse yet, almost as soon as I left her, I found myself wondering whether my visit with Sylvia Vine had been that productive.

I hated to think I'd made the schlep to Long Island for no reason, however. So when I engaged in the usual self-interrogation during that extended little journey, I strained to find something noteworthy I was bringing away with me. Like Sylvia's depiction of her once-upon-a-time friend, maybe?

It certainly contradicted everything I'd heard from Ben and Cassie about the deceased. Plus, it was at odds with the apparent devotion of both of Bessie's sons. Still, I could appreciate that there was at least *some* basis for this damning portrayal.

I mean, while Bessie may have had what she regarded as a legitimate reason for stopping payment on that check, it would, nevertheless, have been a lot more considerate if she'd first notified her cousin of her intention. And as for Sylvia's characterization of the victim as hypercritical and overbearing, it was probable there was some truth in that, as well—

although I did question the extent to which these traits intensified once Bessie had reneged on that loan.

Anyway, my take on Bessie Herman was that while she might not have been goodness all tied up with a pretty red ribbon, she was basically a nice person who, like all of us, didn't always do nice things.

Naturally, I also gave some thought as to how Sylvia stacked up as my killer. The truth is, though, I didn't regard her as too likely a prospect. *But you've been wrong before, you know,* I countered by way of encouragement. *Also, keep in mind that the woman wasn't able to account for her whereabouts during the critical period.* Still, Sylvia's beef with Bessie dated back to August. And why wait four months to send her tumbling down those stairs?

Nevertheless, I finally concluded that today's meeting had been worthwhile after all. If nothing else, it had produced Richie's address and phone number—and I considered him a much more promising suspect than his mother was.

It was after two when I reached Manhattan, and that being the case, I decided there was no point in putting any pressure on myself to get to the office. (Don't ask me to explain this reasoning, because I can't.) So before heading for work, I stopped at Little Angie's, where they make the best pizza in the entire world—I swear. Unless, that is, you have some kind of weird prejudice against a thin, crispy crust, an incredibly tangy sauce, and the kind of delectable toppings no other establishment even comes close to duplicating.

I attempted to sneak past Jackie's desk. Fat chance! "Where *were* you?" she scolded. "I was beginning to think that this Mrs. Vine was holding you hostage."

Anxious to avoid any further questions—and to guard against her spotting any telltale pizza fixings on my person—I was determined to hurry by. So I responded while still in motion, "Um, there were a couple of stops I had to make."

"Hold it. Guess who phoned you about a half hour ago."

I reversed direction. "Who?"

"Take a guess, will you?"

"Okay. Tom Selleck."

"Not even close. Care to settle for Nick Grainger?"

"Really?"

"Really." Then, with a triumphant grin: "*And* he says to call him"—a significant pause here—"at home."

I practically ran down the hall to my cubbyhole. Without stopping to remove my coat, I dialed Nick's apartment. He answered on the first ring.

"It's me. Is anything wrong?" I asked.

"No, everything's fine. I wanted to come back a little early, that's all."

"The bracelet is just beautiful, Nick. I can't tell you how much I love it."

"Really?"

"Are you kidding? I was so thrilled when I opened the box that I wanted to pick up the phone that very minute. I even got your folks' number from Information. But then I figured that in view of the way things are with Derek—"

"I understand."

"Anyway, I'm crazy about that bracelet. I feel terrible that I didn't get you anything, though."

"Don't be silly. The truth is, it was an impulse purchase. I was shopping with Derek—he was looking to buy his mother a pin—and I saw the bracelet, and, well, I wanted you to have it."

"Thank you," I said softly. "So, when did you get in?"

"A couple of minutes before I telephoned your office. Returning to New York this afternoon was another impulse. For the past couple of days I'd been thinking a lot about how much I would have enjoyed spending New Year's Eve with you. But, of course, I didn't have a prayer of getting on a flight to New York. I also had no idea whether or not you'd made plans yourself. Then last night I was talking to this neighbor of my parents'. Now, Dean—the neighbor—has this obscenely wealthy brother. And Dean casually mentioned something to the effect that it was too bad I wasn't interested in going home tomorrow—meaning today—otherwise, he'd have invited me to join him on his brother's private jet. And before I realized I was going to say it, I told him that, as a matter of fact, I *could* use a lift. Incidentally, Dez, that damn plane's spoiled me forever. It's *beyond* luxurious!"

"Your parents were okay with your leaving early like this?"

"They were fine with it as long as I didn't take Derek with me. He'll be traveling as scheduled. My mother will go to the airport with him to make sure he gets off safely, and Tiffany will be meeting the plane when it lands. She actually *volunteered.*" And now he added haltingly, "Er, look, Desiree, I don't want you to, uh . . . to think I was being presumptuous; I flew back just on the *chance* that you might be available."

"You're in luck."

"You're free?" He was enough of a gentleman to sound incredulous.

"As a bird."

We made plans to have dinner at the nicest Manhattan restaurant Nick could find that wasn't already all booked up. After which we'd return to my apartment for a glass or two of champagne.

I must have had the world's biggest, dumbest grin on my face when I hung up the phone. I could hardly believe it! Nick had cut short his vacation just to celebrate New Year's Eve with me! Well, this being the case, I could certainly expect more than a perfunctory kiss on the cheek tomorrow night.

Or could I?

Chapter 18

I toyed briefly with the notion of skipping work on Tuesday. I mean, after you've spent more than eighteen hours on cloud nine, it isn't easy to even contemplate switching gears to deal with such mundane matters as murder—*possible* murder, anyway.

In the end, though, I showed up at the office around ten, silly grin, fluttering stomach, and all.

"Hi, Jackie," I chirped.

"I wasn't sure I'd see you today, Dez. I figured you might want to stay home and prepare for your date."

"The thought did cross my mind. But I have a bunch of notes to transcribe—what else is new?—so I figured I'd come in for a few hours at least."

"And besides, you've got a beauty parlor appointment only a couple of blocks from here. Correct?"

"How did you know that?"

"Call me psychic."

"No, seriously . . ."

"Emaline telephoned about fifteen minutes ago to say she had a cancellation at noon. She wanted to find out if you could make it then, since she'd like to leave early." Jackie raised an eyebrow. "The woman doesn't exactly slave away over those tinted little heads, does she?"

"Look, don't knock my Emaline. What other beauty salon could you phone the afternoon before New Year's Eve and still be able to get an appointment for the big day?"

"I don't suppose you've ever wondered why there's always an opening," Jackie remarked sarcastically.

"Actually, I haven't. I *know* why. But it's like this. With Emaline doing my hair, I set the bar pretty low, so I'm never that disappointed with the results. But I'd better give her a call."

"Can I tell you something, Dez?" Jackie shouted to my rapidly disappearing back. "You're certifiable!"

I had just finished advising Emaline that she could expect me at twelve, when I was contacted by—of all things!—a prospective client. I almost fell off the chair. I mean, forget about hen's teeth; lately, clients have been *really* rare—around here, at any rate.

Anyhow, the individual on the line was calling because she'd come across my name in the Manhattan Yellow Pages, and it sounded like the right name for the job. (???) It seems she needed evidence that her husband was sleeping with her sister's best friend.

Well, peeking into windows isn't exactly my thing. Plus, I'm not too handy with a camera. Besides, I was so tied up with Aunt Bessie's murder that I didn't see where I could take on anything else just then.

"I have an associate that's an expert on matters like this," I told the woman. "If you like, I'll have him get in touch with you, and you can make all the arrangements directly with him, Mrs. ?"

"Smith. Mary Smith. And it's my real name, too. What's *his* name—your associate's?"

"Harry Burgess."

"Harry, huh? It doesn't sound as if he's too imaginative. On the other hand, it has a kind of solid ring to it. Okay. Tell him to call me."

As soon as we hung up, I got in touch with my old friend Harry, a semiretired PI from Fort Lee, New Jersey. I asked about his availability.

"You need me, I'm yours. Hey, it gets me out of the house. Whenever Midge"—she's Harry's wife—"lays eyes on me she's got some friggin' chore needs my immediate attention. I don't know how she dreams up all those jobs for me, either. She's a friggin' magician."

"I should warn you that this woman—Mary Smith—seems like a genuine cuckoo bird."

"No problem. I got nothin' against birds."

"Listen, Harry, I'm all tied up on another case right now, so I'm not involved in this. You make all the arrangements directly with her."

"Okay, but naturally I'll give you a percentage."

"You do, and I'll phone Midge with a few home-decorating ideas."

Less than ten minutes later I heard from my client.

"I wanted to wish you a very Happy New Year, Desiree."

"Thanks, Ben, the same to you," I said, waiting uncomfortably for him to state the real reason for his call.

"And, er, also a healthy one."

"You, too."

"Uh, I don't suppose you have anything to report yet." Well, there it was.

"Unfortunately, no. I'm still in the process of gathering the facts. Incidentally, I was out to see Sylvia Vine yesterday. She gave me her son Richie's telephone number, and I intend to try reaching him today."

"Good. Donnie told me about Richie's call to Aunt Bessie, and I'd like to strangle the little twerp. Anyway, you'll keep me posted on the investigation, won't you?"

"Absolutely. I'll contact you the instant I learn anything."

"Thanks. And, Desiree?"

"Yes?"

"My main purpose in phoning you today *was* to wish you a Happy New Year."

Now, I ask you, is this a nice man—or what?

I silently vowed I'd learn the truth about his beloved Aunt Bessie's death—or bust.

Of course, it was very possible Richie Vine was at work. But then again, maybe not. So I dialed the number Sylvia had provided.

He picked up on the first ring with a gracious "Yeah?"

"Is this Richie?"

"Ric," I was informed.

"Uh, well, my name is Desiree Shapiro, and I'm—"

"I know who you are; my mom told me. She's after me to get together with you and give you the facts—the *real* facts—about what happened between me and Bessie Herman." He spat out the name.

"I'd appreciate it if you could spare me a few minutes—whenever it's convenient for you. But the sooner the better, of course."

"You can forget today. I got me an invite to this fab party in Manhattan later, so I'll be doing some shopping this afternoon. My girlfriend's been bugging me to get a haircut and a new pair of jeans." He let out a snort. "Like anyone'll be sober enough to notice what I got on, right? Tomorrow's out, too, naturally—I expect to be hung over pretty good. And Thursday morning I have some stupid interview. It's for a real dead end job, too. But when your mother *and* your girlfriend are constantly on your back, if you got any smarts, you don't put up a fight; you go along for the ride. Know what I mean?"

"Uh, not exactly."

"I'll spell it out for you. As long as my mom and Shirley are convinced that I *wanna* find work, that I'm willing to take almost anything, I'm okay."

"What if—and it *is* conceivable—your mother and Shirley should learn that you turned something down?"

"Jesus! You are so naive! There's no way they can—I make sure I'm not *offered* the job." Richie laughed then, rather unpleasantly.

What an obnoxious little creep! I thought. But I gave him one of my all-purpose "Oh's.

"And listen, what I just told you? That's between you and me, right? My mother would never believe I'd say something like that anyhow."

"It'll be our secret. About our getting together, though . . ." I reminded him.

"Thursday afternoon's good with me. I can meet you near your office around one, and you can take me to lunch."

Talk about chutzpah! "No problem," I responded sweetly. "What sort of food do you like, Ric?"

"Steak."

"There's a steakhouse in the neighborhood that's supposed to be excellent."

"What's the address?"

I gave it to him. "I'll make a reservation under Shapiro."

"Okay, see you Thursday, Dezzie." *Dezzie?* I wanted to gag. "Just keep an eye out for the best-looking guy in the place."

I didn't accomplish a whole lot in the way of work once we hung up. And it wasn't only because I had to leave for my hairdresser's appointment shortly. The biggest stumbling block was my mind. It kept wandering off to Nick and dinner and then what might—or might not—happen after that. . . .

Chapter 19

Emaline outdid herself that day. Low expectations or not, I came close to bawling when I checked the results of her handiwork in the mirror.

I didn't even *resemble* anything human. (Think French poodle that's been dipped in henna.)

As it happens, I hadn't planned to go back to work after the hairdresser's. But if I had, I'd have picked up the phone and informed Jackie that I wouldn't be returning after all. Listen, the fewer people who got a gander at me in this present incarnation, the better.

As luck would have it, I bumped into Barbara Gleason as I was about to enter our mutual building and she was rushing out. "Hi, Dez," she said. "Gotta run. But Happy New—" She took a good look at me then and stopped short. "What the *hell* happened to you?" she blurted out.

"I had my hair done."

"Is that what you call it? You ought to sue."

"I'll take it under advisement," I responded stiffly.

"Sorry. I shouldn't have said that; it's really not so terrible. It'll be fine by tomorrow. Honestly. And since you don't plan on going anywhere tonight—"

"As a matter of fact, I do," I broke in.

"But last week you said—" She bit her lip. "Listen, I had the same thing once." (I didn't believe this for a second.) "The curls will brush out. But if by some chance they don't, a quick shampoo will definitely do it."

"That's the only reason I haven't killed myself—

and my hairdresser. By the way, Barbara, you look great." She did, too. She was decked out in a beat-up old jacket and baggy jeans. She wasn't wearing a trace of makeup, either. But her cheeks were pink and her eyes were shining and, I don't know, she had a kind of *aura.*

"How can you *say* that? I didn't even bother to put on lipstick today, and I'm dressed like a real schlump."

"It has nothing to do with your makeup or your clothes; you're happy, and it shows." (I had bumped into Barbara at the incinerator on Christmas Day, and she'd gone on and on about how special Sandy was and what a fantastic time they'd had together the previous evening.)

"So tell me, what are you doing later?" she asked.

"I'm having dinner with Nick."

"Nick from upstairs?" She pointed heavenward.

"Yep."

"But I thought he was going to be in Boca Raton until after the holidays."

"So did I, but he came home a little early."

"Well, well," she teased, "I don't suppose it has anything to do with his wanting to spend 'the big night' with you."

"No, it doesn't."

Now, yesterday Jackie had pretty much demanded I tell her why Nick had called. To be honest, though, she didn't have to lean on me very hard. I was actually bursting to give her the report. In fact, right after that, I spoke to Ellen to clue *her* in, too—I couldn't contain myself. But then I decided that enough was enough. I realize there's an excellent chance that this will sound totally off the wall, but I'll level with you. I was afraid that if I went around blabbing my good news to everyone who'd listen, the Fates would punish me for being such a big mouth by putting the kibosh on things. (God! I was almost as bad as my client!)

"Anyway," Barbara was saying, "I'd better get a move on. I'm running over to the store for some club soda; Sandy and I are having drinks at my place before we go to dinner. Happy New Year, Dez. And have a wonderful, *wonderful* evening."

"You, too, Barbara."

We hugged and bussed each other on the cheek before heading our separate ways.

There was a message from Nick when I got upstairs. He'd made a nine o'clock reservation at a French restaurant and would be picking me up around eight-thirty. "I hope that's okay with you," he concluded. "You can reach me at the shop if there's a problem."

I glanced at my watch: three-ten. Good. I'd have plenty of time to attend to things.

I threw on some old clothes and—figuratively speaking—rolled up my sleeves. First, I prepared the hors d'oeuvres, having picked up the ingredients I needed on my way home from work last night. After dinner, when Nick and I returned here, our champagne would be accompanied by chilled mushrooms stuffed with liver pâté. And, of course, there'd also be the ever-popular cheese and crackers. But that was it. I mean, being that we'd have just eaten what I assumed would be a full meal, I decided that anything more would be overkill.

This attended to, I tackled the apartment. I'm not claiming I was all that thorough—the place certainly couldn't have passed the white-gloved mother-in-law test—but it wound up looking pretty damn clean. If you didn't look all that closely, that is.

And now I was ready for the really tough chore: me.

Following a leisurely bubble bath, I spent almost ten minutes with hairbrush in hand, attacking that ridiculous headful of curls. The effort helped some, but still, when I saw myself in the mirror, I felt I should be walking around on four legs and answering to the name Fifi. So I finally washed out what could laughingly be termed my coiffure, and once the hair was dry, I set it in large rollers. A half hour later, when I took out the rollers and applied the brush again, I was okay with the outcome. Not ecstatic, you understand, but at least I was no longer tempted to bark at my image.

I allowed myself a short break at this point in order to grab a snack that would tide me over until dinner. After this I was back at the bathroom mirror.

My makeup went on with only one minor mishap (for which, under the present circumstances, I could at least blame my nervous excitement). What happened was, before I realized what I was doing, I'd begun to fill in my eyebrows with my coral lip liner pencil. But fortunately, while the result was slightly bizarre, the damage was easily rectified.

It was when I was about to get into my clothes that I had to cope with a problem equal to the one on my head.

For starters, I was far from thrilled with anything currently in my closet. Believe me, if I'd had the slightest inkling a couple of days earlier that I'd be seeing Nick tonight, I would have spent every available minute frantically combing the stores for the perfect outfit. But I hadn't, so I didn't. If you follow me. Anyhow, the night before, after a lengthy internal debate, I'd settled on a beige silk shirtwaist that I accessorize with a beige, brown, and turquoise scarf. It's a couple of years old—okay, around eight—but they tell me it's very flattering. ("They" being one woman friend and Ellen.) Not that I expected the dress to cause Nick to go into heat at the sight of me, but I consoled myself (sort of) with the thought that nothing I wore was likely to have that kind of an effect on the man.

At any rate, I was all ready to step into the thing when I noticed that one of the seams had opened. It was a small opening, though, and while I'm no whiz with a needle, how adept does a person have to be to sew up an inch of fabric? I soon found out.

As it happened, I actually did an okay job. Only in the process I pricked my finger—ever so slightly. And suddenly I was bleeding all over the dress!

Now, most women have one outfit they turn to when

they don't know what else to wear. In my case it's a light blue A-line. And while I wasn't too thrilled to be relegated to old reliable, at least it didn't have any busted seams. I checked—twice.

I had just fastened my charm bracelet when Nick rang the doorbell. It was eight-thirty on the nose.

He was wearing a navy suit with a white shirt and a navy-and-red paisley tie. A navy overcoat was draped over his arm. In this woman's opinion, he looked absolutely *gorgeous*. And it wouldn't have been any big surprise to me if on seeing him right now, plenty of females with a more mundane taste in men than my own were to share this assessment.

He wrapped his arms around me and kissed me enthusiastically—on the cheek. As was characteristic of him, he had some kind words for my appearance when he stepped away. "You're a real knockout tonight, Dez."

"So are you."

He laughed. "I suppose there's something to be said for dating a woman with impaired vision." He handed me a bottle of champagne then—Dom Perignon, no less. "Would you mind putting this in the refrigerator?"

I didn't mind at all.

Georgette's was located in the East Seventies. And it was a truly elegant restaurant, with a soft pink and brown color scheme, mirrored walls, shimmering crystal chandeliers, and handsome French provincial furniture. What's more, the food turned out to be absolutely delicious.

It was really a stroke of luck that we'd gotten a reservation here.

A friend of Nick's had recommended the place to him after all the others he'd tried were completely booked, or else the line was constantly busy, or nobody bothered to pick up the receiver. We'd have struck out at Georgette's, too—if they hadn't had a cancellation only moments before Nick's call. Apparently, rather than take the trouble of going to their waiting list, they'd chosen to accommodate us.

We both began the meal with escargot in a puff pastry. (And I have a tendency to get rhapsodic about almost anything that arrives at the table in a puff pastry.)

Practically all my other favorite edibles were also on Georgette's menu. For an entrée, I had roast duckling with orange sauce, accompanied by wild rice with mushrooms and broccoli topped with hollandaise sauce.

Nick chose the steak au poivre (very tasty—I know, having sampled it), which was served with crispy *pommes frites* and glazed baby carrots.

For dessert, we shared a profiterole that was filled with vanilla ice cream and then lavished with a thick hot fudge sauce.

I'm pleased to report, however, that in spite of gorging ourselves on food and wine, we managed to carry on a conversation throughout the meal.

I wanted to know how Nick had enjoyed Florida.

"It was great spending time with my parents, but I'll take New York over Boca Raton any day," he told me.

"How does Derek like Florida?" I forced myself to inquire.

"That's a whole different story. Derek's crazy about it down there. He loves the water, and he can go swimming just about every day. Plus, he's always eating at different restaurants, which he also loves." Nick grinned. "Listen, I can see my son making a living as a food critic a couple of years down the road."

We were both having the escargot at this juncture, and Nick dipped a piece of bread into the sauce. After which he murmured, "I appreciate your asking about him, Dez."

I was attempting to frame a response (I mean, "That's all right" didn't quite do it for me), when he laid the bread on his plate and placed his hand over mine (the one that wasn't involved with the escargot). "It couldn't have been easy, considering how he treated you."

Again, I was all set to say something—although I hadn't the vaguest idea what I intended to say—but I was spared the necessity of taxing my brain. "It's still difficult for me to believe that a son of mine could have acted like such a miserable little stinker," Nick put in, grimacing. "He was so *devious,* too. But I honestly believe the therapy is helping him. That, and the fact that when he stays with his grandparents, Derek is in a very loving environment, and it appears to have a positive effect on him."

"Then it's good that he went to visit them."

"Yes, it is. But don't get me wrong: I'm not claiming he's suddenly evolved into an exemplary human being. However, he did seem a lot more open this past week. And lately he appears to be genuinely contrite about his behavior toward you. Still, his therapist feels that Derek has issues that need to be dealt with—most of them, I'm afraid, a by-product of the divorce." Nick shook his head slowly back and forth. "If Tiffany and I had been able to work things out . . . Maybe if we'd both tried just a little harder . . ." For a moment he looked close to tears. Then, with an obvious effort, he brightened. "But enough about me and my problem child. What's been going on in your life? I want to hear about your latest case."

I gave him a brief run-through, wrapping things up with, "So I'm fumbling around trying to figure out whether Aunt Bessie herself was responsible for that fall, or whether somebody helped her out a little."

"Which do you think it was?"

"Beats me."

"Not for long, though," he said, sounding for an instant like a male Ellen.

After this we touched on a whole variety of topics, covering everything from Tiffany's latest boyfriend— who Nick asserted had barely left his teens—to the relative merits of Agatha Christie versus Sir Arthur Conan Doyle. (And don't ask me how we got around to that one.)

"No contest," I declared.

Nick grinned. "I agree with you. Listen, I don't dispute that old Aggie was a talented lady, but Conan Doyle was a *genius*. His stories have such fascinating twists, such *atmosphere*."

"Yeah? Well, whenever I can't fall asleep, I take my Sherlock Holmes out of the bookcase, and in a few minutes I'm off to dreamland."

"You'll say anything to win an argument, won't you?" Nick accused good-naturedly. "The truth is, there isn't a single Sherlock Holmes *in* your bookcase. I looked."

"Have you considered the possibility that it's very often on my nightstand for the purpose I just stated? Believe me," I said, groping for a title, "*The Hound of the Barkervilles* is better than Sominex."

"Baskervilles," Nick corrected wryly.

"That's what I meant."

"I don't imagine you'd mind showing the book to me when we get back to your place."

Oh, hell, I should have figured as much! "It will be my pleasure," I replied loftily.

The instant Nick and I walked into my apartment, I tensed up. I didn't have a clue what to expect—romantically, I'm talking about.

It wasn't that I was even contemplating anything major. I mean, it would be acceptable if the man gave me a kiss that lasted longer than a wink—and if, for only the second time, it was my lips that were on the receiving end. But suppose he merely revisited my cheek—what then?

I attempted to reassure myself. This wasn't too likely—not after the pains he'd taken to be with me tonight. And let's not forget my beautiful bracelet. Nevertheless, what if we didn't make it past the starting gate yet again? Should I finally question him? Or should I spare us both a whole lot of embarrassment by simply accepting that regardless of the gift and his presence here in my living room right this minute, whatever interest Nick did have in me, it certainly wasn't physical?

Well, I could decide about that later—if I had to.

Anyhow, Nick took a seat on one of the club chairs, while I got out the stuffed mushrooms and the cheese and crackers.

"I suspected it all along," he proclaimed when I placed the two serving platters on the cocktail table.

"Suspected what?"

"That you, Desiree Shapiro, are a crazy person. After our substantial dinner, you're serving *more* food?"

"This is to line our stomachs for the champagne that's soon to follow."

"Oh, I see." He made an effort not to smile.

"What would you like to drink in the meantime?"

"A Coke, please—if you have it."

"Two Cokes, coming up."

When I returned from the kitchen, I handed Nick his soda, then perched on the edge of the sofa cushion with my own.

After we'd been chatting for a little while (during which time this crazy person observed Nick helping himself to two stuffed mushrooms and some cheese), he glanced at his watch. "It's almost ten of. I think it might be a good idea if we opened the champagne, don't you?"

"Definitely."

He followed me into the kitchen and uncorked the Dom Perignon, pouring it into the waiting flutes. Then we carried the glasses into the living room and set them on the coffee table, where they were to remain untouched until the magic moment.

And now Nick sat beside me on the sofa, leaving, I might add, not all that much space between us. "Shall we?" he asked, his hand on the remote control.

"But of course."

He clicked on the TV, and we joined Dick Clark and the hundreds of thousands of eager celebrants—most of them with balloons and noisemakers—who had come to Times Square all revved up to welcome the brand-new year just minutes away.

At last the much-anticipated tradition began. We watched, mesmerized, as the huge Waterford crystal ball commenced its sixty-second descent from atop One Times Square, while the visual countdown in a corner of the screen showed the remaining seconds of the old year slipping by: "Fifty-nine . . . fifty-eight . . . fifty-seven . . . fifty-six . . . " And soon we were on the threshold of two-thousand-three. "Ten! . . . Nine! . . . Eight! . . ." the revelers shouted, ticking off the seconds in unison, their voices growing louder and louder as the incoming year grew closer and closer. "Three! . . . Two! . . . One! . . ." they screamed at the top of their lungs—right before they *really* erupted, and the sounds of noisemakers and earsplitting shrieks of "Happy New Year!" filled the early morning air as confetti rained down from the rooftops.

Turning to me, Nick said softly, "Happy New Year, Dez."

"Happy New Year, Nick."

And then we were kissing, and I mean *kissing*. Maybe it's because I'd been deprived for so long, but I couldn't remember anyone ever kissing me like that before. Not since Ed, I mean. And that was almost a lifetime ago.

We came up for air, sipped some champagne, and kissed again . . . and again . . . and again.

Eventually we relocated to the bedroom. Which is all I intend to say about that night.

Except that Nick never did get around to asking for that phantom Sherlock Holmes.

Chapter 20

Nick picked me up at one o'clock on New Year's Day. I thought the smile on his face was on the shy side, which kind of reflected my own feelings at the moment.

We were going out to brunch at a neighborhood restaurant, so we were both dressed casually. Nick had on a wine-color polo shirt and chinos (and, needless to say, he looked positively adorable). While I was wearing a black cashmere turtleneck and a black wool skirt (an outfit that I insisted to myself was remarkably slenderizing).

Anyway, from the moment we were seated until I'd polished off my French toast and was well into my second cup of coffee, I kept trying to broach the subject that had been on my mind for, lo, these many months. But I couldn't seem to force the words out. I finally took the plunge when Nick was in the process of relating a funny story about some annoying customer. I was so intent on working up my courage that I ignored the fact that he was in the middle of a sentence—possibly even the punch line.

"So what took you so long?" I demanded.

"To do what?" he asked, obviously—and understandably—confused.

"I'm, uh, talking about last night."

"Oh," he responded, reddening. (I have no doubt my own complexion had just taken on a goodly amount of color, too.) I waited uneasily for him to say something more. At last he murmured, "It's hard to explain, Dez."

"Try, okay?" I gave him a wistful little smile.

There was another pause before Nick spoke again. "Okay," he told me stoically, "I'll do my best." And now his forehead pleated up, and two deep parallel lines materialized above his nose.

"When we first met, I liked you—I really did," he began. "Only with my marriage having gone down the drain in the fairly recent past, I wasn't very interested in dating. But, I don't know, then I decided it might be nice to have some pleasant company at dinner. I had no intention of getting involved in anything long-term, though. And that being the case . . . Well, the fact is, I'm just not a hit-and-run type of guy. Listen, is this making sense to you?"

I nodded.

"That's good. Anyhow, while at the outset I didn't figure we'd be going out more than two or three times, I'd always find myself looking forward to our spending another evening together. So the two or three dates turned into, well, quite a few more—as you're aware. And somewhere along the line, a funny thing happened. At first I steered clear of our having any kind of a physical relationship because I felt it was unfair to you. But the longer we continued seeing each other, the more concerned I became about the effect our making love might have on *me.* I wanted to avoid anything that would intensify my feelings for you." He managed a grin. "For a while now, though, I've recognized that I was fighting a losing battle."

"I'm glad you finally threw in the towel," I told him, feeling my cheeks burn again.

"Who could resist you?" he teased. "But let's cut the conversation before I scare myself to death." Then noting my expression, he put in quickly, "Just kidding. I'm glad I threw in the towel, too." And reaching across the table, he took my hand.

*   *   *

Nick had said there was some paperwork he needed to take care of. And I'd claimed it was practically an emergency that I spend what was left of the day transcribing my notes—although I had no intention of even switching on the computer. The truth is, I was overwhelmed by this sea change in our relationship, and I had to have some time to myself. I suspected that Nick might be feeling the same way.

Practically the minute I was back in my apartment I plopped down on the sofa, kicked off my shoes, and leaned back against the cushions. Then I reached for the remote.

It didn't take long for the television to lull me to sleep. I was awakened by the phone.

"Happy, *happy* New Year, Dez, dear. May two thousand and three be filled with happiness and robust health." And with a titter: "A little improvement in your finances wouldn't hurt either." The tone was so unlike her that it took a few seconds before I recognized that this was my good friend from across the hall and that the ebullient delivery was the result of her imbibing more than her usual ration of holiday cheer.

"The same to you, Harriet. And to Steve," I added, referring to her very nice husband. "I hope this is also a great year for Scott," I threw in generously, Scott being Harriet's not-at-all nice, spoiled-rotten son. "Likewise for Hyacinth," I tagged on, figuring it was only polite to include her colorless, almost inert daughter-in-law. "And . . . and, naturally, the little one."

"You never can remember his name," Harriet scolded mildly. "It's Graham. Just think of the crackers," she advised, following which she hiccuped. "Pardon me, Dez. We just got back from a fancy breakfast thrown by one of Steve's co-workers. And a very liquid little gathering it was, I might add. Hey, you didn't mention Baby—thought I wouldn't notice, didn't you?"

"Baby, too," I all but hissed. Now, Baby is Harriet's

Pekinese—and the only member of the family more repellent than Scott is. I mean, that vile creature would like nothing better than to inflict bodily harm on me—I'm convinced of it. But due to my having considerable poundage on him, he's settled for another way of communicating his animosity toward me: Whenever he's given the opportunity, he nonchalantly lifts his leg and pees on my shoes!

And now Harriet's voice took on an unmistakable edge. "By the way, how was your date with *hic* Mr. Wonderful upstairs."

Uh-oh. "Who told you about it?"

"I came up in the elevator with Barbara a few minutes ago. Why are you asking? Wasn't I supposed to know?"

"Of course you were. As a matter of fact, I intended to call you tonight. I had no idea Nick was even back in town until Monday. Anyway, we had a lovely time."

"Glad to hear it."

I couldn't tell whether or not Harriet was being sarcastic, but I thanked her anyway. "What did *you* do?"

"Oh, we also had a delightful time." This time I *knew* she was being sarcastic. "We went to some restaurant in the East Village with the Winklers—you've met them." (I hadn't.) "The food was putrid, and Lila Winkler started to feel sick and excused herself to go to the ladies' room. But she didn't make it. She wound up tossing her cookies in the middle of the dining room. But I'd better get going now; I have to see how Steve's doing."

"Why? Isn't he feeling well?"

"He'll live. He managed to survive last night's festivities okay, but today's breakfast party is a different story. I tried to get him to cut back on the Jack Daniel's. But you know how Steve is; he doesn't listen. And he never *could* hold his liquor."

A loud *hic* concluded the statement—and the conversation.

*   *   *

My eyes were already at half-mast when the phone rang again. "Happy New Year, Aunt Dez."

"And a Happy New Year to you and Mike."

There was a perfunctory thanks before Ellen pounced: "Well? How did it go last night?"

"I had a wonderful time. We went to—"

"Stop! You'll give me all the details when you come over for dinner tomorrow. Is around seven okay?"

"Gee, Ellen, what with New Year's Eve and everything, I'm terribly backlogged. Also, tomorrow I'll be having what I'm sure will be a very filling lunch. Look, why don't we make it sometime next week?"

"Because for one thing, both Mike and I are off tomorrow. And for another, you'll tell me that you're too busy with work next week, too. Besides, I don't think I can hold out that long. C'mon, Aunt Dez," she cajoled. "I'm dying to know what happened with Nick. I'm really anxious to show you our wedding gifts, too."

"And I'm anxious to see them, but—"

"If we don't get together on Thursday, we probably won't be able to do it until after the honeymoon."

To give you a little background on that honeymoon . . . Six days before the wedding, Mike's old college roommate—and closest friend—was in a pretty scary automobile accident. At first the doctors were concerned that his injuries might even be life-threatening. So as soon as they got the news, Ellen and Mike postponed their scheduled trip. To everyone's relief, however, none of Seth's injuries turned out to be that serious. While the poor guy was pretty banged up, he was not only able to attend the wedding but to serve as best man as planned. And now the bride and groom would soon be taking off for Barbados.

"Incidentally, we'll be ordering Chinese food," Ellen was saying. (Surprise, surprise!) "What would you like?"

Just then this old expression popped into my head. And while I believe it originated in reference to poker, it was certainly applicable here, too. It (more or less) goes: "You have to know when to hold and when to fold."

"The sweet-and-sour pork, I guess," I answered resignedly.

Chapter 21

At the office on Thursday everyone went around wishing everyone else a Happy New Year, so I didn't make much headway with typing up my notes. And I'd come in early this morning, too. (Early for me, anyway.) Then before I turned around, it was time to meet with my obnoxious thirty-year-old suspect—who'd sounded on the phone like he was on the cusp of sixteen.

I left work at quarter to one and hiked the four blocks to the restaurant. I was a little taken aback when I walked in—O'Brien's looked more like an Irish pub than a pricey steak house. I mean, not only were there checkered tablecloths and cozy booths, but I was almost ankle-deep in sawdust.

A maître d' in incongruously formal attire showed me to a booth. My lunch date was already there.

Now, remember Richie's telling me to "keep an eye out for the best-looking guy in the place"? Well, damned if he hadn't been speaking the truth!

The first thing to strike me about Richie Vine was his beautiful green eyes, which were framed with these dark, sweeping lashes—the kind you'd be tempted to kill for. Or I would, at least. He also had a straight nose and a nice mouth—not too small and not too wide. His face was tanned and his sandy shoulder-length hair liberally streaked with blond highlights. (Listen, it's *possible* it was the sun. Who's to say he hadn't just come back from Aruba?) The guy was hardly what you'd call a hunk, though. He had a slight build—trust me, a strong wind, and Richie was airborne. Plus, even in a sitting position, he didn't appear to be very tall. (When he stood up at the end of the meal I judged him to be all of about five-six.) Still, in spite of his very un-Schwarzenegger-like physique, I imagined that a great many misguided young females must find Richie Vine extremely appealing.

He made practically no attempt to rise when I got to the table. (I granted him the "practically" because he shifted his behind on the seat a couple of times.) I noticed then that he was wearing torn jeans and a faded plaid sport shirt—with the sleeves rolled up. And unless there'd been a change in plans, Richie here had come to lunch straight from a job interview. Well, if the position wasn't for a bike messenger, his claim about seeing to it that he doesn't get hired was no idle boast.

"You must be Dezzie," he said.

I flinched, after which I responded, "And you're Ric." (I almost added the "hie" for spite but then thought better of it.)

"That's me, all right."

The waiter appeared at this moment and handed us the menus. "Would you care for something from the bar?" he inquired.

The words had barely left the man's lips when Richie responded, "Scotch, neat. Wait a sec, huh? Make that a double."

"And the lady?"

"I'll have a glass of Merlot, please."

Richie was already going through the menu by then. And now I took a look at it myself—and gasped. (If I hadn't been on an expense account, I would no doubt have fainted.) The prices were stratospheric! I could only hope I'd learn something from this little jerk that would make my client's expenditure worthwhile.

Richie had quite a meal for himself, too: shrimp cocktail, onion soup, and a twenty-four-ounce porterhouse steak, along with side orders of creamed spinach, French fries, and onion rings. (This last a huge serving that he didn't even offer to share.) Plus, between bites he managed to squeeze in another double scotch. Then later, I was sitting there marveling at how much had just been packed into that narrow torso, when he ordered hot apple pie à la mode for dessert! Me? I was so appalled by what this metabolic mutant was costing Ben that I put the brakes on myself, limiting my consumption to a sirloin steak (the small size), a baked potato, and—I admit it—chocolate mousse. (After all, there's a limit to how much you can deny yourself.)

Anyway, during the course of the meal, I asked Richie a pretty fair number of questions, all of which he answered grudgingly. But this is understandable, if for no other reason than that the necessity to respond slowed down the speed with which he could bring his fork to his mouth.

I kicked off with, "Tell me about your relationship with Mrs. Herman."

"It started out okay and wound up lousy."

"What changed things?"

"Why're you asking me that? You already know the answer."

"Yes, but I'd like to hear it from you. You say you two got along at one time?"

"That's right. My mom and her, they used to be real close—like sisters almost. When me and my brother Myron were kids, we used to call her Aunt Bessie. And after I grew up I still didn't mind her too much. But then I got what I thought was gonna be my big break, see? What happened was, these two guys were giving me a chance to buy into their auto dealership. They said they were getting too old to put in the hours they'd *been* putting in—one of those assholes was past fifty, and the other one—Christ!—he coulda been pushing sixty. They told me they didn't wanna just *hire* somebody; what they were looking for was a junior partner. Somebody who'd have a *reason* to work his butt off. They made it sound like anyone who went in with them would end up practically rolling in the green stuff. And they asked me was I interested.

"I saw it as a no-brainer. The only trouble was, I didn't have any dough. And Mom . . . well, she isn't exactly a Mrs. Trump. My old man was a nice enough guy, but as a businessman he was kinda pathetic, and he didn't leave her a helluva lot when he died. Also, my mom had recently coughed up a pretty big chunk of change to help out with her grandson's college tuition—Myron's kid wanted to go to Princeton. NYU wasn't good enough for the little hump, right? But anyhow, she said she still had a few thou in the bank and that she'd try and borrow the rest from some friends in her development."

"She didn't consider going to the deceased?"

"If she did, she never said so to me."

"Got any idea why she might not have wanted to ask her close friend to lend her the money?"

"Hey, what am I, a mind reader?"

"Sorry. Please continue."

"Okay. This one day my mom's on the phone with Bessie, and she goes and mentions that partnership opportunity to her—real casual-like, I'm talking about. And just like that"—Richie snapped his fingers— "Bessie pops up and says she'll lend me five thou. Mind you, nobody asked that old bitch for a dime; it was *her* idea. Figuring she'd keep her word—after all, this was my *Aunt* Bessie, wasn't it?—me, like a schmuck, I sign an agreement and ante up a two-thousand-buck deposit for the partnership. And then what does *Auntie* do? She stops payment on the check!"

"She had a reason for that, though—or thought she did, at least."

" 'Thought she did' is more like it," Richie grumbled. "She weaseled out the minute she got wind of this little misunderstanding I had with the cops. You'd think she'da waited to hear my side of things before doing something like that, right? Wrong!"

"How *did* you get into that trouble?"

He made a face. "It's a talent I have, I guess. How it went down was, my buddy—if you can call him that—gets on the horn to me a while back and claims he's raising money for this charity—the Battered Children's Foundation, Flip says it's called. He tells me he needs me to give him a hand and that he'll pay me for it—although my share was hardly enough for groceries even." (Considering the appetite Richie was displaying then, I wondered how much it would take to cover this kid's food bill.) "That's legit, in case you don't know it—people who work for charities don't do it for nothin'."

"Yes, I realize that."

"Anyhow, I wasn't too keen on the thing, but Flip kept pestering me, and my Unemployment had just run out, so I finally told him okay. Well, believe me, lady, I busted my tail for maybe three, four weeks. I addressed a zillion envelopes and I musta made hundreds of phone calls. We scrounged for donations at a bunch of malls, too, Flip and me. He even got some church in Brooklyn to let us hold a fund-raiser there— I think that's how the cops found out the thing was a scam, which, I swear, I didn't have the slightest idea of. But anyways, right after that interview at the automobile place, I say to Flip that he should look for someone else to help him, because I probably won't be able to do this much longer.

"Then only a few nights later the cops show up at my door. There's no such charity as the Battered Children's Foundation, they tell me. Whadda kick in the head! Flip, that piece of garbage, fooled me the same as he fooled everybody else. And never mind that I'm a hundred percent innocent; I still get saddled with six friggin' months of friggin' community service!"

"And to top it off," I murmured sympathetically, "this is when Mrs. Herman decided not to come through with that loan."

"Yeah. And without giving me a chance to explain, either."

"You were able to buy into the company anyway, though."

"Oh, sure, lucky me. Less than three months after I did, Leonard Brothers Motors lost their dealership license and went belly up. Seems the Leonard brothers didn't always walk a straight line, if you follow me."

It took a moment for this to seep in. "Are you saying they were crooked?"

"Got that, didja?" Richie responded, looking pleased with himself.

"By the way, the rest of the money you needed—the five thousand dollars that was supposed to be supplied by the victim—where did it finally come from?"

Richie's fork stopped in midair. Then, his suddenly pink cheeks intruding on his tan, he answered almost defiantly, "My mother borrowed it from friends, just like she intended before Bessie Herman opened her yap."

"Er, one more thing. I was told you phoned the deceased about a month ago to tell her what you thought of her and that you became abusive."

"I don't know where you get your information from, Dezzie, sweetheart, but that's a goddamn lie."

"Apparently someone was with Mrs. Herman when she heard from you," I improvised. "Someone who swears it was you on the other end of the line."

"That's bullshit! If somebody *did* trash old lady Herman that night, it wasn't Ric Vine."

"Um, how do you know the call was made at night?"

Richie's chin jutted out. "I'm a good guesser."

"Listen, Ric, this individual had no reason to make this up. But while I don't think much of the tone of your call, I can see why you'd be extremely angry with Mrs. Herman. After all, she should have heard your side of things before stopping payment like that. In fact, it's a little hard for me to understand why you waited so long before letting her know how you felt about the way she handled the situation. Was it the subsequent bankruptcy of the place that set you off?"

"That's *totally* dumb. If anything, she almost wound up doing me a favor by not lending me the money to buy into that shit dealership—excuse my language. Yeah, she stiffed me. But if I hadn't had the lousy luck to get the cash somewheres else, all I woulda been out was the two thousand I put down for a deposit. Listen, if there *was* a call like that, I'm not the one who made it." Then, almost defiantly: "And I don't give a fu— I don't care if you believe me or not."

I let it go at that.

"I gotta ask you something," Richie put to me then. "My mom says Bessie's death could have been an accident."

"That's certainly a possibility."

"So why are you bustin' chops before you know what's what?"

"Because the sooner you check into something of this nature, the better your chance of determining what actually occurred. That's the reason I'm talking to everyone who might have had a motive, however slight, for murdering Mrs. Herman."

"I admit I was pissed at her—plenty pissed, okay? But I don't go around pushing old ladies down the stairs. It's not my style."

"Incidentally—and this is merely for my records—can you tell me where you were between three thirty and seven on December fourteenth, the day Mrs. Herman died?"

Richie glowered at me. "How am I supposed to remember something like that? That had to be around three weeks ago, right?"

"Almost. And it was on a Saturday," I prompted.

"I suppose I was just sitting around my living room, watching TV. Saturday's like my day off."

I was incredulous. His day off! *From what?*

At this moment Richie spotted our waiter presenting the check at a table within shouting distance of ours. He captured the man's attention with a high-volume "Yo! Waiter!" Then the instant the fellow turned around, Richie placed his order. "Another double scotch here!" he apprised the entire room.

Never before—and never since—have I experienced such an intense desire to become invisible.

Chapter 22

On the way back to the office I replayed my lunch with Richie. I had no idea whether he'd been the one to give Mrs. Herman a helping hand down those stairs or not. (Which, unfortunately, was also the case with all the other suspects I'd questioned so far.) There *was* something I was virtually certain of, however. Richie Vine was responsible for that intimidating phone call to the victim—although the timing of it did trouble me a little. I mean, I could see him placing it soon after she'd elected not to lend him the money. But months later?

I decided that in spite of the rationalization Richie had presented to me, it must have been the closing of Leonard Brothers Motors that precipitated his eruption.

It was Mike who opened the door that evening, and as soon as I crossed the threshold, he bent down from his towering six-feet-plus to plant a kiss on my cheek. "Happy New Year, Dez."

"You too, Mike," I said affectionately.

"Ellen's in the kitchen getting dinner ready," he notified me as he was helping me off with my coat. (Translation: She was busy opening a bunch of containers from Mandarin Joy.)

"Here. My small contribution to the meal." I handed him a bag containing two quarts of Häagen-Dazs: Belgian chocolate, Ellen's favorite, and macadamia brittle, my own personal addiction. (Mike insists he *has* no favorite, that anything's fine with him—as long as it's ice cream.)

"Thanks, Dez. And have a seat," he directed. "I'll be back as soon as I put this in the freezer. Oh, incidentally, red or white?"

"Red or white?"

"Wine." He smiled that warm smile of his. "What's the matter, can't you read minds?" Then, holding up his palm: "Anyway, don't tell me. You'll have the red, as usual."

"Either one's good, Mike, honestly—whichever you two are having."

"Both!" he called out as he made for the kitchen.

I was about to settle on the sofa when I glanced over at the folding table, which was presently occupying a good part of the small living room. It was covered with what appeared to be a particularly lovely cloth. I went over for a closer look. Not only was the cloth absolutely exquisite, but so was everything on it. The dinnerware was the Limoges pattern Ellen had chosen when she and Mike got engaged—several place settings of which had been a joint shower gift from her mother (yecch), her mother-in-law, and me. I also recognized the Wallace sterling flatware—another item that had been on her bridal wish list. Ditto the crystal glassware. The fact is, Mandarin Joy's sweet-and-sour pork couldn't have asked to be more lavishly presented.

At that moment Ellen hurried into the room.

"Aunt Dez!" she exclaimed as if she hadn't seen me for years. She gave me a hug—a fairly gentle one, for once (like Jackie's, sometimes Ellen's embraces are a little too enthusiastic for my own good)—and we exchanged Happy New Years again.

I gushed a little about the elegant table she'd set, and then we sat down side by side on the couch. "Dig in," she commanded.

Directly in front of us, on the coffee table, there was a wooden board with a variety of cheeses and, of course, the requisite crackers to spread them on. Next to this, set on a warming tray, was a Lenox serving platter (also part of the shower loot, if I'm not mistaken) containing about two dozen bread roll-ups wrapped with bacon.

I indicated the roll-ups. "You didn't make these." As soon as I uttered the words, I realized this sounded almost like an accusation.

But Ellen wasn't in the least perturbed. "Are you kidding? Mike did."

"I wasn't aware that Mike could cook."

"Neither was he," she responded with one of her trademark giggles.

I figured he might finally be getting a little fed up (forgive the pun) with Chinese food, when Ellen elaborated. "Last week some woman doctor at the hospital shoved the recipe in his hand. Apparently she'd run off an extra copy or something, and Mike happened to come by. 'Your wife might like to make these one day; they're really good,' she said to him. I don't think he'd ever have attempted them, though, if when he was halfway down the hall she hadn't hollered after him, 'And easy, too!'"

Mike returned at this juncture with a small tray holding a white wine and two glasses of red. After distributing the red to Ellen and me, he plunked himself down on an adjacent club chair.

As I reached for an hors d'ocuvre, Ellen grabbed my forearm. "Nick's bracelet!" she squealed.

"No, it's mine," I corrected facetiously, right before she came out with three "Oh, my God"s.

I'm not exaggerating when I say that Ellen was almost as excited about my present as I was. "Have you *seen* this?" she asked Mike, twisting my arm to afford him a better view.

Fortunately for the arm, he was kind enough to get up and walk over to the sofa. "It's beautiful, Dez," he commented, peering down at my wrist. "Wear it well."

He hovered over me while I helped myself to a roll-up.

"This is delicious, Mike," I said appreciatively.

My recently acquired nephew beamed. Following which he resumed his seat and immediately challenged his bride. "What about you, El? Too chicken to try one?"

"Not anymore. Not with Aunt Dez having survived." And with this, she, too, sampled one of Mike's tidbits. "Hey, this is delicious! I mean it."

And now Mike's smile seemed to stretch across his entire face. "Maybe I can teach you how to make them sometime." He hesitated a moment. "But on second thought, probably not."

Evidently in complete agreement with this conclusion, Ellen tittered. The next instant she focused her attention on me. "All right, Aunt Dez, let's get down to business. Tell me about New Year's Eve."

"It was just wonderful. We had dinner at this marvelous French restaurant on the Upper East Side—Georgette's. Later we went back to my place and watched the ball drop in Times Square—that never fails to send chills down my spine. And once the New Year had officially arrived, we celebrated with a little Dom Perignon."

"Sounds like a perfect evening," Mike commented.

"It was," I said, feeling my face get hot.

"It's happened!" Ellen cried gleefully. "Am I right?"

Mike and I responded almost simultaneously.

"Ellen!" he exclaimed.

"I have no idea what you're talking about," I mumbled.

"Come on, Aunt Dez," my niece persisted.

This time Mike's "Ellen" was quiet—but firm.

"I guess I'll heat up the food for a couple of minutes," his chastised bride groused.

You've got to hand it to Mandarin Joy—they really know their stuff. So it didn't matter that I'd been treated to pretty much this same menu (give or take a dish) whenever I came here to dinner—something

I'd been doing on a fairly frequent basis for a good long while. I was, however, less than enthusiastic about my fortune cookie. I mean, not only was this the fourth straight time I'd gotten that exact message, but they do call it a *fortune* cookie, don't they? And, I ask you, what kind of a fortune is YOU HAVE GOOD HEART?

But maybe I'm being picayune.

Anyhow, during the meal, we chatted about the wedding, of course, with Ellen relating a couple of very amusing incidents—one of them involving an inebriated female guest and an elderly man named Calvin Strong. (Remember, him?) She went on to talk about a new co-worker of hers—Ellen's a buyer at Macy's. It seems that practically everyone in the department (my niece being one of the few exceptions, I'm happy to report) was convinced that the woman drank. And get this: Their suspicions were founded almost entirely on the unusually large quantity of breath mints the lady consumed every time she returned from lunch. Naturally, I saw this reasoning as being badly flawed—*asinine,* if you want the truth. Nevertheless, I have to admit that I fleetingly considered cutting back on my Tic Tacs.

Mike spoke for a few minutes about the talents of Dr. Beaver, the cardiologist he works under at St. Gregory's and a man he dubs a "genius." Then he updated me on his friend Seth, the one who'd been in that terrible accident. "He's really doing fine, Dez, thank God. For a couple of days, though, I didn't figure there was the slightest chance that he'd be able to come to our wedding, much less act as best man."

As for me, I did an uncharacteristic amount of listening and tried—not always successfully—to keep my mind from wandering. Thanks to Nick, I have a feeling I smiled in quite a few inappropriate places, too.

Later, over ice cream and coffee (I know; but Chinese food or not, we voted out the tea), Ellen asked if there'd been any new developments in the Aunt

Bessie investigation. Her response to my "I'm afraid not" was predictably Ellen: "Well, that's okay, Aunt Dez. You'll get to the bottom of things yet."

And now, after forcibly restraining me from clearing away the dishes, she dragged me into the bedroom to admire the wedding presents.

It was quite a haul, too—everything from a Cuisinart and an espresso machine to a sterling silver coffee service, a huge crystal punchbowl complete with a dozen glasses, and additional place settings of both her china and flatware. "At this rate, you could host a banquet," I observed.

"You're right. Isn't it wonderful?" a delighted Ellen agreed. "The gifts are still coming in, too. We received the espresso machine only yesterday."

She began repacking the bounty. "I really have to find a permanent place for all this stuff." And with a sigh: "But I always promise myself I'll do it tomorrow." Suddenly she looked up—and I could see from her expression that I was back on the hook. "Um, about New Year's Eve, Aunt Dez, one question: Yes or no?"

I laughed—I couldn't help it. "Maybe."

"I always tell *you* everything," she rejoined, pouting.

"True. But now that you're happily married, it's become a lot less interesting."

It wasn't until the three of us were at the door saying good night that something occurred to me.

"Uh, Ellen, do you think you might be talking to your mother soon?"

"Sure, why?"

"Well, someone used a word recently that sounds familiar, but I'm not certain of the definition. I have this impression that the word could be Yiddish, though."

"What is it?"

"*Courva.*"

"Does it have to do with the investigation?"

"Only vaguely, and I doubt if it's important. Mostly, I'm curious."

"Well, I've never heard it, but maybe my mom has. If not, she can check with her neighbors. I'll give her a ring in the morning." Then, as if reading my mind: "Don't worry. I won't mention that you're the one who's asking."

"You can forget phoning your mother," Mike interjected emphatically. Both Ellen and I gaped at him. "Listen, when Seth and I were at college his mom used to visit him pretty often. And she inevitably wound up cursing her ex-husband's new wife. Guess what she used to call her?"

"A *courva*?" I ventured.

Mike nodded. "A *courva*."

"Well?" I said impatiently. "What does it mean?" But even before I asked the question, I kind of knew the answer.

"It means whore."

Chapter 23

In the cab on the way back to the apartment, I couldn't seem to stop myself from repeating the word *courva* over and over again in my head. Was it possible that when referring to Sylvia this way, the woman was being *literal*?

Nah! The old biddy just didn't approve of how her flamboyant neighbor dressed. Or maybe she was aware that Sylvia (evidently) had a slew of male friends (at least one of whom apparently enjoyed *Playboy* and *Sports Illustrated*). I mean, the fact that some tart-tongued female used this nasty little epithet to describe Sylvia Vine was certainly no reason to accept it as gospel.

It wasn't until I was about five blocks from home that, out of the blue, something occurred to me that led me to think I might—with the emphasis on the "might"—owe the tart-tongued female an apology. I'm talking about the timing of Richie's bitter phone call to the deceased. (I had no doubt—although even today I have no confirmation—that it was Richie who made this call.) Anyway, follow me for a minute.

Now, since that verbal attack took place months after Bessie Herman had gone back on her promise to lend him five thousand dollars, I'd already determined that it was highly improbable this was what incited the boy to ream her out that evening. Then during my lunch with him, I became convinced it was his frustration at that dealership's going belly up that had set him off. Listen, who better to pin his troubles on than the individual who'd let him down to begin with? But mulling things over a couple of hours later, I found myself giving some credence to Richie's argument that if he hadn't been unfortunate enough to obtain funding elsewhere, Bessie's bailing out on him as she did would have prevented his sinking additional money into that ill-fated venture. So grudgingly, I accepted that it was also unlikely that the bankruptcy had sparked his tirade.

But if it wasn't that, then what was it?

Okay. I know this will sound bizarre—it does to me, too. But a long time ago I came to the conclusion that just about anything is possible. At any rate, suppose Bessie's reneging on her offer had prompted Sylvia to charge for what, until now, I suspected that she'd been cheerfully donating to the gentlemen of her acquaintance. And further suppose that somewhere along the line Richie discovered that his dear, seventyish mama was selling her favors—and worse yet, on his behalf! (Suddenly I had a mental picture of the flush on Richie's face when I inquired about where he finally got the funding to buy into that dealership.) Well, I could see where he might lay the blame for his mother's fall from grace on the already despised Aunt Bessie.

By this same reasoning, when that old woman used the word *courva* with regard to Sylvia, she could have been a hundred percent correct in her assessment.

But naturally, all of this was only a theory.

I walked into the apartment to find a message from Nick on my machine.

"Hi, Dez. Sorry I missed you. I realize this is short notice, but what else is new, right?" An embarrassed chuckle here. "Anyhow, if you're free on Saturday, I just learned that I am, too. Derek was supposed to be staying with me for the weekend. But this afternoon Tiffany's folks made plans to come into the city on Saturday, and they haven't seen him for more than a month. So Tiffany won't be dropping him off here until Sunday morning. Anyhow, I'll . . . uh . . . check back with you tomorrow. Bye.''

He'd sounded a little nervous, a state I could certainly relate to. Only I was maybe a little more than a *little* nervous. Tuesday night's intimacy was something I'd been hoping for—and dreaming of—for months. But since reaching this new plateau, I'd been feeling as if I now had an even bigger investment in the relationship. And I was both exhilarated and frightened by the thought. I imagined that Nick must be, too.

I had trouble sleeping that night. To keep from dwelling on Nick, I wound up lingering over the Sylvia/Bessie thing. And I honestly believe I gained some insight into what struck me as a pretty strange friendship.

Why hadn't Sylvia even *approached* Bessie about providing monetary assistance for her son? I wondered.

Considering how close the two had been at the time—ostensibly, at any rate—I would have expected Sylvia to be more comfortable borrowing from Bessie than going to her neighbors for the loan. This, according to Richie, being what she'd had in mind prior to Bessie's volunteering the five thousand dollars. Now, maybe Sylvia was already engaged in that ancient profession by then, and this was *really* how she intended funding her son's business opportunity. On the other hand, though, it could be that it wasn't until after Bessie's check bounced that Sylvia began extracting payment from the recipients of her affections (which, as you know, is what I theorized that Richie believed). I had to remind myself that I wasn't sure that Sylvia was a prostitute at all. She might simply have been an elderly lady who'd been saddled with or—depending on how you look at it—blessed with the libido of a woman forty or fifty years her junior.

But there was another reason Sylvia might have

avoided broaching the subject of a loan with her distant cousin and very good friend. She may have been unwilling to admit to Bessie her inability to provide the financing herself. This notion caused me to speculate about the possibility of a rivalry between the two—on Sylvia's part, at least. I mean, that sort of thing is often the case with close buddies.

I decided that this rivalry might also have been what induced Sylvia to tell Bessie about that dealership in the first place. After all, she was finally able to brag that her son was embarking on a promising career.

By the same token, if the two were in some kind of competition, it would explain Sylvia's reluctance to turn to Bessie for emotional support when Richie wound up in trouble with the law.

The more I considered it, the more I warmed up to the idea that Sylvia's bitterness wasn't merely the result of a broken promise. It seemed fairly obvious that on some level she'd always resented her cousin and that one of the reasons for this, very likely the principal one, was Bessie's financial security—and her own lack thereof. For Sylvia, Bessie's stopping payment on that check had simply been the most egregious—and final—offense.

Through with all of the conjecturing now, I asked myself if, in the event Bessie Herman had been murdered, any of this amateur psychology of mine was apt to bring me even one step closer to identifying her killer.

I had to concede that it was doubtful.

However, right before I dropped off to sleep, I remember consoling myself with a few of my favorite words: "But you never know."

Chapter 24

I'd been on the case for eleven days now. But I was no closer to finding out what had caused Aunt Bessie's death than I was the day Ben hired me. And I couldn't seem to shake the thought that perhaps I'd unwittingly allowed my personal life to interfere with my professional commitment. So over a quick Cheerios breakfast late Friday morning (I'd consented to give myself a little time off from the office), I determined that if I ever expected to arrive at the truth here, I'd have to redouble my efforts.

Now, I was hardly up to date as far as typing up my notes, so this would necessitate my being practically tethered to the computer for a lot of hours—maybe well into Sunday. It would also mean that I'd have to abandon one of my most counterproductive work habits: attempting to absorb the material while I transcribed it. Not an easy habit for me to break—but a must, since even without that, my normal typing speed ranges between slow and slower.

And getting my notes in order was the easy part of the weekend itinerary I'd laid out for myself.

Once everything was in the computer and I had my hands on the hard copy, I'd immediately begin poring over the pages—again and again, if necessary—in the hope that I'd overlooked something and that I'd finally catch whatever it was I'd missed.

The only break I planned on taking during the next few days was tomorrow evening, when I'd be enjoying the company of one Nicholas Grainger. (Listen, there's just so much dedication a person can expect of herself.)

He phoned as I was putting away the dishes.

"Hi, Dez."

"Hi, Nick."

"You got my message, I suppose." He appeared to be much more relaxed than he'd been yesterday.

"I did."

"So are you by any chance free on Saturday?"

"As a matter of fact, I am." Then for some elusive reason, I giggled.

"Was it something I said?" His tone was perplexed, but amused.

"Uh-uh. I have no idea why I did that." (Actually, I *did* have an idea: It was probably nerves.)

"Okay." I could almost see the shrug. "Anyway, I figured it might be nice if we went to a movie first— if you feel like it, that is—and had something to eat later on."

Now, I wouldn't have passed up the chance to be with Nick tomorrow for anything. But I'd assumed that, as was usually the case, we'd be going out to a restaurant. Period. (I didn't allow myself to think about what might transpire after that.) And I really wasn't keen on unleashing myself from the computer a couple of hours early in order to take in a movie, too. I mean, it's not as if we'd be able to carry on a conversation in the theater—at least, not without getting our heads handed to us. But I decided it was best not to share any of this with Nick. "Sounds good to me."

"Is there something in particular you'd be interested in seeing?"

"I don't even know what's around now."

"There's this film— Wait. Someone's coming into the shop. I'll call you back as soon as I free up."

It was about two o'clock when I heard from Nick again.

"Would you be disappointed if we skipped the movie and just had dinner Saturday night?"

Hallelujah! "No, of course not," I told him, trying not to sound relieved.

"I won't be able to make it much before eight-thirty, though. Is that all right with you?"

"Sure. But is something wrong?"

"Emil wasn't feeling well"—Emil, if you recall, being the man who works for Nick—"so I sent him home. I don't expect him to recover by tomorrow—I think he may be coming down with the flu. And with Emil out, I'll have to hang in until closing time. Anyway, where would you like to eat?"

"You choose."

"Only if you help me. Are you in the mood for French, Italian, Chinese—what?"

Now, we'd been to Georgette's three days ago, so I scratched French. As for Chinese, I wasn't prepared to look another dim sum in the face quite yet. "Italian kind of appeals to me. What about you?"

"Sold. I was leaning that way, too. Uh, Dez?"

"Yes?"

"I'm really looking forward to tomorrow evening."

"I am, too."

I wouldn't allow myself a single minute for day-dreaming. So as soon as Nick and I hung up, I made a quick call to Ellen to thank her for feeding me last night. And then I was right back at the computer.

I was moving along at a semi-decent clip, too, when I was interrupted by the phone at a few minutes past three. Bessie's older son, Don, was on the line.

"I tried to reach you at your office, Desiree, but I was informed that you wouldn't be in today." He sounded almost shy. "I hope you're not ill."

"Not at all. I thought I might accomplish more by working at home."

"That's very likely true." There was a rather awkward pause before he added, "Listen, if it's not convenient for you to talk right now, don't hesitate to say so. I can telephone you again whenever you suggest."

"No, this is fine; I was about to take a break anyway," I lied.

"I . . . er, spoke to my cousin Ben yesterday, and he tells me you haven't turned up anything definitive as yet."

This was a rather considerate way of phrasing it, I thought. He *could* have put it that even after all this time I hadn't come up with squat. Or that I hadn't moved off the dime. Or that I was still at the starting gate. Or . . . But you get the idea. "It's taken a while for me to persuade a couple of people to cooperate," I told him. "So I'm not quite finished questioning everyone who might have had a motive for harming your mother or," I quickly tagged on, "who *imagined* they did." Then in an attempt to deter the man from looking at this lack of progress as a reflection of my ability, I threw in, "I want to be certain I cover all the possibilities."

"I appreciate that. Uh, I trust you won't resent my inquiring about this, Desiree. I realize the fact that I'm not your client might—"

"Please. This is about the death of your *mother*. So ask me whatever you like."

"That's very kind of you. Let me first make clear that at this juncture I'm still vacillating between whether she fell down those stairs—or was thrown."

"To be honest, I am, too, Don."

"Yes, well, whenever I consider the possibility that Mom *was* murdered, Richie Vine immediately springs to mind. And ever since I wore you out with that interminable long-distance briefing, I've been on edge, wondering if you've had an opportunity to meet with him."

"I sat down with him yesterday."

"And—?"

"He denied having made that abusive call, which I have no doubt is a lie. He also insisted he had nothing to do with the tragedy—which at this point I'm in no position to challenge."

"So you, er, feel that he *might* have been responsible for her taking that fall?"

"He might. But then again, he might not. I'm still at the information-gathering stage, remember."

"Just one more question," he said now, stealing my line, "—assuming, of course, that you're able to spare me another few minutes."

"No problem. What's the question?"

"Nigel—the tailor I mentioned? Have you managed to persuade him to see you?"

"I called the store, and evidently he's on vacation. He's expected back on Monday, though, and I plan on contacting him the early part of next week."

"Good. I have my suspicions about that gentleman, as well." Then, after a barely perceptible pause: "Uh, I'm genuinely sorry if I've disturbed you, Desiree. And I want to thank you for being so gracious about what you could easily have construed as my interfering with your investigation. I loved my mother very much, however, and if someone *did* have a hand in her death—" He broke off, apparently to collect himself. "I suppose the problem is," he continued a few seconds later, "that I can't seem to divest myself of the thought that he or she could simply walk away from the crime."

"I can understand how you feel, and believe me, I'll do my best to see that this doesn't happen."

And now, immediately after murmuring his thanks, Don came out with another of my lines: "One more thing."

"What's that?"

"I'd be grateful if you wouldn't mention this conversation to Ben. He assured me he would keep me advised as to your progress, which was a polite attempt at discouraging me from contacting you myself. Obviously he was concerned that Joel and I might besiege you with calls. I can't claim that I disagree with his thinking, either. But I was extremely anxious to speak to you directly."

"Our conversation will remain between the two of us."

"May I take this to be a promise?"

I'll be damned! If it weren't for that stilted way he had of putting things, I might have been talking to Ellen!

"Absolutely."

But before he could ask if I really, *really* meant it, I said good-bye.

Chapter 25

On Saturday I was at the computer practically all afternoon—the "practically" relating to a quick bite of lunch and a not-so-quick conversation with my friend Harriet.

When she phoned at around five-thirty, she was distraught. Baby, her attack-Pekinese, had struck again.

It seems that a short while earlier Harriet had taken the little darling out to do his business, and Baby—who's a he—had met up with an alluring female. "A cockapoo," Harriet apprised me by way of describing the canine temptress.

"A *what?*"

"Don't tell me you've never heard of a cockapoo!"

"Okay, I won't," I retorted.

"There's no need to be so snippy, for heaven's sake. A cockapoo, Desiree, is part cocker spaniel and part poodle. It's really a very attractive mix."

"All right. So what happened?" I was anxious to get in some more work before starting to dress for the evening. Still, I couldn't *not* ask.

"The thing is, Baby did, well . . . you know, what dogs do. He went over and sniffed the cockapoo's private parts—Felicity, her name is. It's possible he might have been a tad on the aggressive side, but—"

"What you're saying is that he sexually assaulted the unfortunate Felicity."

"You're a riot, Desire. Did anyone ever tell you that? These are *dogs* we're talking about! Anyhow, I started to pull Baby away, but he's strong for a little

fellow, and he was sort of resisting. Well, before I had
a chance to make any headway with him, the cockapoo's owner, a sour-faced dowager who was wearing
a diamond ring the size of a bowling ball and a really
stunning full-length mink coat—every one of those
minks must have been better-looking than she was,
too—acted foolishly. She kicked Baby in order to grab
up her dog. Naturally, Baby was upset, so he gave her
the tiniest nip. And "

"Baby nipped the dowager, not the dog," I interrupted, seeking clarification.

"That's what I said. Anyhow, he hardly broke the
skin. Really. I swear, you would have needed a micro-
scope to see the blood. But still, that horrible woman
announced that she intends to sue me. Personally, I
don't think she has much of a case, but, well, do *you*
think she does?"

"I'm certainly no legal expert, Harriet. Besides, it's
hard to answer that from what you've told me. Be
honest now. How much blood *was* there?"

"A thimbleful, tops."

So much for "the tiniest nip." "Let me ask you
something else. Was Baby on a leash?"

"Of course. I never walk him without his leash. If
Felicity had also been on a leash—"

"Are you saying she wasn't?"

"That's exactly what I'm saying."

"And this was on a public street?"

"Certainly it was. It happened on Seventy-ninth
and Second."

"Then I seriously doubt that you have anything to
worry about. First off, it's against the law to walk your
dog on public property unless you have him on a
leash."

"Are you positive about that?"

"Yes." (Listen, Bessie Herman wasn't the only one
who watched Judge Marilyn.) "And when you take
into consideration that the woman *kicked* Baby before
she was bitten, I'd say you're in pretty good shape,
Harriet. But do you want my advice?"

"Sure." It was obvious, however, that she didn't mean it.

"If I were you, from here on in I'd have a muzzle on that dog when he went out of doors."

"Don't be silly! Baby was a tad overexcited today, that's all. And just because of this one small incident—"

"*One* incident?" I challenged. "I have two words for you, Harriet: Mrs. Bauer."

I imagine some background information is in order here. Mrs. Bauer is currently the Goulds' every-other-Thursday cleaning lady, her immediate predecessor, Denise, having left one afternoon never to return. And while it wasn't actually established that Baby had been the cause of Denise's abrupt departure, I have my own thoughts on the subject. Anyhow, not long ago Mrs. Bauer had announced her intention of finding other employment unless something was done to prevent Baby's sharpening his teeth on her ankles. Well, this also fell into the category of what my friend regarded as little nips—only in Mrs. Bauer's case, Harriet referred to them as *playful* little nips. Mrs. B., however, was apparently in no mood for fun and games, going so far as to suggest that the Peke be either muzzled or gassed—the latter alternative not even acceptable to yours truly, in spite of my lack of affection for the miserable creature. (And to set the record straight: I love dogs. Honestly. It's just that circumstances forced me to make an exception in Baby's case.) At any rate, in order to prevent Mrs. Bauer's following Denise out the door, Harriet had consented to outfit Baby with a muzzle.

"Look, he wears a muzzle when Mrs. Bauer is in the apartment, doesn't he?" I put to her now.

"Not anymore." Her tone became accusatory. "You *said* he'd get used to it, that soon he'd hardly be aware he had it on. But Baby simply isn't able to tolerate a muzzle. I finally decided that when Mrs. Bauer is here, I'd confine him to the bathroom until she finishes with the other rooms, then close him in the kitchen so she can do the bathroom. He scratches the hell out of my cabinets, of course, the poor thing."

"The poor thing?"

"Well, how would *you* like to be shut up in some teeny tiny room?"

"You *have* seen my office, haven't you, Harriet? Anyway, you might want to at least consider trying the muzzle again when you take him outdoors." I made this suggestion mostly out of sheer spite. The truth is, I was still smoldering over the fate of my once brand-new and gorgeous Italian faux-crocodile pumps. Which Baby, in his own inimitable way, christened on their very first outing.

"All right, I'll consider it," Harriet responded—but not very convincingly.

By the time the conversation was over, it seemed kind of late to start working again. So I shut off the computer, turned on the bath water, and proceeded to prepare for my date with Nick.

Chapter 26

Nick arrived at eight-twenty—and I all but hyperventilated. I mean, that gap-toothed smile positively melted me. Plus, he was wearing a really nifty blazer that I'd never seen him in before.

"That's a great jacket," I said.

He grinned. "It is, isn't it? A Christmas gift from my parents." He went on to compliment *my* appearance, as he unfailingly does. "You look wonderful tonight, Dez; that's a very becoming outfit."

I lapped up the flattery—although it did require a bit of self-deception.

As appeared to be a pattern with me lately, once again I'd run into a problem when dressing. Actually, right after getting into that suit, I was very tempted to get out of it. Only it was obvious I'd be in for a struggle, and I was expecting Nick within minutes.

Now, I'm aware that when people blame their dry cleaner for an item's no longer fitting the way it once did, the accusation is apt to be viewed with skepticism. But I assure you that in the case of this particular two-piece chartreuse, the problem wasn't that there was presently more of me (I was as svelte as ever), but that there was suddenly less of *it*. Listen, just two weeks ago, before dropping off the suit at the cleaner's, I'd tried it on and everything was fine. What was handed back to me, however, was an abridged version of same.

In fact, a few minutes earlier, I'd taken a last look

in the bedroom mirror—and immediately cautioned myself to pull the skirt way down when I sat—or risk revealing my dimpled knees. (And believe me, this is not where I'd have chosen to have dimples.) Plus, if I didn't want to split any seams, I'd better be sure, too, that I curbed my appetite. Well, at least the color was becoming—chartreuse goes very nicely with my glorious hennaed hair.

We went to a neighborhood trattoria, a place we'd visited twice before. The seats are comfortable, the owners are gracious, and their linguini with portobello mushrooms and white wine—the entrée we both ordered—is sensational. But as for atmosphere, there isn't any. As far as Nick and I were concerned, though, it didn't matter; we seemed to have brought along our own that evening.

We gazed into each other's eyes, held hands between courses, and even shared a brief kiss at one point. It was like I was sixteen again! (Or so I'm assuming, since I can't exactly remember that far back.)

Of course, we managed to get in quite a lot of talking, too.

Nick wanted to know about my investigation, and I confessed that I was still completely in the dark as to who—or what—had caused Bessie Herman's death. "But I intend to finish typing up all my notes tomorrow—I've been lax about that—and then I'll sit down and review them. With any luck, I'll come across something that'll point me in the right direction."

"I get the impression you're leaning toward the woman's having been murdered. Am I right?"

"You are. But that's how I feel this minute. And I tend to fluctuate in my opinion, so who knows how I'll feel tomorrow? Irrespective of how I, personally, regard this, though, I have to go on the premise that a crime was committed here. You see, the only way I can find that Bessie Herman took that tumble on her own is if my investigation indicates that it's highly unlikely anyone pushed her. It's kind of like arriving at a diagnosis by eliminating all but one of the possible causes."

"Assuming it *was* murder, do you have any idea yet who might have killed her?"

"Oh, I could name a number of people who *might* have killed her. I have no idea who actually did, though."

"Well, hopefully one of your suspects made a slip of some sort."

"While you're hoping, also hope that I'll be able to spot it."

Nick smiled encouragingly. "I'd bet on it."

Nick was considerate enough to hold off mentioning his son until we'd polished off the dessert we were sharing: a large, luscious slice of pecan pie à la mode. (In deference to my outfit, however, I limited myself to two or three bites—five, tops.)

"I spoke to Derek this morning," he said. Well, I knew the name had to come up sometime tonight, so I wasn't taken by surprise.

"When did he get home, by the way?"

"He flew back the day before yesterday. He asked me about you, Dez; he wanted to know if we'd been out together New Year's Eve. And I said that we had."

"He was aware that we're seeing each other again?"

"I told him weeks ago that we were. Do you know how he responded? He said he understood now that what he'd done was really terrible and that he was glad he hadn't messed things up for us permanently."

Well, his doting father might convince himself that Derek was sincere, but that little stinker was hardly the apple of *my* eye. And awhile back I'd finally concluded that I couldn't afford to buy a single thing that kid was selling. Something that should have been evident to me from the start.

Apparently, though, I was now expected to comment (favorably) on the new and improved Derek. But for the life of me, I couldn't come up with anything positive to say. Fortunately, I suddenly remembered a discussion that had taken place during that disastrous evening at my apartment. And this allowed me to avoid lauding The Kid From Hell without totally ignoring his existence. (Which, as you know, I'd have been most pleased to do.) "Speaking of Derek, I've been meaning to ask you: How was his acting debut?"

"Acting debut?"

"When the two of you were at my place the night that's best forgotten, we talked about Derek's having a part in his school's production of *Our Town*. I remember how nervous he was about it."

"That's right! I'd forgotten we even mentioned it then. Anyhow, he was really good, if I say so myself. Of course, it's not as if he were playing the Stage Manager; his part was definitely on the skimpy side. But he managed to make the most of it. Actually, I believe he has a kind of talent for acting."

You can say that again! I told him—although not out loud.

And now it occurred to Nick that in view of my history with his son, it was hardly necessary to point this out, and he smiled weakly. "Uh, you're not thinking what I'm afraid you're thinking, are you, Dez."

"Of course not," I answered solemnly.

We both laughed.

Predictably, on the walk back to our mutual building, my nerves kicked in. In spite of his display of affection in the restaurant, I wasn't really sure what to expect now. What if, at that very moment, Nick was having second thoughts and, in an effort to slow things down, decided it might be a good idea to end the date in our prior-to-New-Year's-Eve mode?

I resolved that I'd either kill him or myself. Whichever seemed more practical.

I needn't have been concerned.

Nick accompanied me into the apartment and took a seat on the sofa. I poured us two apricot brandies and parked myself beside him—*close* beside him. We sat like this for maybe fifteen or twenty minutes, chatting and sipping our liqueurs.

Then after that . . . well, things just kept getting better and better. And better.

Chapter 27

When I opened my eyes on Sunday Nick was gone.

"I'll probably be out of here by seven," he'd informed me the night before. "Tiffany expects to drop off Derek early in the morning, and I want to be sure I'm home when she does."

"Wake me when you get up, and we'll have breakfast."

"Don't be silly. You've been working hard; you need your sleep."

"Listen, I can go back to bed for a while after you leave—or I can be really smart and get in some much-needed extra hours with my notes." I could see that he was hesitant, so I added what was meant to be a practically irresistible "Please?"

I got a grudging—and, as it turned out, untruthful—"Okay" in response.

Glancing at the clock on my night table now, I was stunned to see that it was nearly twelve. I actually bounded out of bed (well, it was a reasonable facsimile, anyway) and hurriedly dressed (if you consider a schlumpy bathrobe "dressed"). Then I went into the kitchen. Nick had left a note on the table.

I DIDN'T HAVE THE HEART TO DISTURB YOU, DEZ—YOU LOOKED SO PEACEFUL. CUTE, TOO. I'LL TALK TO YOU SOON. There was a PS: ARE YOU AWARE THAT YOU SNORE?

I made a face. "The man lies!" I announced to absolutely no one. "I *never* snore!"

Concentrating on the investigation that day required a willpower I wasn't sure I had. But somehow I managed to pluck Nick—and last night—from my mind.

Blessedly, at a few minutes past two I finally finished transcribing every word I'd jotted down on the case, beginning with my initial conversation with Ben Berlin and going straight through Thursday's little tête-à-tête with Richie—oops, Ric—Vine. Here I took a short break with a peanut butter sandwich and a cup of coffee. Following which I went to the computer again and printed the whole thing out.

And now I settled down at the kitchen table with my typewritten notes. I studied them very carefully—and when I was done, I studied them even more carefully a second time. But no lightbulb went on in my head. If there was anything to be found there—and I had to proceed on the assumption that there was—I just wasn't finding it. It was past six at this point, though, so I decided that maybe I'd have more success after a little nourishment.

Shoving the papers to one side, I set the table. Then, not having given much thought to this evening's menu, I searched the freezer for inspiration. I lucked out. Hiding behind some steaks and a container of Bolognese sauce was a casserole of chicken with artichokes and mushrooms. The chicken had been there for so long I couldn't remember when I'd prepared it. I briefly contemplated tossing it—after all, I warned myself, you can't keep food indefinitely, even in the freezer. But in the end I elected to take my chances, since the one thing I did remember about that dish was that it was really tasty. Anyhow, to round out the meal, I boiled up some rice and made a salad, throwing in whatever I laid hands on in the refrigerator that hadn't shriveled up or turned moldy. Dessert was a couple of scoops of macadamia brittle—which I felt I deserved—along with two cups of my miserable coffee—which no one deserves.

An hour later I was ready for another go at my notes. But now I proceeded so slowly that it was almost self-defeating; I came close to lulling myself to sleep.

By the time I put down the last page, I was thoroughly frustrated. I mean, I was no more enlightened than I'd been after my first two read-throughs.

Well, to paraphrase Scarlett O'Hara, there was always tomorrow.

Jackie was on the phone when I got to work on Monday, so I waved and headed straight for my cubbyhole. It took her only three minutes to join me.

"I never really had a chance to talk to you on Thursday. How was New Year's Eve?" She plopped down on the chair.

"Great."

"You told me *that* much. Did anything . . . *special* happen?"

"What happened was that Nick and I went out to a lovely French restaurant. Then we went back to my apartment and watched Dick Clark on TV. And after the ball dropped in Times Square, we celebrated with some Dom Perignon."

"Dom Perignon, huh? My, my. If Derwin ever sprung for that stuff, I'd faint."

"So would he."

We giggled in unison, after which Jackie said, "Well, you *know* what I'm asking you, but if you'd rather not say, that's all right." Her pout was barely noticeable.

I responded with, "How was *your* New Year's Eve, Jackie?"

She took the rejection with what, for Jackie, was unusual grace. "Not too bad. Kinda nice, in fact. We went to this cousin of Derwin's. She had about twenty people over for a potluck supper."

"What did you bring?"

"Lasagna."

Now, in Jackie's kitchen, about the only edibles that don't get tossed in the broiler come in a TV dinner. But before I could raise an eyebrow, she added, "Store-bought, but you'd never guess. I swore to Der-

win that if he let it slip that I didn't make that thing
with my own two hands, I'd tear out his gizzard."

Once Jackie left, I occupied myself with paying
bills—some even before they were due. The primary
purpose of this being to postpone what I feared would
be another fruitless stab at my notes. Then, at around
eleven, I received an astonishing telephone call.

"This is Janet Stark, Ms. Shapiro. I'm the bookkeeper at Seymour Real Estate."

"The bookkeeper, did you say?"

"That's right. We nearly met about a week ago
when I inadvertently interrupted you while you were
here questioning Cliff Seymour. Mr. Seymour didn't
see fit to introduce us, however."

Oh-h-h. This was the tall, attractive brunette who'd
burst into Cliff's office and handled his rudeness to
her with such self-assurance. "Yes, of course. How are
you, Miss Stark?"

"It's Mrs.—I'm divorced. But call me Janet, and I'll
call you—what is it you like to be called? Desiree?
Dez? Dezzie?"

I laughed. "Anything but Dezzie."

"Okay, Dez. The reason I'm phoning is to tell you
that Cliff Seymour's alibi for the time of that woman's
death is absolutely worthless. His schedule that day?
Those letters he dictated in the evening? Complete
fabrications! He didn't show up at work at all that
Saturday."

My eyes must have doubled in size. "How do you
know this?"

"Because Valerie Kranepool told me."

I cautioned myself not to get too excited, but I
wouldn't listen. Maybe things were looking up after
all!

"Uh, Janet? It would be preferable if we could have
this talk in person. Is it possible for us to get together?
We can do it whenever it's convenient for you and
any place you suggest."

"I doubt that's necessary. What I have to tell you is pretty straightforward, and it won't take long."

"All right." What else could I say? "I assume that you and Valerie are fairly close." This seemed unlikely, but it was the only explanation I could come up with for the secretary's sharing that sort of information with her.

"We never *were*. But we now have something in common."

"What's that?"

"Cliff dumped us both."

"Oh."

"Let me tell you how we suddenly came to bond. This past Saturday I had to go in to work to pull some figures together. Neither of the Seymours was around—Chad was out of town and Cliff was God knows where. But Valerie was at her computer. As soon as I walked in, I saw that her eyes were all red and puffy—I'd have had to be blind to miss it. Obviously, she'd just done some serious bawling. She wouldn't say what was wrong, though, so I left her and went to crunch some numbers. At about one o'clock, when I was through for the day, I passed her desk again, and she still looked positively terrible. I advised her to go home and take it easy, but she insisted she had some letters to get out. So I said, 'Have lunch with me first—my treat. I'll even throw in a martini.'

"The kid laughed. She realized I was aware that she doesn't drink. But anyhow, she finally agreed to the lunch. And after a bit of small talk and a glass of wine that I pretty much had to force on her, she let me in on why she was in such a state.

"Cliff, it seems, was not only cheating on his wife with Valerie, but for a while now he'd been cheating on *Valerie* with somebody else. Val actually met her rival once. (This, incidentally, was before the woman was promoted to being Val's successor.) What happened was, late one afternoon two or three months ago, Cliff's newest sweetie put in what I can almost guarantee was an unexpected appearance at the office. Cliff had her ushered into his inner sanctum, and after about five minutes the two of them drove off in her car. According to Val, the woman's older—but when you're twenty-three, who isn't older? She's also thin and very blond. Anyway, when he came in the next morning, the lying slime told everyone who would listen that yesterday's visitor was his cousin. But Val had to be the only one who believed him.

"Then this Thursday Cliff summoned the poor kid to his office and notified her that they were through, finished—kaput! Of course, in the process, he made himself out to be practically a martyr. She couldn't *imagine* how difficult this was for him, he told her, but over the holidays he'd come to recognize how selfish he'd been. She deserved better than a man who wasn't able to celebrate Christmas or New Year's Eve with her. His instructions to Valerie were to find a nice young fellow who wasn't encumbered by family obligations, someone who was free to share the important times in life with her. *Blah, blah, blah.*

"I confided to Val that once upon a time Cliff had fed me pretty much the same garbage. Only I didn't mention that he left out the 'young' when he'd advised me to get myself another guy." She managed a half-hearted laugh.

I wasn't quite sure how to respond to all of this, so I clucked my tongue in sympathy. After which I determined that a gentle reminder might be in order here. "Um, about Mrs. Herman's death . . ." I said softly.

Janet was clearly embarrassed. "God! I am *so* sorry! I got carried away. The fact is, Cliff outdid himself there. He concocted an alibi that made it impossible for him to have been in Queens when the old woman went down those basement stairs. And he persuaded Valerie to go along with his little fairy tale. He convinced her that if she didn't help him, there was a chance he could wind up in prison for something he didn't do."

"After throwing her over like that, though, Cliff has to be at least *somewhat* concerned that she'll give him away."

"Apparently not. He must feel that he's got her pegged—and he's right. You see, Valerie's convinced of his innocence. And there's not a vindictive bone in that great little body of hers—this is a very sincere individual we're talking about. So in spite of how he treated her, she's not about to get him in hot water."

"He really lucked out," I observed wryly.

"You can say that again. I doubt that Cliff has been giving nearly as much thought to Valerie's having backed up his story as she has herself. You see, although she's still determined to stick to it, ever since you were here she's been nervous that if anyone learned she'd lied for Cliff, she could be in trouble. I had to point out to her that it wasn't as if she'd told the lie under oath or even to the police—no offense, Dez."

"I take it Valerie has no idea that you're phoning me."

"No. And I don't want her involved in this. If you confront Cliff—and I'm assuming you will—I'd appreciate it if you'd just tell him that I was your source. I can always claim that I'd overheard him talking to Valerie." Janet's tone softened. "Her mother hasn't been too well, and I'd hate to see that poor kid lose her job."

"What about you? Are you still employed there?"

"I am—much to Cliff's annoyance. But remember, I keep the books for the company—and you're familiar with that old saying about knowledge being power. Besides, I've been considering leaving anyway. I'm sure I wouldn't have any problem connecting with another firm. I'm a damn good bookkeeper, if I say so myself."

"One more question, Janet. I'm curious. Do you

believe Cliff murdered Mrs. Herman? I suppose what I'm really asking is whether you regard him as being capable of such a thing."

"I sometimes think that anyone is capable of murder, given the right circumstances. And these might have been the right circumstances for Cliff. He's a very ambitious man, Dez. And Seymour Real Estate and Development Company isn't doing nearly as well as he tries to convince people it is. That property of Mrs. Herman's could make a real difference in the company's bottom line. Still—and it pains me to admit it—I can't picture him pushing an old woman down the stairs. But, hey, what do I know?"

"If he isn't guilty, though, why would he go to all the bother of phonying up an alibi?"

"Probably because he's afraid that his past could work against him. Years ago he was sent to jail for nine months on an assault and battery charge. Then not long after he got out, he was responsible for a hit-and-run."

"Well, in any event, I'm looking forward to having another talk with that employer of yours. And I can't thank you enough for getting in touch with me. I—"

"Oh, hell. Don't give me too much credit. For almost three years now I've been waiting to send a little grief Cliff's way.

"And today, Dez, is payback time."

Chapter 28

Janet Stark didn't quite live up to that old adage—you know, the one about hell having no fury like a woman scorned.

True, her purpose in phoning was to use me to put the screws to Cliff. (And I was only too happy to oblige her.) But in admitting that she didn't actually believe him capable of murdering Aunt Bessie, she evidently stopped short of wanting the man to be treated to a lethal injection.

Poor Janet. Cliff had obviously put her through the wringer.

And poor Valerie. Almost certainly she was still carrying the torch for that lowlife.

Don't misunderstand me, though. The fact that I sympathized with these women doesn't mean I condone taking up with a married Don (or Donna) Juan. Of course, this could be because I've never fallen head over heels for anyone who already had a spouse. On second thought, though—and you can call me old-fashioned or prudish or, if you insist, a sanctimonious prig—I wouldn't feel right about playing house with somebody else's honey. No matter what.

At any rate, I wasn't prepared to confront Cliff about his bogus alibi yet. And I certainly wasn't in any mood to revisit my notes. So I did the only sensible thing: I went out to lunch.

A coffee shop had recently opened up diagonally across the street from the office, and the advance word was pretty good. I was seated at the counter, enjoying a cheeseburger and some really crispy fries, when someone tapped me on the shoulder.

I turned toward the tapper—the woman occupying the stool to the left of mine. "Don't I know you?" she asked.

Putting down the cheeseburger, I took a good look at her. She was a large middle-aged woman with black hair—and I mean *coal*-black—that was frizzed out to *there.* "I don't think so," I told her with a polite smile.

"Are you sure?"

"Well, as sure as I *can* be." Hair like that I wouldn't have forgotten.

"You're not a friend of Lovey La Barre's?"

"I'm afraid I've never heard of her," I said, attempting to turn away so I could concentrate on my food.

The woman placed a heavy hand on my forearm. "Oh, Lovey isn't a she, dearie. He's a *he*—a female impersonator. Also," she elaborated with obvious pride, "he's my best girlfriend's cousin's cousin. It's hard to believe you never heard of him."

"I'm sorry, but I never have."

"Lovey's a *sensational* performer. And he's appearing in this terrific revue over on Ninth Avenue— the papers all gave it raves. You can catch it any weekend through the nineteenth. It so happens I got discount tickets to it, if you'd like a couple."

"That's very nice of you, but I expect to be working really long hours for the next month or so."

The woman's already narrow eyes narrowed further. "You saying you work Saturdays and Sundays, too?"

"Yes, from home," I snapped, my spine automatically stiffening at her tone.

"Hey, don't get mad, dearie. I was just curious—I never did learn to mind my own business. But let me give these to you anyway." She pulled a stack of tickets from her coat pocket and deposited two of them alongside the plate holding my waiting and rapidly cooling burger. "Listen, you never know. Maybe you'll decide to give yourself some time off to relax and have fun—and believe me, this show is just the ticket." She chuckled at her own cleverness.

I took the easy way out. "Thank you," I said, turning away and shoving the tickets into my handbag.

My new friend leaned over for some final words. "Try and see it—I promise you won't be sorry. But if you positively *can't* get away for a couple of hours, maybe you can let someone else take advantage of that discount, okay?"

"I'll do that."

As I bit into my now ice-cold burger, I heard my former buddy say to the man seated on the other side of her, "Don't I know you?"

I had to smile. The whole incident was just *so* New York.

When I returned to the office I still hadn't decided on the best way to deal with this Cliff thing, so I figured I'd leave it alone for a bit and let it percolate in my brain. I also managed to give myself an out for not taking another crack at my notes yet. The fact was, I hadn't questioned all of the suspects. And I should at least wait until I heard what the terrible-tempered dry cleaner had to say before tackling that intimidating pile of papers again.

Now, today was supposed to be Nigel's first day back at the shop. And my original intention had been to hold off contacting the man until tomorrow to give him a little time to settle in. But the thing is, I couldn't come up with another productive way to occupy myself this afternoon.

I lifted the receiver.

"Dependable Cleaners," a woman informed me.

"Is Nigel available, please?"

"He's not in. May *I* help you?"

"No, thank you. I really have to speak to him directly. I understood he would be home from vacation on the sixth."

"Well, he *is* home—he flew in yesterday. But he's

got an awful case of jet lag, and he couldn't drag himself in here this morning."

"Oh, that's too bad."

The woman laughed. "Don't feel *too* sorry for him; he spent five weeks in Europe, touring England, Spain, and France. And he enjoyed himself immensely. I'd put up with a little jet lag for a trip like that, wouldn't you?"

It wasn't until a couple of minutes after I hung up the phone that what I'd just been told impacted on me.

Nigel had been abroad for five weeks! And Aunt Bessie died on December fourteenth—which was only about three weeks ago. So unless he'd interrupted his holiday to fly home and do her in—and then turned right around and flew back across the Atlantic—he couldn't possibly have been responsible for Bessie's demise. Which I considered unfortunate. I mean, judging from Don's depiction of the man, I wouldn't have minded nailing him for the crime. Not even one little bit.

Nevertheless, it looked like I'd have to scratch Nigel's name off my list. And mentally, that's what I did.

Unable to dream up another excuse not to, I had a protracted go-round with my notes after that—with predictable results. Which prompted the decision to stash them away until next Monday. Of course, it would be a miracle if my brain were to sharpen during the interim. But at least I'd be studying the contents with fresher eyes.

I was just gathering my things prior to beating it out the door when Nick phoned.

"Dez? I wasn't sure I'd still catch you. I wanted to say hi and tell you how much I enjoyed Saturday evening."

"I did, too. I wish you'd wakened me when you got up on Sunday, though; I'd have liked to fix breakfast for us."

"I know. But I couldn't bring myself to drag you

out of that deep, peaceful sleep. Listen," he said, sounding a shade uncomfortable, "I was hoping we might do something over the weekend. But this Friday Tiffany is off to Boston for a three-day visit with her girlfriend, so Derek will be staying at my place until Monday morning. If you're not too busy, though, maybe we can get together during the week."

"Which night do you want to make it?"

"How does Thursday sound? Emil will most likely be back to work by then, so I can leave the shop an hour or two earlier."

"I was just about to ask you about Emil. How is he feeling?"

"A lot better, he claims. Fortunately, it wasn't the flu—only a very bad cold. But about Thursday . . ."

"Oh, Thursday's good." And to convince him I meant it: "Great, in fact."

"I'll call you, and we'll make arrangements."

The truth is, it rankled that I wouldn't be seeing Nick on the weekend, when we'd have been able to spend more time together. And I was annoyed at myself for *being* annoyed, if you follow me. I mean, I realize that your child has to come first. Still, being relegated to a Thursday would have been a lot easier to take if the reason for it wasn't named Derek.

Chapter 29

I'd had the forlorn hope of being able to come up with some brilliant scheme that would induce Cliff Seymour to own up to those lies of his. But by Tuesday morning there'd been no epiphany. I managed to take it in stride, however. In fact, the second I was ensconced in my office, I was not only ready but eager to challenge the man.

I could barely recognize that it was Valerie who answered the phone; only a trace of the singsong remained in her voice. "Cliff Seymour, please. This is Desiree Shapiro," I said.

"Oh . . . uh, Ms. Shapiro. Please hold on a moment." The girl appeared to be uneasy—but could be I was projecting or something.

She was back on the line almost at once. "Umm, I'm sorry, Ms. Shapiro, but Mr. Cliff is in conference."

"Then I'd appreciate your giving him a message for me."

"Certainly."

"Tell him I have *proof* that his alibi doesn't hold water. Have you got that?"

"'. . . proof that his alibi doesn't hold water.' Yes, I've got it."

"Good. Thanks a lot, Ms. Kranepool."

"Uh, Ms. Shapiro?"

"Yes?"

"Am I in trouble?" This time she spoke so softly that it was a challenge to make out the words.

"No, you're not. So don't worry."

Valerie's response was most likely "Thank you." But her voice had dropped even lower, so I wouldn't swear to it.

It took less than ten minutes for Cliff to call.

"What the hell's with you?" he railed. "You have poor Ms. Kranepool thinking she's about to be dragged off to the guillotine."

"Whatever Ms. Kranepool thinks, you've got yourself to thank for it. *I* didn't have her phony up an alibi for *me*."

"What makes you so sure it's phony?"

"Because I know the truth."

"Which is—?"

"Which is nothing I intend to discuss on the telephone."

"Listen, maybe I wasn't a hundred percent up front with you. But I wasn't in Ozone Park that day, and I can prove it."

"Not on the phone you can't."

"All right. Let me come to your office."

About two hours later Cliff Seymour put in an appearance, the scent of his hair gel preceding him into my cubbyhole by a good three seconds.

He was dressed casually, in faded, baggy jeans. As soon as he removed his down jacket, I was struck by the handsome silver-and-turquoise buckle on his western-style belt. I didn't have long to admire it, however; the buckle disappeared under the fold of his ample stomach the instant he sat down.

Looking at him closely now, I was struck by how pale he was, how subdued. There was none of the arrogance, none of the bluster I'd found so off-putting during our first meeting. In fact, the man was like a whipped dog. Only there was no way *he* could play on my heartstrings.

Cliff began the conversation even before I had a

chance to offer him a cup of coffee. "I want to make it clear that I had nothing to do with Bess Herman's death," he announced.

"Then why the lies? I've discovered that you never went into work at all that Saturday."

He seemed to have turned a shade paler. "I suppose you badgered Valerie into telling you that."

"Who?"

"Ms. Kranepool."

It was my turn to lie. "I can't remember ever hearing her first name," I said. "But anyway, the information didn't come from Valerie. I don't imagine it's occurred to you that someone might have been anxious to see you that evening. Anxious enough, in fact, to stop by your office—twice. And incidentally, the first time was about five o'clock. There was, however, no one around."

"Oh." Beads of sweat were dotting Cliff's forehead now. He took a tissue from his pants pocket and wiped his brow before asking, "Who came by?"

"For the purpose of our discussion that doesn't really matter, does it? What matters is that your story about being at work during the critical time period is no longer valid. In other words, Cliff, you've been busted. And after you went to all the trouble of faking that correspondence, too."

"Actually, the correspondence wasn't fake. That Thursday, after you informed me of Ms. Herman's death and we made arrangements for you to drive down to my place, I just went to the computer and changed the original dates on the letters to December fourteenth. Then I ran them off again."

"I don't understand why you felt so compelled to furnish yourself with an alibi."

Cliff ran his tongue over his lower lip. "Two reasons. One: I'm a very vulnerable suspect. And two: I'm a coward." Here he took a pathetic stab at a smile.

"What makes you so vulnerable?"

"To begin with, there's my history. I used to be a wee bit on the wild side, Desiree, and I had some run-ins with the law. Nothing major and nothing recent, I assure you. Still, the fact remains that I've got a record. I also had what could be regarded as a strong motive for disposing of Bess Herman. The acquisition of her property is important to Seymour Real Estate and Development—obtaining that land would enable us to build a very profitable shopping mall. And I'll level with you. The company isn't exactly riding high just now. We need a big boost if we're going to keep afloat. At any rate, in spite of all the inducements that were presented to her, it didn't appear that Bess could be persuaded to sell. But, of course, there was a fairly decent likelihood that her sons would see things differently."

"Let me ask you something, Cliff. Are you under the impression you're the only suspect in this investigation?"

"No, not at all."

"So wouldn't it figure that the rest of the suspects would have their motives, too? Otherwise, they wouldn't be suspects."

"I understand that. But I'm sure not everyone else's motive is that clear-cut, whereas my desire, my *need* for Ms. Herman's property is pretty compelling—and hardly a secret. Also in my case, there are . . . well . . . other factors that come into play."

"Such as?"

Cliff moistened his lower lip with his tongue again. "Recently my wife of eight years walked out. And ours was not one of those ultracivilized 'we'll always be pals' partings, either. Irene learned that I've been seeing another woman, and *furious* doesn't even begin to describe her reaction. We have two children, and I'd bet everything I own that she's out to ensure that I'm denied visitation rights. For over a month now I've been sick with worry that she might manage to pull it off, too. You see, Irene comes from a wealthy family. And in addition to having *mucho* bucks, these are very influential people. My father-in-law's a state senator, and Irene's first cousin is an assemblyman. Her second cousin—the two of them grew up together, incidentally—is a federal prosecutor. Trust me. If that clan ever found out that I was under even the slightest suspicion here, they'd do whatever they could to see that regardless of who committed the murder, I'd be the one to pay for it."

The man sounded paranoid. "Do you honestly believe they'd go that far?"

"Absolutely," he said firmly. "You probably think I'm paranoid"—he had that right, anyway—"and you could be a hundred percent correct. Nevertheless, I'm convinced that once Irene gives them an earful of my cheating ways—if she hasn't done it already—well, you can rest assured that I have no intention of helping them load their guns. Figuratively speaking, naturally—I'm not *that* paranoid."

"Did you ever consider reconciling with your wife? It would most likely be to your advantage to have a family like hers on your side."

Cliff shook his head vigorously. "I was relieved that she wanted out. Less than a year into the marriage, I was toying with the idea of leaving *her*. Only I didn't have the guts to do it. And then once the kids were born, I was concerned about what a divorce might do to them. But I've come to the conclusion it's in their best interests that their mother and I go our separate ways. After all, it wasn't as if we were providing them with a loving home to grow up in. A couple of words in my own defense, though. I admit that I wasn't the best husband in the world, but Irene's far from the warm, caring type. Try getting close to that woman— I'm not only speaking physically, either—and you're likely to wind up with frostbite.

"So there you have it. In light of both my past and my present circumstances, when you notified me of the possibility that Bess Herman was murdered, I decided I'd better have a damn good alibi in place." He eked out a grin. "Like I said, I'm a coward."

"I've got one more question for you, Cliff."

"Shoot."

"You gave this vague story about driving around Pennsylvania for most of that Saturday. In contrast, though, you put a lot of effort into establishing that you were in the office between four-thirty and seven o'clock, having this falsely attested to by Ms. Kranepool and supported by that altered correspondence. So I have to wonder: If you didn't commit the murder, how could you know what hours you might be asked to account for?"

"Joel told me," Cliff reluctantly confessed. "I know, I know. I claimed I hadn't been in touch with him, but. . . . uh, I lied. Right after you phoned me that Thursday, I gave him a call—Bess had once mentioned where he worked. I said that I wanted to offer my condolences, and in the course of our brief conversation, he supplied me with the particulars about his mother's death. But let me ask *you* something now, if I may."

"Go ahead."

"If I'd killed Bess, why would I need to find out from Joel when she died?"

"That's easy. You're smart enough to realize that it was unlikely the autopsy could determine the exact time of her death, so you needed Joel to fill you in on the outside perimeters: when she was last seen alive and exactly when her body was discovered."

"It wasn't like that; I swear."

"Maybe not. But that's certainly a reasonable explanation."

"Reasonable but wrong," Cliff grumbled.

"One more question," I promised again. "When you called me back before, you said something about being able to prove you weren't in Queens that day."

"That's right."

"Then where were you?"

"With Gwen, the woman I've been seeing for the past five months. We spent the entire day together."

"Would you mind telling me how you spent it?"

"I'll give you our complete itinerary. I was at her house by ten that morning, and we sat around and talked for close to an hour. At about eleven we went out to brunch. And after that we took in a movie—it was an oldie: *Rear Window*, with James Stewart and Grace Kelly. From there, we returned to Gwen's house and watched some TV. Around six o'clock she started preparing dinner for us, while I watched *more* TV—she didn't want me in the kitchen. It was a great meal, by the way: steak, baked potatoes with sour cream and chives, onion rings—the works. I'm a meat and potatoes guy, and on those rare occasions when Irene did condescend to cook, a lot of bean sprouts and tofu were involved. Among other things, Irene's a vegetarian." He made it sound like a dirty word.

"And you left Gwen's place when?"

"At ten the following morning."

"Do you think Gwen will confirm all of this?"

"I know she will."

I waited until my meeting with Cliff was over before contacting his ladylove. She echoed his account of that Saturday right down to the evening's menu, to which she made one small addition: "And we had chocolate cream pie for dessert."

Then, a contemptuous note in her voice, she declared, "His *wife* doesn't believe in dessert."

Chapter 30

Over a BLT and a Coke at my desk, I decided that I wouldn't be ejecting Cliff from my suspect list à la Nigel. As far as I was concerned, my good friend Cliffy was still a major player.

The thing is, I wasn't at all convinced that he'd leveled with me. I mean, forget the alibi Gwen had provided for him. How could I be certain she hadn't been moved by Cliff's charm (the nature of which totally eluded me) to swear to his lies—just as Valerie had? I could almost *hear* him telling his newest conquest that, innocent as he was, he could, nevertheless, wind up behind bars without her help.

At any rate, it was then that I resolved to try another strategy with regard to the investigation. After all, I was hardly getting anywhere with my notes. Which led me to speculate as to whether the reason I hadn't found a single clue in that whole damn stack of papers was because there was simply no damn clue to find. (This, of course, was preferable to placing the blame on my being obtuse.) Maybe the thing to do now was to canvass the residents on Bessie's block. Could be that *somebody* would remember seeing one of the suspects in the vicinity on the crucial afternoon—and with luck, that blessed individual might even recall the time.

But the truth is, I wasn't too optimistic. After all, Aunt Bessie's death occurred weeks ago. And with no suggestion of murder at that point, it wasn't likely any comings and goings that day would have remained fixed in the mind of even a single neighbor. Still, doing a little snooping in Ozone Park was preferable to sitting around in my cubbyhole pulling out my glorious hennaed hair—or, worse yet, rereading those notes.

And now, having consumed the last speck of my sandwich, I picked up the receiver.

Janet Stark was first on my list.

I asked if she'd be able to get her hands on a picture of Cliff and if so, whether she could fax it to me.

She could.

And, almost before I blinked, she did.

Joel was next.

He was maybe on the chilly side of cordial, but only marginally—at the outset, anyway.

After disposing of the amenities, I said casually, "I understand you received a call from Cliff Seymour about a week and a half ago."

"Yeah. He wanted to offer his condolences on my mother's death. He said that he'd only just heard about it."

"I suppose he was interested in how it happened."

"I guess so."

"Did he mention your mother's summer home?"

"Why? Does it look like he had something to do with her fall?"

"I wouldn't say that, Joel. But if I'm going to do my job, I can't disregard the possibility."

"I know. But I really can't stop to talk. I have an appointment all the way across town in fifteen minutes. Matter of fact, you caught me as I was putting on my coat."

"I won't keep you long, I promise. If you could answer that one question . . ."

"Okay. Yes. He brought up the subject. He assumed I'd inherited that property—which I had. Anyhow, he started to go on about what a great deal he was prepared to offer me if I sold to him, but I cut him off. I told him I wanted to wait a decent interval before doing anything about that, and I said I'd contact him when I was ready to discuss it. Donnie and I can't bring ourselves to dispose of the house in Ozone Park yet, either," he added sadly. "Mom left that to the two of us."

And here I (nervously) posed the question that was almost certain to be met with antagonism. "How does Frankie feel about your decision regarding the place at the shore?"

I was right about the antagonism. "Why are you asking me that?" Joel all but snarled.

"I had this notion that she might be anxious to keep it," I improvised. "You know, it's pretty nice to own a home at the beach, especially if you plan on having children."

"For chrissake! Frankie and I haven't even set the date yet!"

"So, uh, she would just as soon you'd sell right away?"

"She says it's up to me."

Yeah, I'll bet. (Listen, I'd seen that little lady in action.) "I understand." It kind of popped out under its own steam.

"No, you don't. For your information, Frankie has really delicate skin, so there's no question of our ever making use of the house. That's why she thinks that the sensible thing is to unload the place while this guy Seymour is still so hot for it."

For a sharp little girl like Frankie, pulling Joel's strings must have been a piece of cake. *I'd* even gotten him to spit out an admission he'd been reluctant to make.

Dare I ask him now for photos of himself and Frankie or not? I wondered.

"Listen, I'm sorry, but I *really* gotta split," he announced, sparing me the necessity of wrestling with this decision.

I didn't do too well with Sylvia Vine, either.

To my request for photographs of both her and her

son, she responded, "I vould give to you if I have, only I have not."

I attempted to persuade her that the photos could help eliminate them as suspects, but before I was able to finish my spiel, she interrupted with a firm, "Must go—dentist appointment."

And that was that.

I had nothing to lose by trying Richie, although I wouldn't have given you two cents for my chances of success there. Which shows you how much *I* know.

I wasn't surprised to find him at home. (It was extremely doubtful he'd be at work anywhere.) What *did* surprise me was that once I told him what I wanted and why, he was actually fairly pleasant. "There's this snapshot my girl took at Thanksgiving—it's of me and my mom together."

"That would be great! If you could put it in an envelope, I can arrange for a pickup."

"No sweat."

"And thanks a lot"—I managed to catch myself before the *Richie* slipped out—"Ric," I said loud and clear.

"That's okay, Dezzie. Knock yourself out."

Well, this left Joel and Frankie. Actually, I didn't figure Frankie's picture was too important. After all, she'd already admitted to being at the victim's house that afternoon. Of course, she might have lied about the time—although I couldn't come up with a reason for her misleading me about that. Anyhow, Don would probably be able to help me out with the photos. But since I didn't have the number of the high school he taught at, I'd have to wait until tonight to phone him.

Having set up this new agenda, I was a little less depressed about things. Ten minutes later, however, the new agenda bit the dust.

There was no longer a need to show around a bunch

of photos. Or pore over my notes for the umpteenth time. Or beat myself up for not having solved the case.

Because just then, that's exactly what I did. Solved the case, I mean.

Chapter 31

So what took me so long?

Well, aside from the obvious answer (my being incredibly slow-witted), to discover who murdered Aunt Bessie, it was necessary to compare the statements of two individuals. In other words, it was only by taking into account what one of them had revealed that I was able to determine that the other was a bald-faced liar.

Naturally, though, the interviews had been written up—and, therefore, studied—in the order in which I'd spoken to the people involved. And because other conversations had intervened between the two that are relevant here, I'm ashamed to admit that I'd neglected to make the connection that should have hit me between the eyes.

At any rate, it wasn't much past four when I was through phoning about the photographs. Nevertheless, I was pretty spent by then, so I'd decided to call it a day—only my bottom refused to leave the chair. (No, it wasn't a premonition, just out-and-out laziness.) And, in spite of my fervent wish not to, I wound up going back over the case in my mind.

Thinking about the motives of the various suspects, it seemed to me that Sylvia Vine's was the weakest. Would she have killed Bessie for reneging on a five-thousand-dollar loan? Very unlikely, unless, of course, she felt that Bessie's breaking her word was what had led to her—Sylvia, I mean—putting a price on her affections. That whole prostitute thing, though, was kind of iffy. And even if it was true that Sylvia had entered the profession, would she have murdered her cousin because she, Sylvia, had elected to begin charging for what she'd probably been donating to the needy for years? Of course, the woman did have another grievance against her relative, one to which I concede that I'd given short shrift: Bessie's supposed desire to run her life. Among the examples Sylvia had ticked off for me were the victim's badgering her to wear less makeup, attend school to improve her English, and *keep a kosher home*. But it was even more difficult to accept that any of these had earned Aunt Bessie a broken neck.

What it all boiled down to, I guess, was that I didn't really feel Sylvia Vine was my killer. On the other hand, though, I can't say I was a hundred percent convinced that she wasn't.

At any rate, immediately after turning my focus away from Sylvia, I moved on to Frankie—probably because they were the only two female suspects.

Now, here I had a more likely candidate. I mean, it was a fact that her fiancé's mother wasn't too keen on her. Also a fact: This was a girl who was used to getting what she wanted. And what she wanted was to marry Joel.

Well, suppose Frankie had been less than truthful about the outcome of her visit to Mrs. Herman. She claimed that her dropping in on Mrs. H. as she did had turned things around. Why, Frankie informed me, Bessie had even wanted the two of them to come to dinner that evening. It had been the deceased's intention to prepare a Russian specialty for the occasion, too: *beef Stroganoff*.

And that's when, at long last, it gelled.

I slapped myself on the side of the head. My God! How could I have missed it! *Beef Stroganoff in a kosher home?*

At that moment I was so exhilarated that I felt like turning cartwheels. (Which is probably the most ludi-

crous reaction I've ever had to solving a crime—
particularly when you consider where I rank on the
fitness scale.) I settled for pressing the intercom.

"What?" a put-upon Jackie inquired.

"Are you busy?" I didn't wait for a response. "Can
you come in here for a few minutes?"

"Okay. Anything wrong?"

"No. It's finally right."

"I figured out who killed Aunt Bessie!" I squealed
the instant Jackie appeared in the doorway.

She was a good enough friend to be excited for
me. "No kidding! Who?" she demanded, leaning over
my desk.

"Just have a seat and listen." Jackie sat. "Now,
Frankie—Joel's sweetie, remember?—says that on the
day of the murder, she stopped by to see her future
mother-in-law and that Bessie invited her and Joel to
have dinner there that night. According to Frankie,
Bessie mentioned that she'd be serving beef Stroganoff." I paused for effect before dropping the zinger
on her. "Only Mrs. Herman is kosher!"

Jackie peered at me blankly.

Well, considering that her interest in food is restricted to consuming it, I should have expected as
much. "Beef Stroganoff is made with sour cream."

"Ohhh," Jackie murmured.

"And if you're kosher, you don't mix meat and
dairy."

"I know *that,* for crying out loud," she retorted
huffily. "Anyway, congratulations!"

"Thanks, Jackie."

She jumped to her feet and scooted around the
desk. I figured if I stood up it would be like asking
for one of her trademark hugs, which almost invariably result in my taking an inventory of my ribs. This
way, she had to bend down and be content with bussing my cheek.

"So are you going to the police with this, or what?"
she demanded.

"I don't see how I can. The Stroganoff isn't really what they'd regard as *proof* that Frankie pushed Aunt Bessie down those stairs."

Plopping down on the chair again, Jackie mused, "Then she hadn't been invited to come over later at all."

"Correct. If Frankie went there that afternoon to ingratiate herself with Mrs. Herman, this was evidently one time she struck out."

"Still, she wasn't the only suspect who lied to you about something, was she?"

"Hardly. But the others did it to divert suspicion from themselves once they learned that Mrs. Herman was dead. Frankie, however, told *her* whopper *before* it was established that the woman was no longer with us. She phoned Joel to inform him that she'd just been to his mother's and that they'd had such a nice talk that Mrs. Herman extended that dinner invitation. The girl didn't worry about whether she'd get away with this piece of fiction, since she had firsthand knowledge that Bessie Herman was no longer around to contradict her."

"You'd never have realized she was making this up if she hadn't thrown in the beef Stroganoff, would you?"

"It's quite possible I wouldn't. But the nice thing about so many murderers is that in an effort to be convincing, they tend to embellish their stories. In Frankie's case, though, I'm surprised she even bothered. I'm sure she believes that whatever leaves her lips will be regarded as pure, unimpeachable truth. I had the privilege of seeing her in action, and that's one superconfident little cookie."

"Well, if *I* ever decide to rub someone out, I'll have to remind myself to steer clear of the embroidery," Jackie declared, grinning.

"Same here."

And not mentioning any names, I suddenly had a mental image of the planet's most obnoxious nine-year-old boy.

Chapter 32

Before leaving the office on Tuesday, I got in touch with my client.

"I have good news and bad news," I announced.

"Start with the good news; I can use some of that today."

"I know who killed your aunt, but—"

"What did I *tell* you?" Ben erupted. "I was *certain* you could do it!"

"The problem is—and this is the bad news part—I don't have any proof."

"But you're confident you're right."

"Yes."

"You'd better say who it was before I burst."

"Frankie."

The response came slowly. "You mean *Joel's* Frankie?"

"I'm afraid so. I just hope . . ." I couldn't quite finish the thought."

"What?"

"That Joel wasn't in this with her."

"Never! Joel loved his mother. They may have squabbled occasionally—what families don't? Most of the time, though, they got along extremely well. Aunt Bessie was a very loving mother, and Joel was a devoted son. Trust me on that. But what led you to determine that it was Frankie who shoved my aunt down those stairs?"

I was about to respond to the question when it suddenly occurred to me that it might be wise to first verify one all-important point. "Uh, Ben? Your aunt Bessie—she was still keeping a kosher home when she died, correct?"

"That's right." He sounded puzzled.

And now I let out my breath (it wasn't until this instant that I even realized I'd been holding it) and proceeded to outline the facts.

"Good God," was all Ben said when I'd finished. Then after a few moments he murmured incredulously, "And Frankie murdered my aunt for not being delighted with the prospect of having her as a daughter-in-law? It boggles the mind."

"I don't believe it's quite as simple as that. I think there are other factors that entered into Frankie's decision to do away with your aunt Bessie. First of all, it's apparent that Mrs. Herman was fairly well off financially. And from everything I've gathered, this is a very mercenary young lady we have here. At the same time, it could also be that she's truly gaga over Joel.

"At any rate, Frankie was anxious to get her hands on Mrs. Herman's money—I don't have much doubt about that. But the exact reason for her resorting to homicide is a little less clear to me. One possibility is that it was because she was afraid Joel might be persuaded by his mother to break off the engagement. But Frankie's so damn cocksure of herself that it's conceivable she never even considered such a thing. Perhaps the two women had an argument that afternoon that ended in violence. Or perhaps Frankie was so eager to improve her financial situation that she was unwilling to wait around for your aunt to die a natural death."

"Whatever her reason was, she . . . she killed her." Ben's voice shook as he said the words. "Uh, hold on a second, will you?" In the background, I could hear him blowing his nose.

He was back on the line about a minute later, his tone more even now. "I suppose Joel should be told about this."

"I'd say so."

"Er, I hate to ask." *Uh-oh.* I was hoping I was wrong about what was coming next—only I wasn't. "But listen, would you mind letting Joel know what you've concluded? I'm sure you'll do a much better job of explaining things than I could. Also," he put in with an embarrassed little laugh, "I'm not at all certain I have the heart to break this to him."

And I do? Still, it wasn't as if I'd never been saddled with that unpleasant task before. Besides, if Joel should turn out to be furious with the messenger (which was very likely), it was preferable that the messenger not be a member of his own family. "All right," I agreed with zero enthusiasm.

"Thanks. Thanks a lot. And Desiree? I'd like it if you'd continue on the case. I have faith that, given more time, you'll come up with the necessary evidence against Frankie."

"Of course I'll continue. And I promise you, Ben, I'll do everything I can to put that girl where she belongs."

The truth is, I'd have attempted to uncover that evidence even if I weren't being paid for it. I mean, I have this *thing* about anyone's getting away with murder.

Was I nervous about talking to Bessie's younger son?

I'll tell you how nervous I was: so nervous that I could barely think about food. (For me, *that's* nervous!) And forget about my actually preparing anything. Unfortunately, though, I get a headache when I skip a meal. I also wind up with an irritable disposition. Plus, not eating makes my brain fuzzy. (I swear.) So passing on supper wasn't an option.

That's why, on my way home from work that evening, I did the unimaginable: I picked up a TV dinner! I vowed, however, that Jackie would never know.

At eight o'clock, after feasting on pasta that tasted like cardboard, I went to the telephone, my hands suddenly moist. As I began dialing Joel's number, I crossed my slippery fingers that Frankie wasn't with him.

"Joel? This is Desiree." My mouth was so dry that I made this peculiar clicking sound when I spoke. "Am I disturbing your dinner or anything?"

"No, that's okay." (Which meant that I probably was.)

"Uh, are you alone?"

"Why do you ask?" He seemed to be a little wary.

"I'm just concerned that this might take awhile. And if you have company, I could call back later."

"There's no company, so go ahead and ask your questions."

"I didn't call to *ask* you anything; I called to tell you something."

"What's that?"

"Your mother didn't have an accident, Joel," I informed him as gently as I know how. "She was murdered."

Three or four seconds ticked by before the boy said in a near-whisper, "Are you sure?"

"Yes."

It took him even longer to manage the "Who?"

"It would be best if I explained something first."

"But—"

"Honestly, it's the only way you'll be able to understand how I arrived at the judgment I did." I didn't allow any time for further discussion. "Your mother kept a kosher kitchen, I understand."

"Yeah, that's right," Joel responded impatiently.

"Well, are you familiar with beef Stroganoff?"

"That's the thing Mom told Frankie she planned on making for us that . . . night."

"Did your mother ever serve this to you before?"

"I can't remember, but she must have—only she probably never said what it was called."

"It's very unlikely you ate that dish at your mother's, Joel. Have you any idea what the ingredients are?"

"How should I know? I'm no cook."

"It doesn't seem as if Frankie is, either."

"What do you mean?"

"Beef Stroganoff is prepared with sour cream."

There was a protracted silence before Joel found his voice again. "You think Frankie *lied* about what we were having for dinner? That doesn't make any sense," he scoffed.

"Look, Frankie wanted to convince you that as a result of her visit, the ice between your mom and her had thawed a bit. And the proof of this was that supposed invitation. Apparently, Frankie was under the impression that by mentioning what was on the menu, she was giving her story some added credence. And I imagine she must have decided that with your mother being Russian-born, the Stroganoff lent kind of an authentic touch."

"You're telling me that my mom *didn't* say anything about our coming to dinner?"

"Exactly."

"Well, you're wrong. Frankie would never have made up a thing like that. She's a truthful person. A *very* truthful person. She's also the sweetest, the most compassionate . . . I must have misunderstood about our having beef Stroganoff."

"There was no misunderstanding; Frankie referred to the same dish in a conversation I had with her."

"Well, then she didn't remember what it was Mom actually told her. Or maybe she didn't hear her right."

"I don't believe that. And I have a feeling that, deep down, you don't, either."

"Hold it. Ask yourself *this*, why don't you? If we *weren't* expected, why did my mom set the table for three people? That's something I saw with my own eyes, you know."

"Are you so positive it was your mother who set the table?" I put to Joel quietly.

"Well, I'll tell you one thing," he retorted. "It wasn't Frankie." Then, in desperation—and perhaps as much for his own benefit as mine: "Look, Frankie *couldn't* have done this—physically, I mean. You never met my mother, but she wasn't really that small a woman—not nearly as tiny as Frankie is, anyway. Frankie doesn't have the kind of strength it would have taken to throw her down those stairs."

"Something like that wouldn't require much strength at all, particularly if your mother was caught off-guard. Also, Frankie *was* a lot younger and undoubtedly in better physical condition." And when there was no immediate response: "I'm terribly sorry about this, Joel."

"There's nothing to be sorry about—except falsely accusing an innocent person. Frankie didn't murder my mother, Desiree. She was aware of how close the two of us were, and she'd never have hurt me that way."

"I—"

"Hey," he all but snarled, "I didn't think you were much of a PI to begin with. And now I *know* you're not."

A dead line was my clue that the conversation was over.

I had trouble sleeping that night.

Was Joel right? Could I have jumped to the wrong conclusion?

Sure I *could have*. But I didn't.

Frankie clearly told me Bessie had intended making beef Stroganoff. And it wasn't because the girl had a lousy memory or faulty hearing. Uh-uh. Frankie Murray was as sharp as they come. It was just fortunate that she wasn't a cook. Or if she was, that she didn't have any idea that if you're kosher, meat and cream don't mix.

Two seconds later I had another question for myself. How had Frankie managed to lure Aunt Bessie over to those cellar steps, anyway?

It took me only three or four minutes to concoct a possible scenario.

Now, from what Ben had said, that basement was

used to store all sorts of things—including a box of Joel's CDs. So in my little playlet Frankie tells Aunt Bessie that some of their friends—hers and Joel's—are coming over to her apartment that evening and that Joel had suggested she stop by and pick up a few of his old CDs. Would Mrs. Herman mind showing her where they are? she asks.

Mrs. Herman responds that, no, she wouldn't mind—just give her a minute to run upstairs and change her shoes. Frankie, however, is anxious for Bessie to be found dead in high heels—after all, that's what had tripped her up the year before. So she assures her intended victim that she needn't worry. "I'll hold on to you," she promises. To further discourage a change of footwear, she might even have put in that she was in a terrible hurry. Her company is due at six, she could have said, and she's not yet through preparing for them.

Of course, Frankie most likely employed an entirely different ruse to lure the victim over to that staircase. But I was satisfied. Listen, just now, on the spur of the moment, I'd managed to get Bessie Herman right where Frankie wanted her. So this would hardly have presented a challenge for such a motivated—and manipulative—young lady.

At any rate, in my scenario's final scene, the deceased is standing on the landing, with Frankie close behind her. And now the girl reaches out—and it isn't for the older woman's arm, either.

Our Frankie is about to see to it that poor Aunt Bessie has one final tumble down those treacherous steps.

Chapter 33

As eager as I was to continue on the case and uncover the proof needed to nail poor Bessie's killer, there was one problem: I hadn't the slightest notion how to go about it.

On Wednesday morning and for a good part of the afternoon I kept challenging my sluggish brain to devise an ingenious little scheme of some kind. But all I was able to come up with was an Extra-Strength Tylenol headache. I finally decided that—at this point, anyway—there was only one way to proceed. (Doubtless because it was the only way I could think of.) I would fall back on the same type of game plan I'd intended on pursuing originally—before zeroing in on Frankie, I mean.

I phoned my client and told him I needed to reach his cousin Don.

"Has anything happened?"

"Nothing—except that I spoke to Joel last night, and he refuses to believe that his fiancée murdered his mother."

"That doesn't surprise me."

"It wasn't exactly a shock to me, either. But the girl hardly deserves his loyalty. She didn't even spare him *unnecessary* grief, for God's sake."

"What do you mean by 'unnecessary'?"

"Look, it's horrible enough that Frankie deprived the man she professes to love of his mother. But to set the whole thing up so that *he'd* be the one to discover the body? This makes my skin crawl."

"Oh, God," Ben muttered. "That hadn't even occurred to me."

"Frankie's an original, all right," I muttered back.

"There's something that's been troubling me since yesterday, Desiree. Not that it makes any difference, but it's been on my mind a lot."

"What is it?"

"Did Frankie go to the house for the express purpose of killing my aunt? Or did she stop in there hoping to win her over, but then, when that failed . . ." He didn't bother completing the sentence. "I'd really like your opinion."

"I honestly don't know, Ben, and I probably never will. The reason I'm calling, though, is that I intend visiting your aunt's block and showing Frankie's picture around. Could be somebody saw her that afternoon, and if they did, perhaps they noticed something a little suspicious. Naturally, I can't expect Joel to hand over a picture of her, but I'm hoping Don will be able to help me out."

"The photo's a good idea," Ben said kindly—if not entirely truthfully. I mean, since there wasn't another idea in my head, I had no choice but to go with it. However, I didn't actually believe it had escaped the man's notice that it wasn't much of an idea at all.

"I'd like to talk to Don as soon as possible, but I don't have a daytime number for him," I explained.

"Let me try him at the school and have him contact you."

"Thanks, Ben."

"Incidentally, Desiree, I told Donnie all about your conclusion with regard to his mother's death."

"What did he say?"

"That your reasoning made perfect sense to him and that he's very grateful to you for identifying his mother's killer. As you can appreciate, though, he's upset for his brother that it was Frankie who turned out to be the assailant. And to be honest, so am I."

"As a matter of fact," I admitted, "I'm not too happy about it, either."

*   *   *

Following my conversation with Ben, I sat at my desk for a few minutes, staring absently at the likenesses I'd requested previously—which had almost immediately turned out to be totally unnecessary. There was Cliff Seymour flashing a supercilious smile. And Sylvia and Richie Vine (who were slightly upstaged by the handsome turkey on the table in front of them), standing side-by-side and gazing fondly at each other. At least I *thought* it was fondly, the camerawork of Richie's girlfriend being so shaky that the snapshot was too blurred for me to be certain. It was obvious that if either of the Vines had turned out to be the culprit, that picture would have done zilch to help the investigation along.

Anyway, after this I went out to Jackie's desk to chat for a little while. The phone was ringing when I returned to my cubicle. It was Don Herman, who was both pleased and saddened.

"I can't thank you enough for uncovering the truth, Desiree. Naturally, I won't claim that I'm delighted with your findings. I ache for Joel that the girl who ended the life of his wonderful, caring mother—and mine, as well, of course—is the same individual he'd chosen to be his wife."

"I wish the outcome had been different, too, Don."

"Ben tells me you'll continue checking into things. What do you anticipate will be your next step?"

"I have to uncover some evidence to corroborate my findings. That's why I wanted to talk to you. Would you, by any chance, happen to have a picture of Frankie?"

"I would. When she and my brother became engaged, Frankie had a photograph taken to submit to the newspapers, and Joel mailed me a print. She looked so open, too—so *innocent*. That old adage about appearances being deceiving is certainly a truism in this instance," he remarked dryly. "But why are you interested in acquiring her photo?"

"I want to show it to your mother's neighbors. It's

possible someone will recall seeing Frankie doing something that day that was, well, a bit questionable."

Unlike his cousin, Don made no pretense of being enthusiastic about my lame agenda. "Do you think there's much chance of that?"

"No, but like I said, it *is* possible."

"I suppose it is." But he sounded doubtful. "Unfortunately, I won't be home until fairly late this evening. However, I'll send the photograph out to you in the morning by Federal Express, priority overnight. You should receive it on Friday."

And now we speculated a bit about whether in the absence of further proof (God forbid!), Joel would ever accept the fact of his fiancée's treachery. (I'd pretty much determined by then that Bessie's younger son had played no part in her murder—although I still wasn't quite ready to stake what there was of my reputation on that.) Immediately following this exchange, Don had a final question for me.

"Look, I would never impose upon you by requesting that you keep me advised of your progress, but would it present a problem if I were to call *you* from time to time?"

"No, not at all."

I never dreamed I'd hear from him again only hours later—and that I'd be left with yet another puzzle to solve.

Chapter 34

On the way home from the office on Wednesday, I stopped off at D'Agostino's—and wound up leaving a hefty part of my available funds behind.

I was either low on or completely out of everything from tarragon to toilet tissue. Into the shopping cart (with its two bum wheels) went spices and paper goods and salad fixings and meat and chicken and coffee and fruit and . . . Actually, practically the only essential I currently had in decent supply was my macadamia brittle. But to avoid a Häagen-Dazs crisis anytime soon, I decided I'd better bolster my inventory. (Look, you never know when you'll come down with beriberi or something and be unable to make it to the supermarket.)

The phone was ringing when I walked into the apartment. I managed to snatch up the receiver before the answering machine kicked in, thus sparing both the caller and myself from listening to a message delivered by a Minnie Mouse sound-alike. (While I still maintain that this irritating tone is the result of some glitch in the machine, having to hear it is, nevertheless, very depressing to a person who regards her voice as being not that far removed from Lauren Bacall's.)

Anyhow, it was Nick on the line, with some less than wonderful news for me. "I'm really sorry, Dez; I'll have to cancel our date. I just spoke to Emil. He's had a kind of relapse, and he can't make it in to work tomorrow after all."

"I'm sorry, too—about both Emil and the fact that

we won't be getting together tomorrow night. I was looking forward to it."

"Not any more than I was. Listen, I'll call you over the weekend, and we'll set something up for next week. Okay?"

"Sure. That's fine, Nick." But, of course, it wasn't. I mean, while the postponement couldn't be helped, "fine" was definitely pushing it.

At a few minutes before ten, I heard from Don Herman.

"I hope I didn't awaken you, Desiree," he said, sounding tentative.

I laughed. "It's very rare that I make it to bed before midnight."

"The reason I'm telephoning you now is because only a few moments ago I recalled something. It may have no significance whatever with regard to your investigation, but I felt you should be the one to make that judgment."

"What's this about?"

"My mother's watch—it's missing. But perhaps Joel already mentioned that to you?"

"No, he didn't. When did you become aware that it was gone?"

"Immediately following the funeral. My whole family had flown in from California—even my twelve-year-old son and ten-year-old daughter had come to pay their respects." Don's tone took on a more somber note here. "And after the services, we all went back to what had been my mother's home for many, many years—and Joel's and mine, as well. A group of us were sitting in the living room, talking, when suddenly Eloise—my irrepressible daughter—blurted out that she wanted to see her grandmother's wristwatch.

"I should explain what prompted that outburst. A long while back—before Eloise was even born—my father gifted my mother with this elegant and, I'm certain, costly timepiece. It has a Swiss movement, and the face is bordered in a design of eighteen-karat gold.

Moreover, there's an eighteen-karat-gold bracelet that must be at least a half-inch wide."

"In other words, this wasn't something you'd wear to the supermarket," I remarked.

"I wouldn't think so."

"But you were saying . . ."

"Well, Eloise, who has always been a very feminine little girl, has coveted that watch since she was a toddler. And last June, when my mother was in California for a visit, she promised Eloise that it would be hers on her sixteenth birthday.

"At any rate, when my daughter said she wanted to look at the watch, my wife and I admonished her—we were absolutely mortified. After all, this was the day of my mother's funeral. Joel, however, overruled us. He took Eloise by the hand, and they went upstairs to the master bedroom. After about ten minutes they rejoined us. Apparently, Joel had been searching all the obvious places for that watch, but without success.

"Well, both he and I assumed that it would resurface eventually. There was nothing to indicate that someone had broken into the house, you understand—it wasn't as if the room were in disorder or anything of that nature. But then the following week—I'd already returned home by then—my brother conducted a second search. On this occasion he also wanted to ascertain whether all of Mom's other jewelry could be accounted for. Not a difficult task, by the way, since she had only a few valuable pieces. At any rate, as far as he was able to determine, nothing else was missing. As for the watch, it hasn't shown up to this day."

And now Don put in hastily, "I trust you can appreciate why, at the time, I would fail to link the disappearance of the wristwatch and my mother's death. The truth is, I still have no idea whether there's a connection. Nevertheless, when it came to mind this evening, I felt I should bring the matter to your attention."

"Thank you, Don. I'm glad you did. Do you know if a report was filed with the police?"

"Well, after hunting for it that second time, Joel assured me he planned on contacting them."

"You don't sound too convinced that he did, though."

"That's because my brother has always been a world-class procrastinator, Desiree. And incidentally, I have no doubt that if he did fail to pursue the matter, this was the reason—the *only* reason. Keep in mind that we became aware that the watch was missing weeks ago, when it was a rather iffy proposition that our mother had been murdered at all. Moreover, even if this had already been established, the last person Joel would have suspected of killing her—and perhaps also stealing the watch—was the young woman he loved. But I'll check with him tomorrow and remind him to file that police report—if he hasn't already done so. I *did* question him about it once, and he promised to see to it the very next day. Knowing Joel, however, I may well have been remiss in not keeping after him."

"From your description, it sounds as if that watch should be fairly easy to identify," I said.

"Absolutely. Mom's initials—BLH—are even engraved on the back of the case."

"Incidentally, was Frankie also at the house on the day of the funeral?"

"She went to the services, but she had to be at work afterwards. She came by later—in the evening."

"I imagine Joel would have told you if the watch had since turned up somewhere."

"Now, *that* I'm certain he would have done."

"This whole thing is pretty strange," I commented. And then I had a couple of thoughts. "Of course, the watch may not have been stolen at all. For all anyone knows, your mother might have misplaced it days— perhaps even *weeks*—before she died. But she didn't mention it because she chose not to enlighten her nearest and dearest as to how careless she'd been."

Don chuckled. "That sounds like Mom."

"Or if there *was* a theft," I went on, "it could have

occurred while your mother was alive—only she might have attributed the loss to simply forgetting where she'd put it."

"So the fact that the watch seems to have disappeared doesn't necessarily have anything to do with her death," Don murmured.

"Probably not. Still, it *could*. Although, frankly, right now I don't see how."

Which is just one more example of how myopic I can be.

Chapter 35

Last night I'd gone to bed too tired to think straight. In fact, I was so tired that even the sorry state of the investigation failed to prompt any tossing and turning. I must have drifted off right after my head made contact with the pillow.

This morning, however, almost as soon as I sat down to my Cheerios with banana slices, it appeared that the cobwebs had been miraculously swept from my brain while I slept. If only long enough for me to appreciate how the missing watch could be tied to the crime. Even if I was on target, however—and I couldn't be sure that I was—whether my sudden burst of smarts would eventually lead to Frankie's landing behind bars was a big question mark. All I could do was to get in touch with Don. And then cross my fingers, and my toes, and my eyes . . .

I quickly dialed his home—no answer. Well, I still didn't have his number at the school, so I spoke to the answering machine:

"Listen, Don, in retrospect, I don't feel that it's a good idea for you to talk to Joel about reporting the theft. I mean, my conversation with him on Tuesday left him with enough to deal with right now—whether he's willing to accept my conclusion or not. Anyway, there's an off chance that providing the police with the information on the watch could wind up being important. So I strongly suggest you contact them yourself—today, if possible—and ask them to notify *you* if it's found. I'd also mention that you suspect

Frankie of having pilfered it. Oh, in the event Joel's already called them about the watch, don't worry; there's no harm done." But I had my fingers and all those other appropriate parts crossed when I said that.

In the evening I telephoned Ellen and Mike to wish them a happy belated honeymoon. They were leaving for Barbados the next day, and they were both busy packing, so the conversation was brief. I didn't say anything about solving the case, because this would have required a fairly lengthy explanation—something I hadn't the inclination to provide just then and neither of them had the leisure to listen to.

"I'll bet you have the answer to who killed Aunt Bessie by the time we return from Barbados," Ellen declared.

"You could be right," I agreed. "I'll let you know when you get back."

Don phoned a few minutes later, while I was in the shower. "I wanted to give you an update," he explained to my machine. "I spoke to Sergeant Spence about the watch this afternoon. I attempted to impress upon him that there was a great deal of sentiment attached to this watch and that my mother had bequeathed it to my ten-year-old daughter. He inquired whether I had an idea as to who might have taken it, and I replied that I was convinced it was my brother's fiancée.

"Then he asked if I had any actual evidence to this effect, and when I conceded that I did not, he appeared to be somewhat skeptical. At this juncture I felt that it was necessary to sacrifice truth to expediency. I hope I didn't compromise the investigation in any way, Desiree, but I claimed that not long ago I'd had a conversation with Joel that led me to determine that Frankie had stolen the watch. I told the sergeant that apparently she'd made a comment to my brother about wanting *her* new watch engraved with the same kind of old-fashioned script used on my mother's watch. And in the course of our talk, Joel made some offhanded reference to this. He didn't appreciate the significance of what he was telling me, of course. It took me a while to recognize it, as well, I said to Spence. But it finally occurred to me that, in view of the coolness between Frankie and my mom, it was extremely doubtful my mother had ever removed the timepiece from her wrist to show the engraving to that young lady. Furthermore, I said, I found it even less believable that my mother had invited Frankie to view the objects in her jewelry box.

" 'Have you discussed this matter with your brother?' Sergeant Spence asked me. I answered that it wouldn't have served any purpose, that my brother was so enamored of his fiancée, so convinced of her estimable character, that he'd insist she'd come by her information honestly, perhaps suggesting that someone had alluded to the engraving in her presence. Which is nonsense. 'There's even a strong possibility that if the police were to question him about this,' I said to Spence, 'he'd deny having spoken to me about anything like that in the first place.'

"Well, the sergeant pointed out that Frankie's remark notwithstanding, he couldn't simply ring the girl's doorbell and search the premises. However, he feels that in light of her impending marriage to my brother, it's highly improbable she would have held on to the watch anyway. According to Sergeant Spence, it's far more likely she either sold it—and unless I could give him some clue as to a potential buyer, it would be next to impossible to trace the sale—or she pawned it. He told me that the best he could do was to check out the pawnshops near both Frankie's home and place of business. With a little luck, he said, perhaps the watch will turn up."

Amen, I responded softly.

Frankie's picture was delivered on Friday, as Don had anticipated. Which worked out perfectly. What I mean is, the murder had occurred on a Saturday, when there are bound to be more people at home than there are during the week. So tomorrow would, likewise, be the best time to talk to Bessie's neighbors.

Something else of note happened on Friday. Toward evening my client called to let me know that he'd just received word—via Don—that the autopsy results had finally come in. His Aunt Bessie's death had been ruled an accident.

Well, while I wasn't exactly taken by surprise, the findings were upsetting nonetheless. I mean, the way I saw it, this pretty much shut the door on my going to the police with what I already had on Frankie. But I consoled myself with the fact that it wasn't substantial enough for me to conceive of doing that anyway.

At ten o'clock the next morning, I headed for Ozone Park.

On the drive out to Aunt Bessie's neighborhood, it popped into my head that Joel must have alerted Frankie to my having labeled her a murderer. But I reconsidered almost instantly.

Even from my limited knowledge of the personalities involved here, I decided it was doubtful that Joel had repeated anything of our conversation to his betrothed. I just couldn't see him risking the unpleasantness that was almost sure to result from his apprising the very assertive Frankie of my conclusion. I was all but certain, too, that if she *had* been informed of my findings, this "confident, take-charge woman"—as she'd referred to herself when we'd met—would already have picked up the phone to persuade me that I was in error.

For Joel to keep something like this from Frankie, however, he'd have to be a marvelous actor. Either that, or it would be necessary to deceive himself into believing the girl was innocent. My money was on the latter. I mean, I didn't figure he'd simply ignore the terrible truth that his future wife had murdered his mother. Besides, Joel Herman didn't impress me as giving Robert De Niro any reason to break out in a rash.

And now I began to contemplate the task ahead of me. I tried to be optimistic, but history wasn't on my side. I mean, I'd gone this photo route any number of times before, and in almost every instance no one had been able to tell me a thing. Or so they said.

Still, I've always maintained that every investigation is different. Well, maybe today I'd come across somebody who'd prove me right.

Chapter 36

I found a parking space at the end of Aunt Bessie's block. Now, I hadn't planned to meet with Cassie Ross today—we'd already had a prolonged discussion relating to the death of her friend. But just as I was walking away from my Chevy, who should turn the corner toting a small bag of groceries?

"Desiree! Is that you?" Cassie demanded.

"Yep."

I was amazed it had even occurred to her that it *could* be me. The weather was absolutely frigid that Saturday, and I was so bundled up I might have been mistaken for Nanook of the North. In fact, it was doubtful my own mother—may she rest in peace—would have realized that it was her Desiree lurking behind that enormous scarf I'd wound around my neck three times and then pulled up over my chin. And if that didn't make me almost unrecognizable, I was also wearing a knitted cap that covered my entire head, completely concealing my most recognizable—and glorious—feature.

"What are you doing here?"

"I need to speak to your neighbors," I said. "Maybe somebody noticed something unusual that afternoon."

"Have there been any new developments in the investigation?" Cassie asked.

"Actually, yes. The autopsy report just came in, and Bess's death was ruled an accident."

"What about you? What do *you* think? Never mind.

You wouldn't be here if you agreed with the report. Am I right?"

"Yes, you're right."

"So? Got any idea yet who did this to my sweet Bess?"

"I've narrowed it down," I responded evasively.

Apparently Cassie realized I'd told her as much as I intended to, so she didn't pressure me further. And in a few minutes, we were in front of her house. "Listen, why don't you come in for coffee before you get started with your interviews—or even later on?" she invited. "It'll warm you up." And before I could respond, she added enticingly, "I baked yesterday— macadamia nut cookies. They're my specialty."

It pained me to decline. "That is *so-o* tempting. Only I'd better say no—I have a lot of ground to cover. But I really appreciate the offer."

"Well . . . if you're sure." Then: "Say, you know who might have seen something, Desiree? There's a Mrs. Baron who lives directly opposite Bess . . . that is, where Bess *used* to live. It's the place with the black shutters," she elaborated, pointing. "Mrs. Baron's over ninety, with a bad case of arthritis, so she doesn't get out much. And she rarely watches television. 'Too much sex,' she once told me. Mostly, she sits in her chair listening to the radio and looking out the window."

"Thanks, Cassie. Mrs. Baron just jumped to the top of my list."

The door was secured with a chain and didn't open more than about three inches, so I wasn't able to make out the person peering at me through the crack. Holding up my PI license, I explained that I was investigating the death of the woman who'd lived across the street—Mrs. Herman—and asked if I could talk to Mrs. Baron for a couple of minutes.

The door swung open at once to reveal a very old woman in a loose-fitting purple smock, leaning heavily on a cane. Small and stooped, she had a wrinkled face the color of parchment and short, straight gray hair that was too sparse to adequately cover her scalp. "Come in," she said with a hospitable smile. "Lucky for you I kept in my dentures after breakfast—I sometimes don't, especially if I'm not expecting company. And without these choppers, I could scare you out of a year's growth." A sound that was part giggle, part cackle accompanied the words.

I didn't have to be concerned about how to respond, because she quickly introduced herself. "I'm Evangeline Baron, but call me Vangie."

"And I'm Desiree—Desiree Shapiro."

Vangie turned and preceded me—with some difficulty—into the living room. And after persuading me to hang up my coat ("You'll roast if you don't get out of that thing, dear"), she settled into the sofa. When I returned from my trip to the closet, she directed me to a worn, high-backed chair directly opposite the couch. I noted then that there was a matching chair positioned in front of the window—angled toward the street.

"So you're checking into Bess Herman's demise, are you? I suppose that means you don't believe she just *fell* down those stairs."

"No, I don't. And I'm hoping someone might have noticed something—*anything*—that Saturday that might be regarded as suspicious or out of the ordinary."

"All *I* noticed was some little blonde going into Bessie's. And before you ask, I'm certain it was that same day, because when I heard Bessie had had an accident, I wondered if her visitor was there when it happened."

"Can you, by any chance, recall what time you saw the girl?"

"It wasn't much past two o'clock—I'm sure of that, too. The woman who comes in to do for me was supposed to stay until two-thirty, but at two on the button she just picked herself up and left. I know, because I checked my watch soon as she was out the door. Some people have the idea that because you're old, you must be missing most of your marbles, so they figure they can get away with anything. Well, Rosemary didn't get away with that extra half-hour's pay, I promise you that. But you wanted to know about blondie. . . . She came along not even five minutes after Rosemary drove away."

I removed Frankie's picture from my attaché case and, leaning over, handed it to Vangie. "Is this the person you're referring to?"

"Pretty." Then scrutinizing the head shot, she said, "Could be her, but she was all the way across the street. And if it hasn't come to your attention yet, dear, I'm no spring chicken anymore; my eyes aren't as sharp as they were when I was an ingenue of eighty. All I can say for a fact is that Bess's visitor was a tiny thing. I probably could've eaten apples off her head," Vangie boasted playfully. "This blonde here"—she rapped the photo with her knuckle—"is *she* tiny?"

"Very," I answered, reclaiming the photograph she was holding out to me.

"It's likely she was the one, then." And before I could inquire about anything else: "Don't tell me you suspect that bitsy youngster of killing poor Bessie."

"It's a possibility, Vangie. Do you have any idea when she left Bessie's?"

"Not really," the old woman admitted regretfully. "It couldn't have been before three, though. I was sitting over there, looking out the window—I do a lot of that nowadays, and I don't miss much, either. Anyhow, I had the radio on, and before I dozed off I recollect the announcer's saying it was three o'clock. That's something else I do a lot of lately—dozing off. When I woke up it was past five, and I went into the kitchen and had myself some supper. That ended my people-watching for the day." And now, she tilted her head. "When did you become involved in this terrible affair?"

There was no need to stop and think; I was painfully

aware of how long I'd been on the case. "It will be three weeks on Monday."

"You've been a private eye for a while?"

"Yes, for quite a while." I could tell that Vangie was warming up to a full-scale interrogation. But although I felt guilty aborting her efforts (it was obvious she craved both a little drama and some companionship in her life), I had to cut her short. "Um, I'd really better get moving—I'm going to try and talk to all of your neighbors today. Thank you so much for your help, Vangie."

"You wouldn't mind letting yourself out, would you, dear?—the door locks automatically."

"Of course not."

As I was shrugging into my coat, Vangie said, "I should really thank *you* for coming by—I don't have very much company. Listen, if you should get the goods on that blondie—that's how they say it nowadays, 'get the goods,' am I right? Anyhow, will you give me a call?"

"I'll be happy to."

"Promise?"

My God, it was getting contagious! "Promise."

I only hoped I'd have reason to deliver.

After leaving Vangie, I visited the home on her immediate right. A frazzled young woman with a yapping puppy nipping at her heels and a screaming baby in her arms informed me that she'd been in the hospital giving birth on December fourteenth.

"Well, maybe your husband—"

"I don't have one of those useless items anymore. The bastard ran off with some slut when I was six months pregnant, and I haven't seen him since."

A middle-aged couple lived to *her* right. The husband had been out of town when Bessie died. The wife said she *thought* she recalled seeing a young blond woman leaving the victim's house that afternoon. But when I showed her Frankie's photograph, she wasn't able to ID her. And when I pressed for the approximate time of this possible sighting, I had to settle for "Between three and four, I believe. But it might have been a little earlier"—and with an apologetic smile—"or a bit later." Naturally, the woman hadn't been aware of any suspicious occurrence. "Not that I remember, anyway."

No one I spoke to after this was any more helpful than these three had been—until I crossed the street. I was about to try my luck at the large brick dwelling on the corner when, in the distance, I spotted a tall, thin man with a short, fat dog walking in my direction. I waited until they were almost alongside me. "Excuse me, do you live on this block?"

I saw now that the man was fortyish and quite nicelooking (if you like the type). "Why do you ask?" He was appraising me through narrowed eyes, while his bulldog sniffed my shoes. I reached down and petted him for a second—the bulldog, I mean—and he gazed up at me and wagged his tail enthusiastically.

"A month ago, a woman was murdered not far from where we're standing. And I'm questioning the residents here to find out if anyone might have noticed anything . . . well, *peculiar* that Saturday. I'm a private investigator, by the way—the name is Desiree Shapiro."

"Oh. I'm afraid I can't help you, Ms. Shapiro; my place is two blocks west."

I was prepared to resume my bell-ringing when I realized I was being hasty. "Do you often come here with your dog?"

"Pretty often. I like to be sure Caesar gets his exercise." At the mention of his name, the dog's tail was in motion again. "Besides, in my neighborhood the kids are always playing ball in the street, and I keep expecting to get one in the chops." He smiled for the first time now. "Or worse yet, that they might crown my buddy Caesar."

"I have a photograph of a young woman with me, and I wonder if you'd mind looking at it. If you happened to be around on the day of the homicide, it's possible you may have seen her."

"Is she the suspect?"

"One of them." I handed him the picture—which he returned almost at once.

"Oh, *sure.* She was leaving some house—it was on this side of the street, toward the middle of the block—and she stopped to admire my handsome friend." He glanced down at Caesar with an affectionate grin. "She told me she loved bulldogs. This was maybe a month ago—on the weekend. During the week, I'm at work in the afternoon."

"Do you by any chance recall the time?"

"No, I— Wait a minute. It's coming back to me. It must have been around three-fifteen, three-thirty. My wife and I were meeting some people for drinks and an early dinner that evening—we had theater tickets—and I wanted to take Caesar out before I started to get dressed.

"Well, he didn't seem disposed to do anything worthwhile on his own turf, so I kept walking. What sticks in my mind is that when the young lady and I were having that conversation, I was attempting to figure out how to break away. The problem was, Caesar still hadn't taken care of business, and it would be seven o'clock before my son came home to give him another go at it. But just as I was about to excuse myself, she said good-bye."

"When you were talking to this young lady, did she appear to be rattled at all?"

"On the contrary. She was very composed, very charming."

"Can you remember what date this was, Mr.—?"

"Wilder. Howard Wilder. I couldn't say offhand, but I should be able to tell you in a moment." And now he pulled his cell phone out of his jacket pocket and punched in a number.

At this point I noticed that Caesar had begun to tug on his leash, so getting down to his level, I removed my gloves and scratched him behind the ears. I was rewarded with a lot of wet and sloppy—although, doubtless, heartfelt—kisses.

A couple of minutes later, Howard helped me struggle to my feet. "My wife saved the ticket stubs for tax purposes—the couple we were with are clients of hers," he explained. "At any rate, I ran into that suspect of yours on Saturday, December fourteenth."

"Thanks *very* much, Mr. Wilder. Um, would you mind giving me your phone number in the unlikely event I have to contact you about this?"

He hesitated only a moment. (I could almost hear him saying to himself, "Why not?") Then in a matter of seconds he'd taken his business card from his wallet and presented it to me.

"Let me give you my card, too—in case something else should occur to you." Now, being that this required fishing around in my humongous, junk-laden handbag, I challenge *anyone* to produce that thing in seconds.

Everything worked out okay, though. An impatient Caesar did what he had to do then and there.

It was close to five when, after talking to at least thirty-five other human beings and one additional dog, I breathed a sigh of relief and called it quits. The fact is, after Howard Wilder, it had all been downhill.

In three instances nobody was home. And of the individuals I did get to speak to, only a handful could identify Frankie from her photo. One of these, a dapper elderly man, was able to pinpoint the time he'd seen her entering the house—only he wasn't certain of the date. A teenage boy told me he'd caught sight of "that hottie" going up Bessie's walkway—he practically drooled when he said it. He, too, was able to supply the time but came up blank on the date. And two women said they were positive they'd seen Frankie in the neighborhood one afternoon, but neither of them had the slightest idea of the date *or* the time.

Not a soul reported anything odd taking place. But

following my talk with Howard, I was sure this was because there hadn't *been* anything odd. Which was hardly a shock. I mean, if anyone could commit a murder and then immediately afterward act in a totally natural manner, that someone was Frankie. Evidently she'd even gone out of her way to engage Howard in conversation in order to demonstrate—in case he should ever be questioned—how normally she'd behaved.

Well, I hadn't uncovered any "smoking gun." So, would I be back tomorrow to pay a visit to those few people who hadn't been in today?

No. Clearly Frankie's demeanor hadn't raised any red flags. Moreover, I'd been able to verify an important piece of information.

The sticking point was whether I'd ever have an opportunity to make use of it.

Chapter 37

By the time I got back to Manhattan on Saturday, I was starved. And no wonder. This morning I'd been so anxious to talk to Aunt Bessie's neighbors that I wouldn't allow myself the extra few minutes it would have required to eat anything substantial. So all I had with my coffee was a lousy half a corn muffin—I mean, the thing was minuscule! And I hadn't taken any nourishment since. (I don't count that Snickers bar I consumed during the drive back, as its sole purpose was to supply me with the energy to make it home.)

Hungry as I was, though, I was too tired to fix anything for myself. So after dropping my car at the garage, I stopped at Jerome's, a coffee shop right near my apartment building that I frequent every so often.

I spent a very relaxing hour or so here; I simply refused to permit the subject of murder to intrude on my cheeseburger and fries—and certainly not on my chocolate mud pie. I sat there quietly, enjoying the food and, now and then, engaging in a brief, light-hearted exchange with Felix. Felix being the colorful going-on-eighty waiter who's had the exclusive on serving me my burgers at Jerome's for more years than I can remember.

Later that evening, when I was home watching TV (but not actually paying attention), I suddenly had this thought. It had nothing to do with proving that little Frankie was a sugarcoated assassin—I'd be wrestling with that small problem again soon enough. This concerned someone else who was never out of my mind for long.

The thing is, Nick had fed me at any number of worthy establishments, but I had yet to reciprocate. Of course, the blame for this lay entirely with his son and heir, since as I've mentioned, I *had* prepared a meal for us—one that even included a special kid-oriented menu for Derek. So if TKFH hadn't tampered with my boeuf Bourguignon, the three of us would have sat down to a lovely repast that evening. Nevertheless, in view of the Bourguignon's tragic end, I still owed Nick that dinner.

Now, I'm aware that with some men a really satisfying meal can get you more points than a great pair of legs. However, at that moment this didn't even occur to me—I swear. (And who knew if it would be true of Nick anyway?) The point was, I owed him. So the next time we had dinner, I was determined that it would be at Chez Desiree's.

On Sunday I didn't do much of anything except agonize over whether I'd ever be able to—as Vangie had put it—"get the goods" on Frankie. I told myself that I'd have to find some way to trip up the little witch, that's all. But as eager as I was to implement another strategy, just then my poor overtaxed brain wasn't up to the challenge of deciding what this should be. So I also had to tell myself to let things percolate for a day or two. "You'll come up with something, you'll see."

As soon as I set foot in the office Monday morning, Jackie wanted to know how I'd made out in Ozone Park.

"Well, I didn't discover anything earth-shattering, if that's what you're asking. But I did establish that Frankie had leveled with me about when she'd arrived at Bessie's that day and when she'd left."

"You thought she was lying?"

"I was reasonably sure she *wasn't*. All along I'd

pretty much figured that *she* figured her presence in the neighborhood might not have gone entirely unnoticed—which would have made the truth her only option. And as it happens, I learned that when she left Mrs. Herman's house that afternoon, Frankie ran smack into some guy who was out walking his dog."

It must have been another half hour and two cups of coffee later before I reluctantly picked up the phone to give Ben this same update.

Predictably, he was dejected by the not-so-good news. "So we still have nothing to take to the police."

"No, but I'm not ready to throw in the towel, and I hope that's true of you, too."

"Absolutely."

"I'm working on another approach, so give me a couple of days, okay?"

"Of course."

I'd barely put the receiver back in its cradle when I received a call that practically caused my jaw to drop to my chest. A potential client was actually on the line!

The caller—her name was Solange Delong—apprised me that a week earlier she and her antique-dealer husband had hosted a charity dinner at their home that was attended by fifteen prominent, well-heeled couples. And as a reward for their good works, the Delongs were now missing a very valuable eighteenth-century Chinese vase.

Well, in view of the sensitive nature of an inquiry of this kind, Mrs. Delong had been reluctant to bring in the police. But I was highly recommended to her, she told me, by a friend of her daughter's who vouched for both my competence and my discretion. (Incidentally, the friend turned out to be Vicky Pirelli, the teenager who had recently been a client of mine herself.)

I agreed to take the case.

You probably think this was nuts, considering how committed I was to bringing Frankie to justice. But I was fairly sure that any new plan to entrap her would require more brainwork than legwork. Besides, if it should wind up being more time-consuming than I was anticipating, I could almost certainly count on my friend Harry Burgess to help me out with this Chinese vase business.

Anyhow, Mrs. Delong was apologetic. She realized, she said, that ideally I should have had the opportunity to look into the theft immediately after it occurred. However, she had no idea the vase had disappeared until this weekend. Her husband, she added, remained unaware of the crime; the morning after the charity function he'd flown to Europe for a three-week buying trip. And now she added—her tone even more apologetic—that while it was no doubt crucial I visit the site of the robbery, she was presently recovering from a severe attack of the flu. "I'm hoping we can do this by the end of the week, though—if not earlier. Maybe there's still a chance you can locate the vase before Raphael—my husband—returns."

I promised her I'd do my best. "And don't worry. Just take care of yourself. A few more days aren't likely to affect the investigation." (While this might not have been entirely factual, what choice did I have?)

"Good. I wouldn't want to expose you to this bug of mine."

Which made two of us.

In any event, I was extremely pleased to hear from Solange Delong. Maybe it was paranoia, but the calls for my services had been so few since I'd begun working for my current client (try *only one* prior to Mrs. Delong's) that I was beginning to fear he could be my last.

Sometimes it feels really nice to be proven wrong.

Nick phoned at about three o'clock. Emil had come to work today and seemed to be pretty well over his illness. "Could we reschedule for Wednesday?" he asked.

"Sure. And by the way, we're having dinner at my place."

Naturally, Nick protested. And—also naturally—I insisted. And I won.

"All right," he finally agreed, "but I hate having you go to so much trouble—especially considering how busy you are with that murder case."

"I enjoy cooking—honestly; it's like therapy for me. So end of discussion. What time would you like to make it?"

"You name it. With Emil back, I can be there whenever you say."

"How does seven-thirty sound?"

"Perfect. What can I bring?"

"Just your appetite. If you walk in with anything else, I'll feed you gruel. I mean it."

Nick laughed. "I don't doubt that for a minute."

Chapter 38

On the way home from the office I did some of the shopping for Wednesday. And once I was back in the apartment, I was so anxious to roll up my sleeves and get started on Nick's dinner that tonight's supper was a quick one—Progresso's Manhattan clam chowder and a tuna sandwich. Following this, I doled out a really skimpy portion of Häagen-Dazs for myself and practically gulped down the vile coffee accompanying it.

Now, except for the boeuf Bourguignon—which would only serve as an instant reminder of something neither of us cared to be reminded of—we'd be having pretty much the same fare on Wednesday that I'd prepared for Nick that first time. Again, for hors d'oeuvres, I was planning on the mushroom croustades (shiitake mushrooms and herbs in little toast cups), plus a couple of wedges of cheese—in this instance St.-André and Jarlsberg—along with assorted crackers. But for the main course, I'd switched to a veal scaloppine dish, which would be accompanied by rice and a salad. And finally, Nick would now have the opportunity to sample my most special dessert: a chilled lemon soufflé.

Anyhow, that evening I prepared the croustades and froze them. Tomorrow night I'd deal with the soufflé. Then on Wednesday, I'd finish my food shopping and stop off at the liquor store for wine—a bottle of red and a bottle of white.

As soon as I sat down at my desk on Tuesday, I
trained my sights—once again—on nailing Frankie. I
went over a few approaches that could *conceivably*
accomplish this, all of which—like that business with
the photograph—I'd implemented in some form or
other on previous cases. And more often than not,
with disappointing results. If I could only come up
with something just a little less iffy. . . .

At about eleven o'clock I heard from Don Herman.
"I thought you might be interested in learning that I
spent this past weekend in New York."

"*You did*?"

"Yes. Friday, on the spur of the moment, I telephoned Joel to let him know that I wanted to fly out
to see him the next morning. I told him that it had
been a long time since we talked, just the two of us,
and that there was a great deal we should sit down
and discuss. But I emphasized that I wouldn't make
the trip if he had plans of any sort. Of course, he
understood that I had Frankie in mind."

"What was his reaction to the call?"

"Well, I can't be certain of his actual feelings; I
believe he was more surprised than anything else. But
while he didn't appear to be elated by the prospect of
a visit with his older brother, he made no attempt to
discourage me, either."

"Uh, when you got together, what did he have to
say about . . . about everything?"

"Not very much, actually. I was the one to broach
the subject—very cautiously—of his fiancée's having
murdered our mother, something Joel adamantly denied. He was vehement in his insistence that Frankie
was a highly moral person, totally incapable of com-
mitting such a horrific act."

"Did you ask if he'd ever repeated my accusation
to her?"

"I did. But his response was that he wouldn't dream
of upsetting the sensitive Frankie by relaying anything
so preposterous. He insisted that she must simply have
misunderstood whatever it was my mother told her.

In my opinion, Joel has never permitted himself to so much as *speculate* as to the veracity of your conclusion. Moreover—as Ben undoubtedly notified you—according to the autopsy findings, our mother's death was accidental. And Joel regards this as verification of his original contention: that there was never any murder at all.

"Uh, Desiree, about my initiating that meeting with him—it didn't muck things up in any way, did it?"

"I assume you mean with regard to the investigation. And I honestly don't see how it could have."

"I'm relieved. The truth is, that possibility didn't occur to me until I was back in California—although it no doubt should have. When I made the decision to see my brother, however, my primary consideration was to assure him that I was there for him and that I always would be. I was also very anxious to convince him of the validity of your reasoning. Under the circumstances, I just can't *conceive* of his marrying that girl."

"I don't imagine you were too successful—in getting him to accept my reasoning, I mean."

"Unfortunately, no." And now the man added almost sheepishly, "I should admit something else to you, as well. On the flight to New York, it also crossed my mind that I might induce Joel to confront the young woman. I even entertained the thought that should your canvassing of Mom's neighbors on Saturday not achieve the hoped-for results, he might be persuaded to have a go at tricking her into an admission—with your help in providing the script, of course. But once Joel and I began to talk, I realized that there wasn't so much as a minute possibility of his agreeing to this."

"By the way, Don, you were right. That canvassing didn't prove to be any great success."

"I heard—I spoke to Ben last night. I trust this didn't discourage you to the extent that you'd consider resigning from the case, however."

"Absolutely not. I'll just have to come up with something else."

I could have added that enlisting his aid with Joel was one of those iffy strategies I'd been considering when he phoned. But I didn't.

Before leaving the office, I stopped at Jackie's desk to let her know I wouldn't be in tomorrow. What I *refrained* from letting her know was why. Listen, if she'd had any idea it was because Nick was coming for dinner Wednesday evening, as sure as my name is Desiree Shapiro, she'd argue with me over the menu.

"You're not feeling well," she declared.

"I'm fine; it's only that I have some things to take care of at the apartment."

It was as if I hadn't spoken. "I can always spot it when you're under the weather. You should see yourself, Dez; you're white as a ghost. Take a couple of aspirins when you get home. And make yourself some hot tea. Oh, and be sure to drink plenty of juice."

"Thanks, Jackie. I'll do that."

Listen, I can tell when I'm licked.

Chapter 39

That night, as soon as I was finished with supper, I prepared the lemon soufflé. And following this, I got the apartment in company-ready shape. Later on I set up the folding table in the living room (which also pitches in as a dining room, office, and guest room), covered it with my one nice cloth and set out the matching napkins, along with the good silver, china, and glassware.

On Wednesday I went to the bakery for an Italian bread and some cookies, then to the greengrocer's for the salad fixings. My last stop was the liquor store— from which establishment I departed with what the proprietor had termed an "exemplary" pinot noir and a "tantalizing" pinot grigio.

When I came home I made the salad and the dressing, then whipped up some heavy cream and piped it onto the soufflé. Unfortunately, the results weren't nearly as professional-looking as they had been when I'd decorated this dessert for that ill-fated dinner I'd hosted for Nick and son. But I consoled myself with the knowledge that at least tonight Nick would have a chance to eat the damn thing—barring some unforeseen circumstance, that is.

All that was left to do just now was to slice up the Italian bread and pound the veal cutlets a bit. I pretended that it was Frankie I was flattening and did a better than usual job of it.

It was past four when I'd finished the advanced preparations—still plenty of time to indulge in a nice, fragrant bubble bath. But what was intended to be a relaxing interlude wasn't. Not for more than the first five minutes, anyway. Because Derek wormed his way into my head.

You must be crazy, I laced into myself, and hardly for the first—or even the hundredth—time. I mean, with his only child feeling as he did about me, my relationship with Nick didn't have a prayer. Sooner or later, somehow or other, that evil, conniving kid would wreck what we had together. Listen, Derek may have convinced his father and a few other gullible individuals that—thanks to some therapy and the loving environment created by a pair of doting grandparents—he'd become a changed little juvenile delinquent. But I was not a believer. And if I were in possession of even a thimbleful of brains, I'd have broken things off with Nick before getting more and more *and more* involved. But what did I do instead? I cooked for the man, that's what!

At any rate, once I got out of the tub, I didn't dwell on TKFH any longer. I simply refused to allow him to ruin tonight's dinner. Messing up *one* of my dinners was enough for the little creep.

My makeup went on without a mishap that evening—I even managed to restrict the mascara to my eyelashes. And my normally ridiculously stubborn hair didn't give me so much as a second's grief. Plus, when I stepped into my navy-and-cream A-line, I decided that it was really quite flattering. All in all, I didn't look half bad. In fact, if I say so myself—and I do—I looked pretty damn good.

I'd no sooner finished reheating the croustades and arranging the cheese platter when the bell rang.

Nick stood in the doorway wearing one of his handsome tweed jackets and smiling his adorable heart-stopping, gap-toothed smile. It was all I could do not to throw my arms around him then and there.

"You're even prettier than usual tonight, Dez," he said, bussing me on the cheek. Then he handed me a box—a *two-pound* box!—of Godiva chocolates.

"Thank you, Nick. These are wonderful, only—"

He held up his palm and grinned. "I know. But I took a chance that you'd have pity and skip the gruel."

A few minutes after this, when we were in the living room sipping pinot noir and stuffing ourselves with hors d'oeuvres, Nick asked about the investigation.

"Well, I figured out who murdered Aunt Bessie," I replied nonchalantly.

"You're kidding! Why didn't you say anything about this before?"

"Because I wanted to wait until I saw you."

"All right. You're seeing me now, so tell me!"

"It was Frankie." And I explained what had led me to this conclusion, ending my soliloquy with, "The problem is, I have absolutely no hard evidence."

"Now that you know the killer's identity, though, it should be a little easier to come up with something . . . uh, shouldn't it?"

"I wish." I filled Nick in on my visit to Ozone Park.

"You must have been terribly disappointed," he commiserated.

"I was. Even though it went pretty much as I was afraid it would."

"So what happens now?"

"I have no idea."

"Don't worry, you'll think of something. And that's no platitude, either. You *will*."

"From your mouth to *His* ear." And I gazed at the ceiling.

It was about a half hour later that I went into the kitchen to prepare the veal and heat up the rice. And since there's barely enough space for one in there, Nick kept me company from the doorway. He wanted to know if he could do anything to help, and I politely turned down the offer. But when the man posed the question for the third time, I figured he was asking for it, so I handed him the salad bowl and the dressing. "Take these out to the table and toss," I commanded.

At dinner, he was lavish in his praise of the food.

"This veal is *so* good, Dez. No, forget I said that. It's terrific."

"Thanks, Nick," I responded airily, making an effort to convey that I was taking the applause in stride. But I had the feeling I was blushing.

For most of the meal, the conversation was easy and often playfully argumentative.

For example, we got on the subject of movies. Nick's dual favorites are *Saving Private Ryan* and that old classic, *Gunga Din.* I'm partial to *Babe* and *Victor/ Victoria.* (Not exactly in the same ballpark, are they?) At the mention of my choices, Nick feigned shock. "You have to be kidding," he remarked, shaking his head. But I detected a smile hovering around the corners of his lips.

At one point we worked our way around to all-time entertainment greats. We both agreed on Sinatra. But when it came to the ladies, Nick's eyes lit up when he mentioned Barbra Streisand. "There's nobody like her," he proclaimed.

"That's something to be thankful for, anyway," I muttered. "Hey, you want talent? Is the name Judy Garland familiar to you? Never mind. What can I expect from a man who prefers Sherlock Holmes to Hercule Poirot?"

We kept things light over coffee and dessert, as well—for a while, at least. Nick, bless him, said all the right things about my lemon soufflé. But now, too, I didn't want him to see how pleased I was, so I acknowledged the compliment with an offhand "thank you," while in reality I was puffing out my chest. (But unfortunately, only figuratively speaking.) Following this, we chatted about everything from alligators to Santa Claus. (And don't ask me where *those* two topics came from!)

Then, out of the blue, the ax fell.

"Listen, Dez, before I left the apartment tonight, Derek phoned, and I told him I was going to be seeing you. He asked if I thought you'd ever be willing to spend a few hours in his company again. Of course, I said that I couldn't speak for you. The truth is, though, Derek's changed in these last months. I don't claim he's overcome all of his problems—I'm not one of those blindly doting parents—honestly." A shame-faced little grin here. "But I do believe he's come a long way since beginning his therapy, and he appears to sincerely want to make up for his past behavior toward you. Still, I realize his actions were absolutely deplorable, so I'll understand if you decide against his joining us one day. But think about it, okay?"

"Okay." But I felt a little sick. If I said no, there was a good possibility that, in spite of his words, I might be alienating Nick. A yes, however, would be like putting myself on the firing line again.

At any rate, Nick didn't stay too long after this—it was late, and we both had work the next day. But at the door he thanked me, said it had been a wonderful evening, then gave me a long, passionate kiss. "Sleep well, Dez," he murmured.

I can't say I hadn't expected Nick to bring up that dreaded subject one of these days. But I'd been hoping that day wouldn't be quite this soon.

I mean, for Derek to morph into a nice, normal human being would require a lot more than a couple of months of therapy. Trust me, in view of all his hostility, if there were ever to be a new, improved Derek (and you wouldn't catch me betting on that), he was light years away from materializing.

Which left me with some crummy choice! Do I agree to go out, the three of us, and allow the kid the opportunity to implement another nasty little plot to expel me from his father's life? Or should I refuse outright to see him or else keep stalling until Nick finally gave up on the attempt to fashion us into a congenial trio? Which eventually was bound to result in his giving up on me, too.

Well, however this was handled, a breakup was inevitable. But then, there'd never been any doubt in my mind about that.

Chapter 40

It happened on Friday.

The day started out to be ordinary enough. Solange Delong phoned first thing in the morning—it couldn't have been much past nine-forty-five—and I'd just walked into the office, plunked my posterior on the chair, and brushed the sleepers from my eyes. She assured me she was completely recovered from her bout with the flu and wanted to set up an appointment. We arranged that I'd be at her home Saturday afternoon.

Following this, I did what I'd been doing quite a lot of for the better part of a week: I sat there staring into space, waiting for inspiration. I kept hoping a fresh, clever little scheme would pop into my head and enable me to deliver Bessie Herman's murderer to the police. But the only thing that occurred to me was that I had to do *something*. So I began to dust off the old standbys.

Well, one tactic I occasionally employ is to set up a meeting with the perpetrator, to which rendezvous I carry a tape recorder concealed in my handbag. Only yesterday, though, I'd sort of semi-rejected this particular approach because—after careful consideration—I'd concluded that Frankie wasn't a very good candidate for it. I felt that she was too crafty to be trapped into making any kind of admission. But on the other hand, I argued with myself now, she was so damn self-confident—*over*confident, really—that she might give herself away just by being so positive that she wouldn't. If you get my thinking.

I never did reach a conclusion about this, however; I was still toying with the idea when I got back from lunch. And then, just as I'd pretty much decided that it might be worth a try (I mean, what else did I have in mind?), THE CALL came in.

It seemed that the case against Frankie Murray had suddenly developed a backbone.

You couldn't miss the excitement in Ben's voice. "I had a long conversation with Donnie—we just hung up. And you'll never guess what's been located!"

For a moment I had trouble with my breathing, and after that my throat was so tight it was tough getting out the words. "The watch," I croaked.

"Correct!"

The truth is, while I'd attempted to be optimistic, deep down I don't believe I was ever all that confident that Aunt Bessie's treasured timepiece would resurface. But I'd been consoling myself with the thought that it *could* happen. Although on those occasions that I forced myself to be a bit more realistic, I put the chance that it actually *would* happen as not that much better than Publishers Clearing House sending me a check for a number with a bunch of zeros after it.

"The police contacted Donnie about the watch this morning," Ben was saying.

"Where was it found?"

"In a pawnshop not far from Frankie's apartment. The building superintendent brought it in there weeks ago."

"Only until late last week the watch hadn't been reported missing," I commented dryly.

"Right. The police interrogated the super the other night. And from what Donnie was told, here's what happened. One evening—or I should say, *morning*— soon after the theft, the guy returned home from a little imbibing at a local thirst-quenching establishment. It was almost two a.m., and he'd just started walking up the alleyway leading to the rear entrance when he saw Frankie. She was standing right by the garbage cans, looking all around her, apparently to make sure she wasn't being observed—I understand she even glanced up at the windows. At any rate, the girl must have been more than a little unnerved at the super's discovering her there. She said that she'd just come downstairs to throw out an old pair of shoes. And then she left. Incidentally, the trash was due to be picked up the following morning.

"Naturally," Ben continued, "the super considered the whole thing somewhat strange. After all, why go out in the dead of night just to get rid of a pair of old shoes? Moreover, while the area is fairly well lit, it still didn't appear to be a likely hangout for a young woman. The police mentioned something to Donnie about the super's getting it into his head that Frankie could be meeting a lover there, and the man was evidently curious as hell. So after he rounded the corner at the back of the building, he peeked out at the alley; he kept his eyes glued to that alley for ten minutes to see if Frankie would return. And just as he was prepared to give up—there she was. She resumed her spot near the garbage, gave her surroundings the once-over again, and quickly pitched something into one of the cans. Then the super noticed that she had a stick with her and that she was shoving whatever it was she'd tossed in there under some of the other refuse. After which she hurried off.

"Well, by now the man's curiosity was *really* aroused. So he went into his apartment, got himself a cardboard box, and started transferring the discards that were close to the top of the heap into the box. It didn't take long for him to uncover the watch."

"He couldn't be certain that this was the article Frankie had unloaded, though," I observed.

"Maybe not a hundred percent. But one thing he *was* certain of: Whatever Frankie threw away fit in the palm of her hand. And when he was finished shifting some of the contents of the can into that box, this was the only item to qualify."

"So the super dug your aunt's beautiful wristwatch out of the garbage," I murmured sadly.

"That seems to be the case. And apparently he gave his find to a lady friend as a Christmas present. I don't know what the man could have been thinking," Ben muttered. "The crystal was cracked, and the watch wasn't even working. Imagine palming off something in that condition as a gift! And this is no kid I'm talking about, either; I understand the super's in his sixties. Anyhow, the woman wouldn't accept the watch until he had it repaired. But he refused to accommodate her. And the lovebirds got into such a hassle about this that they wound up calling it quits."

"So he pawned the watch," I put in.

"Exactly. And once Donnie reported it missing, Sergeant Spence began canvassing the pawnshops in Frankie's area. I understand he struck pay dirt on his second try."

"Let me ask you something. What time did the watch stop? No, don't tell me. It was around three-fifteen, give or take about ten minutes, right?"

"Right," Ben confirmed. "Okay, here's a question for *you*. Did you suspect all along that this was the reason it had disappeared, or is it something that occurred to you just now?"

"Neither one, really. When Don initially told me his mother's watch was gone, I drew a blank. While it didn't make sense that this was the only valuable piece missing from her jewelry box, the more logical explanation eluded me—until the following morning. That's when I recalled Joel's mentioning that his mother had been dressed to go out the day she was murdered—she was supposed to get together with a friend, but the date was cancelled. Anyhow, her plans had included treating the friend to a birthday dinner. Well, I figured Mrs. Herman had intended that they celebrate at a nice restaurant. I mean, it wasn't likely that she'd be treating the woman to a Big Mac. The way I saw it, there was every reason to assume that your aunt had had that watch on when she died.

"At first, though, it puzzled me that Frankie would take it off her victim's body. I mean, she certainly couldn't risk being spotted *wearing* the watch. Plus, she must have been anxious to get out of that house as fast as possible—even though she did stop to set the table in order to give the impression that company was expected. In any event, it finally dawned on me. Frankie must have stolen that watch because it had stopped—evidently as a result of the fall. And once she noticed this—no doubt while checking to be sure your aunt was dead—she realized that *when* it stopped could damn her."

"I *knew* there was a reason I hired you," my client joked.

"Don't give me too much credit. I'm a real mystery buff. And when there's a broken watch or clock on the scene, its purpose is usually to allow the detective to determine exactly when the murder took place, based on the time it went out of commission. And from there—"

Ben cut me off. "Hold it. You'd *already* identified the assailant, remember? Also, the timepiece *wasn't* on the scene. But when Donnie told you it was missing, you surmised why the watch must have been on Aunt Bessie's wrist that Saturday—and by the same token, why it was no longer anywhere to be found. Listen, remember when I said that fate had put you on the plane that day, Desiree? Well, I'm more convinced of it now than ever. And I'm very grateful to you."

I thanked Ben for the kind words, following which I said, "I'm only happy Frankie took the watch home with her. Thank goodness she didn't dispose of it somewhere between your aunt's place and her own apartment. Although," I reflected, "she probably didn't want to chance being seen—it was broad daylight then."

"And also," Ben suggested, "I doubt that she's

aware of when the sanitation trucks collect the trash in my aunt's neighborhood. And it's not likely she'd have cared to have a watch registering the critical time—one engraved with her victim's initials, no less—sitting around for God knows how many days."

"Good point," I said admiringly. "You—" I broke off; something had just sprung to mind. "Listen, Ben, how do you think Joel will react when he learns about the watch? He's totally smitten with that girl."

"Whenever he hears about it—and Donnie may already have broken the news to him—this won't be easy for Joel to accept. Then, of course, he'll have to deal with Frankie's arrest, which I expect could be imminent. On the positive side, though, after all that's been uncovered, it will be pretty difficult for him to continue tuning out the facts. And coming to terms with the truth will, I believe, go a long way toward helping Joel heal."

And here Ben said tentatively: "Er, one more thing, Desiree. Now that there's finally something tangible to implicate Frankie in the murder, I suppose it would be a good idea if the police heard about the beef Stroganoff. Doubtless they'd also be interested in knowing about the evidence of that fellow with the dog and anything else you have that might strengthen the State's case against that girl. So would you mind giving Sergeant Spence a call and filling him in?"

Would I *mind*? I mean, this was the call I'd been waiting to make for three interminable, nail-biting weeks and four long, frustrating days.

I could feel this dopey grin spreading across my face. "It would be my pleasure," I said.

Desiree's Veal Scaloppine with Mushrooms and Ham

1-½ lb. veal scaloppine, sliced very thin
clove of garlic, cut in half
flour for dredging
¼ cup butter
cooked ham, cut into very narrow strips (about ½" x ⅛")

¾ lb. mushrooms, thinly sliced
salt to taste (approximately ½ to ¾ tsp.)
dash of pepper
½ cup dry white wine
1-½ tsp. lemon juice
Snipped parsley

1. Rub veal with the cut garlic, then coat each side well with flour.
2. In a large skillet, heat butter over a high flame until hot. Add the veal slices, a few at a time, and sauté until golden brown. (About a minute on each side should be enough.) Remove from pan.
3. Put the ham strips in the skillet, giving them a few quick turns. Remove.
4. Lower flame. Return scaloppine to skillet, and heap the ham and mushrooms on top. Then sprinkle with salt and pepper, and add the wine.
5. Cover skillet and cook over very low heat for about 20 minutes or until fork-tender, checking occasionally to be sure meat is moist. If needed, add a tablespoon or two of water.
6. Just before serving, sprinkle with lemon juice and parsley.

SERVES 6.

NOTE: It's not a bad idea to pound the veal a little yourself, so it's *really* thin.

Turn the page for a
preview of the next
deliciously entertaining
Desiree Shapiro mystery
Coming in February 2007

I probably shouldn't admit it.

I mean, while I do okay, I'm not the most successful PI in Manhattan. In fact, to be honest, I'm not even the fourth runner-up. I suppose that's why on those occasions that I do get well compensated for my services, I'm so eager to make a deposit. And not in the bank, either.

Emigrant Savings can wait; Bloomingdale's can't.

The thing is, it makes me feel good to be rewarded for my efforts with something tangible. And that Wednesday not one, but two nice, fat checks had come in the mail as payment for a couple of investigations I'd recently completed: the first involving the murder of an elderly woman and the second the theft of a priceless eighteenth-century Chinese vase. So naturally, I headed straight for the big B.

It was around three o'clock. I was standing at the jewelry counter while the salesperson removed a pair of sterling silver earrings (with an onyx inset) from the case when I heard this terrible racking cough directly behind me. Before I had a chance to turn my head, a firm hand grabbed my left shoulder.

I whirled around. I can't say I was actually surprised to find that it belonged to Blossom Goody—the cough, that is.

"Figured it was you," she told me. "I recognized the hair."

Her tone left no doubt as to her opinion of my

glorious hennaed hair, and I bristled. *This* from a woman with yellow Little Orphan Annie curls? Nevertheless, I managed to eke out a semiwarm hello.

"Hello yourself, Shapiro. Called your place about an hour ago, and your secretary claimed you had an appointment outside the office. Some appointment," she muttered.

"It was canceled," I said quickly. "I got the message on my cell phone right after I left the office."

"*Sure,* you did."

Well, how do you like that! Since when did I have to account to *her* for my time? But I bit my tongue—hard. I know better than to take on Blossom Goody and her mouth. "Uh, so why did you phone me?"

"Because I'd just heard from someone who needs a private eye bad."

Now, I'd acquired a client through Blossom once before—with tragic results. So maybe she thought I might be a little leery about accepting another referral from her. (I wasn't.) Anyhow, she immediately went on the offensive. "Don't hand me a lotta crap about how busy you are, either. You're not too busy to sneak over to Bloomingdale's in the middle of the day." I was about to remind her that she was here now, too, but I didn't get the chance because then she added, "Listen, I told the man that he couldn't get better than Desiree Shapiro."

I barely had time to fluff up my feathers when Blossom hurried on. "I'll buy you a cup of coffee and fill you in," she pressed. "I gotta get outta here now, though—I'm dyin' for a smoke. Meet you in front of the store—the Lexington and Fifty-ninth Street side—in five minutes."

"Listen, Blossom, I may want to buy these earrings, and I—"

"Okay, six," she amended magnanimously. "Just don't dawdle."

It took me five minutes to decide that I had to have the earrings and another five to make the purchase. But to prove to myself I still had a spine, I tacked on an extra three minutes before joining Blossom, who was propped up against the building having a coughing fit.

"Well, you certainly took your sweet time," she groused when she was finally able to catch her breath. "There's a place a coupla blocks from here makes a decent cuppa java." And seizing my elbow, she steered me to the crosswalk. Immediately following which she popped another cigarette in her mouth.

"I'm buyin', so go crazy," Blossom invited when we were handed the menus. "Get yourself something sweet, too—the desserts here aren't half bad."

I took her up on it and, after briefly deliberating between the devil's food cake and the almond torte, I ordered apple pie à la mode to keep my coffee company. Blossom just wanted coffee. "Had a big lunch," she explained. And then, as soon as the waiter left us: "I suppose you'll throw a fit if I smoke." (Unfortunately, while the law banning smoking in New York City restaurants had been signed in December of 2002, it wouldn't be going into effect until the end of March.)

"I don't imagine any of the other customers would be too pleased, either," I pointed out.

"All four of 'em?" she retorted. "Never mind. Gotta go pee anyway. I'll grab a few puffs in the la dies' room."

Watching her walk away, I was reminded of why I don't have a single pair of slacks in my closet. This lady, who is no taller than my measly five-two, matches me pound for pound. Which doesn't exactly make her a little wisp of a thing. Yet here she was, wearing bright purple pants! I mean, Blossom's bottom resembled nothing so much as a giant grape!

She was back at the table just as our order arrived. And in between visits to her coffee mug, she proceeded to fill me in on what she was obviously determined would be my next case.

"Like I told you, Shapiro, this fellow really needs

your help. A few weeks ago there was a terrible tragedy in the family: Byron's younger son was shot to
death. The police still don't have any leads, and Byron's going nuts—like any father would. 'Take it easy,'
I said to him. 'If anyone can find out who was responsible for this, my pal Desiree Shapiro can.' "

"This man's a client of yours?" (Blossom's an
attorney.)

She shook the Little Orphan Annie curls in denial.
"A friend."

"What can you tell me about the murder?" I asked,
my fork en route to the apple pie.

"Nothing. Except that according to Byron, there
wasn't any motive for it. Jordan—the vic—was a great
guy. Married more than twenty years to a woman who
was still nuts about him. Was like a big brother to
his eighteen-year-old son. Had a business partner who
thought he was the greatest thing since Egg McMuf-
fins. Had a trainload of friends. Blah, blah, blah."

I swallowed hurriedly. "Yet somebody killed him."

Blossom frowned. "Yep."

"How did it happen?"

"Byron was too shook up to go into detail when I
talked to him. You need to call him." She reached
down and, retrieving her handbag from the floor, fumbled around in it for what had to be close to two
minutes. Finally, she produced a crumpled scrap of
paper and, after smoothing it out (more or less) with
her fist, placed it in front of me.

"Byron Mills," I read aloud.

"Yeah. I promised you'd give him a ring tonight."

"You did *what?*"

"Keep your panties on, Shapiro. Byron's one of the
best people I know, and this thing's practically de-
stroying him."

I let it go. Glancing at the paper again, I took note
of the phone number under the name. I didn't recognize the exchange. "Where is this, anyway?"

"Cloverton."

"*Where?*"

"It's a little town upstate."

"How *far* upstate?"

"Only about an hour, maybe an hour and a half from Manhattan—and it's a very pleasant drive. The weather's supposed to be pretty decent tomorrow, too."

Now, this was too much! *"Tomorrow?"*

"Byron's anxious for you to start checking things out." And when I scowled: "Whatsa matter, Shapiro? You afraid Bloomingdale's'll go bankrupt if you don't show up for a day?"

A nasty retort was sitting on my tongue, but I wound up swallowing it—because of what Blossom hit me with next.

"Listen, my friend's in bad shape. Only a coupla days ago he lost *another* son, and he said he blames it on Jordan's murder. But don't ask me to explain what he meant by that. Before he could tell me, he started bawling so hard he had to hang up."

Well, I was curious as to how this one murder had resulted in two deaths. So in spite of being put off by Blossom's high-handed manner and that long drive upstate, in the end I wound up taking the case.

The fact is, I'm as nosy as the next person. No. I'm nosier.

Selma Eichler

"A highly entertaining series."
—Carolyn Hart

"Finally there's a private eye
we can embrace." —Joan Hess

MURDER CAN MESS UP YOUR MASCARA
0-451-21430-7
MURDER CAN BOTCH UP YOUR BIRTHDAY
0-451-21152-9
MURDER CAN RUIN YOUR LOOKS
0-451-18384-3
MURDER CAN SINGE YOUR OLD FLAME
0-451-19218-4
MURDER CAN RAIN ON YOUR SHOWER
0-451-20823-4
MURDER CAN COOL OFF YOUR AFFAIR
0-451-20518-9
MURDER CAN UPSET YOUR MOTHER
0-451-20251-1
MURDER CAN SPOIL YOUR APPETITE
0-451-19958-8
MURDER CAN SPOOK YOUR CAT
0-451-19217-6

Available wherever books are sold or at
penguin.com

S316